BERECHIAH
UNDER THE SHADOW OF THE ALMIGHTY

BY

ROBERT HERMANSON

DORRANCE PUBLISHING CO., INC.
PITTSBURGH, PENNSYLVANIA 15222

All Rights Reserved
Copyright © 2000 by Robert Hermanson
No part of this book may be reproduced or transmitted
in any form or by any means, electronic or mechanical,
including photocopying, recording, or by any information
storage and retrieval system without permission in
writing from the publisher.

ISBN # 0-8059-4839-2
Printed in the United States of America

First Printing

For information or to order additional books, please write:
Dorrance Publishing Co., Inc.
643 Smithfield Street
Pittsburgh, Pennsylvania 15222
U.S.A.
1-800-788-7654

Dedication And Thanks

✵ ✵ ✵ ✵ ✵

Dad, have I not listened to your instruction?
And Mother, have I not followed your pursuit of Scripture?
Have you both not taught me discipline
as we try to walk the path of
faith and righteousness?

Thank you for your hands of help and words of love!

Is this not how we stretch out our hands across generations,
from your great-grandparents to our great grandchildren?

This book is for all of us,
about love and faith and family and righteousness—
all things I learned from you!

I want to express my gratitude and appreciation to the following persons: my sister Mary Elizabeth Hermanson, for her insight and hard work in preparing the final manuscript; my wife Brenda, for her love and support; my son Hans, my daughter Johanna, and her husband Steve Flythe, for their hours of lively discussion and assistance; and beyond family, Dr. Gloria Thomas, Rev. Clarence Carmichael, and Rev. Clyde Bauman, who all provided advice, critique, and encouragement. Thanks!

Contents

✷ ✷ ✷ ✷ ✷

Foreword vii

Book One:
    Chapter One: Jerusalem 2
    Chapter Two: Encampment 18

Book Two:
    Chapter Three: Rechabite and Zadikite 30
    Chapter Four: The Gates of En-Gannim 51
    Chapter Five: Visitation 62
    Chapter Six: Josiah and Obadiah .75
    Chapter Seven: Megiddo 95
    Chapter Eight: The Court of Pharaoh at Riblah 109
    Chapter Nine: Jeremiah the Prophet 121
    Chapter Ten: The Fall 134
    Chapter Eleven: Survival 147

Book Three:
    Chapter Twelve: Return to Jerusalem 156

Addenda:
    Historical Setting 162
    Maps 167
    Zadikite Genealogy 171
    Glossary 174

$\mathcal{F}$ORWARD

✻ ✻ ✻ ✻ ✻

The purpose of this book is to suggest, in the form of a novel, theological and social issues which are fundamental to our understanding of our biblically based faith. It explores those issues and roots of issues which are hidden within the complex history of Judah, and within the theological reflections and understandings which have underpinned and interpreted that history. Hopefully the insights you discover will be profound and worthy of discussion, and may even result in changes in attitude and behavior.

The historical setting of this book is from the latter years of the reign of King Josiah (ca. 640 - 609 B.C.) through the Babylonian Captivity, with all action occurring within the divided kingdoms of Judah and Israel and immediate environs. You might find it helpful to briefly review the historical setting; such a review is found within the Addenda.

You will find that becoming familiar with names and their meanings will add a great deal to your reading. For example: Pharaoh Necho states clearly to King Josiah that it is the Holy One of Israel Who has called upon him to be at Megiddo and that Josiah should withdraw from the field. Josiah refuses and is defeated and dies. The state authorities and princely persons enthrone Jehoahaz, but Necho rejects Jehoahaz and places his brother Eliakim on the throne, changing his name to Jehoiakim, meaning "Jehovah establishes." The implication is clear. It is Jehovah who places Eliakim—now Jehoiakim—on the throne. Please notice these details. There will be an added depth of insight, truth, irony, and pun if these linguistic things are noticed.

What is unavoidable is the anxiety caused by name and relationship confusion. Biblical names and lineage lists can be distracting, bewildering, and irritating. This is mostly because of our unfamiliarity with the names and their meanings and our own regrettable disregard of lineage. We also tend to consider lineage lists as unimportant. As you become familiar with names, their pronunciation, and meaning, there will come recognition and comfort.

Since this tale is placed within a historical biblical period, to not use biblical names and lineage lists would be an embarrassment. You, the reader, must recognize the problem as unavoidable, and focus on developing familiarity—and pronunciation—as soon as possible. Saying the name aloud will help; saying the name many times aloud will really help. The use of specific names is intentional due to their meaning. It is one of the points (be it minor) of this tale. It is in names that we find identity, a connection to family, history, our faith, and to our future, our progeny, and their kinfolk.

One of the important names is Berechiah. There are two persons of importance named Berechiah. Both Berechiahs are fictitious in this book. While Berechiah the Zadikite appears first in the book, Berechiah the Rechabite is actually about eighty years old when Berechiah the Zadikite is born. Berechiah means "Blessed of the Lord" or "The Lord has blessed."

This brings up an additional note of importance: Take care to recognize clan membership. One Berechiah, as stated, is Berechiah the Rechabite, that is, Berechiah of the Clan Rechabite. The other is Berechiah the Zadikite, Berechiah of the Clan Zadikite.

The Rechabites are a clan named after a historical figure found in 2 Kings 10 whose special clan deeds are recorded in Jeremiah 35. The Rechabites are a historical clan of Judah.

The other clan of importance in this tale is completely fictitious. The name is Clan Zadikite. It comes from the Hebrew *tsaddiq*, meaning one who is righteous, one who is just, and one who has the authority to cause these to occur, such as, theoretically, a prince. (The Hebrew 'ts' is pronounced as 'z.') The hint is that this is a princely clan, coming out of the leadership of the early kings of Israel, of royal lineage. The clan seeks to be righteous and just.

Another name of importance is Obadiah. Obadiah is a Zadikite, father of Berechiah the Zadikite. His "mentor" is Berechiah the Rechabite.

Other names should be familiar, or, if not familiar, at least infrequent.

※ ※ ※ ※ ※

There is what may seem to be confusion as to specific dates of birth, death, or events. Please consider these all intentional, similar to our Scripture itself, which sometimes differs in terms of specifics. An obvious example is in 2 Kings 24:8, where Jehoiakin becomes king at age eighteen, while in 2 Chronicles 36:9 he was eight when be became king. Why? One can speculate and one can address copying mistakes, or politics, or theological issues, or all of these impacting Scripture. But the question remains. Why?

Another example of differences in the narrative which has a bearing on our story is 2 Kings 23:30 that Josiah's servants carried him dead from the field of battle. It is stated in 2 Chronicles 35:23-24 that he was carried from the field and brought to Jerusalem where he died. What is the difference if Josiah died in one place or the other? There is a difference! Consider the differences.

✳ ✳ ✳ ✳ ✳

Several terms are used which come to us directly from the Hebrew. If I were to say, "He is a chief" or "She is a queen," the words "chief" and "queen" are colored by our modern experiences, perceptions, and training. In choosing a word for the person who would be head of a clan, I chose a Hebrew word that means "leader," "one who goes before," and "prince." Clan leaders were not able to be autocrats. Elders advised them, and the clan consented. To provide a new word without the baggage of 'chieftain' or 'prince,' which are really inadequate and inappropriate, I chose to use the Hebrew word "Nagid." Please be conscious of the limitations of the authority of the "Nagid" of the clan, as well as his designated responsibilities.

Another term I would like you to note is one that means "banner" or "pennant" in Hebrew, but that I would like to expand to mean more. Usually one would consider a banner as only flown at certain occasions, as is a pennant. Today both would have identifying colors and possibly figures on the cloth. The banner therefore identifies who you are. The Hebrew word I have chosen with this special meaning is "dagal." This will designate an identifying banner flown or worn or draped by the person wanting to identify who he or she is. It has colors that identify to all who you are. It would also be used in a personal way, draped over the shoulders, similar to how we use vestments today.

The term for "elder" will be the Hebrew word "zaqen." Again, it is a word that for us has no extra color or negative baggage. It will be used as meaning "one having authority due to age, wisdom, righteousness, and responsibility, as generally assigned by the population."

Another term used is the Hebrew word "Nokri," meaning "foreigner." The Hebrew people considered the foreigner strange, if not even dangerous, and at the same time had responsibility for the foreigner wandering in their land. "Nokri" is used to assist in the feeling of separateness or real difference, as our word "foreigner" seems to have lost some of the uncomfortableness associated with "foreign" or "foreigner" as needed in this book.

✳ ✳ ✳ ✳ ✳

The style of writing is intentional.

I pray you will find enjoyment in reading this tale and that you may be prodded (possibly provoked?) to consider your faith and your beliefs.

ROBERT HERMANSON

Remember to take a look at the Historical Setting, the Glossary, the Maps, and the Genealogy in the back of the book.

May our Lord be with you!

BOOK ONE

✳ ✳ ✳ ✳ ✳

Our story begins ca. 538 B.C. The Babylonian Captivity is approaching an end. Jerusalem remains in chaos. Berechiah, Nagid of the Zadikites, is worshiping within the remains of the temple, which had been destroyed by Nebuchadnezzar in 586 B.C.

Chapter One

✺ ✺ ✺ ✺ ✺

Jerusalem

> "Behold O Lord! I remain in despair,
> My soul is in tumult.
> My heart is torn within me!"

These painful words were spoken by an ancient, righteous, and faithful man.

"Ancient One! Grandfather!" The young man's voice cracked as it does entering manhood, even in the hushed voice. Within his year of celebration of arriving at the fullness of manhood, he had yet to appear to be a man. Haggai was slender, with taut muscles, but frail, as if not having had enough food for many years. As it was not very subtle, the Ancient One recognized the fear in his voice. Good. Fear helps in survival. Without fear, a man loses a sense of his own frailty. Fear marked the beginning of the search for Adonai, the beginning of wisdom.

"Ancient One! Please! Finish our worship! The shadows begin to form!"

"Quiet. We go when all is done." The Ancient One scarcely missed a breath. The words continued:

> "Hear how I groan,
>   There is no one to console me.
> All our enemies have heard our woes;
>   They are pleased that thou hast done it.
> Bring the day Thou hast foretold,

Berechiah

And let them be as I am."

Seven listened, and worshiped, and prayed. Four guarded the gathering in discreet corners amongst the rubble. Four more watched the approaches. All had worshiped. All had prayed, but one: the Egyptian. The Ancient One, the old man, had never moved. He had remained kneeling, praying, thinking all night as if made of stone, like the ones at his side, gnarled, broken, speaking of better days. He had knelt that way since their arrival after dark.

More than one had prayed: "O Lord, may the eyes and ears of our enemies be closed this night!"

The words continued. Most were heard, but it did not make a difference. They, too, knew the Word. They believed. They all felt the Word, knew the Word, believed the Word, and lived by the Word. For them the Word was life itself. For the man-boy, it seemed he had been born whispering in this desolate place; born whispering the words and Word among the rubble. Though he had never seen it as Solomon had, he knew its description by heart. Oh, it must have been beautiful! Oh, it was so desolate!

>"For all these things I weep;
>   My eyes flow with tears;
> For a Comforter is far from me,
>   One to revive my boldness.
> My children are desolate,
>   For the enemy has prevailed.
>
> How lonely sits the city,
>   Once full of Thy people!
> Has she not become as a widow?
>
> She that was royal of the peoples,
>   Once a princess among the nations;
>   Now the font of another's wealth!
> The roads to Zion mourn,
>   For none come to the appointed feasts;
>   All her gates are forsaken,
>   Her righteous groan;
> Our maidens have been dragged away;
>   Jerusalem is bitter.
>
> Jerusalem! Jerusalem! You sinned intentionally and grievously;
>   Those who once honored you, now despise you!

Robert Hermanson

  Yes! Hear her groan
      As she turns away.

  Your prophets have seen for you
      A false and deceptive vision;
  They wallowed in your iniquity
      As you took your fortunes;
  Oracles were seen,
      But they were delusive and deceptive.

  O Lord,
    You have wrapped yourself within anger
      And pursued us, slaying without pity.
    You have made us off-scouring and refuse
      Among all peoples.
    You have wrapped yourself within a cloud.
      Will our prayers ever reach you?

  Let us measure and examine our ways,
    And return to the Lord!

  Let us lift up our hearts and hands
    To the Holy One of Israel!

  We offended and rejected you
    And you have not forgiven us yet."

  "Ancient One! Dawn approaches! You know your command. We must be away." There was authority in this one; apprehension, concern, yes, but no fear—not at that moment.
  "Yes...Yes...." But the Ancient One continued:

  "My eyes are tired of weeping:
    My soul is in tumult;
  My heart is poured out in bereavement
      Because of the destruction of
        The daughter of our people."

  A sigh came from the men; the end was near. In unison they continued, except for the Egyptian at the broken gate, and they said:

Berechiah

"The steadfast love of Elohim never ceases,
    His mercies never come to an end;
        They are new every morning!

Great is Thy faithfulness!
'Elohim is forever my allocation,' says my soul,
    'Therefore I will hope in Him.'"

All turned and looked at the Ancient Warrior. He raised his arms:

"Remember, O Mighty One of Israel, what has befallen us!
    Behold! And see our disgrace!"

With that, the Ancient One, Berechiah, Nagid of the Zadikite, wearily arose. More than four score years had taken a toll, as had ancient wounds—and new wounds—of battle. All wounds were nothing compared to the sorrow and grief carried within his breast. This "Claw of Israel" was a mighty man, a warrior of Israel, of Judah, as had been his father, and his father before him. Berechiah, son of Obadiah, son of Amoz, son of Hezekiah, son of Johanan, son of Nathan, were all Zadikite, all Nagid of the Zadikite. All were without fear of death. There was more! Far more fearful than death was the fear of being found wanting by He Who Is, being found unrighteous, or being found unfaithful!

For Berechiah, fear of pain and fear of death both passed from him in the tent of Necho, Pharaoh of Egypt, as he beheld his slain father and uncles and cousins, and his only king, Josiah. Josiah, the righteous king.

Pharaoh Necho had known his father, Obadiah the Zadikite, the mighty right hand of Josiah. He knew Berechiah the Zadikite. Berechiah had been over a year in Pharaoh's tent after Megiddo at Mizpah.

The king may have been Lion of Israel, King of Judah, but Obadiah, Nagid of the Zadikite, was his Claw. Necho had bestowed that and other titles on Berechiah, Obadiah's son...was it fourteen? What lifetime was that?! Sword in cut hand, Pharaoh Necho had sworn an oath to Berechiah. He had given his seal and *Dagal* as protection, and the title of his father: the Claw. Berechiah would be forever protected, forever honored, forever the bane of the unrighteous, and forever followed by an Egyptian. There had been three so far, over how many years? Was it seventy? Maybe more, maybe less! Berechiah, Nagid of the Zadikites would have to ask Rizpah, his wife, on his return to the caves.

Only in worship did Berechiah depend upon others to be his eyes. The night had been long; worship was imperative. Worship was longed for. As long as he breathed, he would worship. As long as he breathed, he would enter the whore Jerusalem, even if he had to steal in as a thief in the night. Why? He had to. What would he not sacrifice to worship? It was not sacrifice. It was required, just as was eating, or sleeping, or loving his wife.

The Nokri, the traitors, and the governor of this barren city who so feared Jerusalem that he ruled from Mizpah, all had placed a price on Berechiah's head. The governor taxed the remnant in Jerusalem. He taxed the territory, if he could find someone to take tax from, for there were only the poor in Israel. Berechiah paid no tax. He stated he paid tax only to a righteous king. He had not paid tax since Josiah's death. How long ago was that? He would have to remember to ask Rizpah.

The governor wanted his tax. To gain his tax he had his small army. But the experiences of past governors (assassination and recall, and either meant death!) led this one on a different course. He needed his small army for his personal protection. Brigands were his tools of terror. With these he kept his army in check. With these he created obedience. They took and gave him some. He then gave to his army. To be sure, far less was given by all parties than what was agreed. But all parties knew the lie; it was acceptable. All were satisfied, including the King of Bab'el, as long as there were no "problems," meaning no disturbances or insurrection. Berechiah the Zadikite was an old, old "problem." If he were ever caught, they would find out his wealth. But this never happened.

To the governor, Berechiah was not acceptable. He was defiant. He killed. He killed brigands; he killed army; he killed thieves. Those things which were done to keep the populace subjugated, Berechiah defied. Not only did he defy, he encouraged defiance. He believed in some obviously worthless deity whose Temple was defiled and people scattered! How foolish, insane, and dangerous. Also, there may be that oath of Pharaoh—the protection of the pharaoh! While Necho was long gone, each new Pharaoh was obliged to protect Berechiah. Would they? To harm Berechiah might mean to start a war with Egypt! That could not occur!

Some had said the governor knew when Berechiah was in Jerusalem. The cynic smiled. He had to have the people think he knew. But even if he did know, what could he do? Chance losing half his guard? Never. Some then said he knew, and allowed a righteous man his time to worship. The cynic smiled. The truth was the governor could do nothing about it. He had tried and failed. Others had tried and failed. The result was a standing order to assassinate, and he who did would be wealthy beyond his dreams! Those who had tried all died—fools. But the Governor was happy. At least there was a balance, and only fools died.

Few would have known the Ancient One's titles except 'the Claw.' Few would have cared much. Berechiah cared for but one title: Word Protector. Only his *zaqen* of his clan and his offspring knew this title. May Adonai protect the Keepers of the Word! Berechiah would search for Word possessors only when in direst need. Now he knew only the regions where they were: Shechem, the Rechabite tents of what was once southern Edom; with the Sukkiim; one in Egypt; and in captivity. And was there still one in Tirzah, the place of his twin sister's family?

Berechiah, Nagid of the Zadikites, had sent for them. They had not come. If they could have come, they would have come. Berechiah's grief was beyond compare. His own most recent find and charge was Haggai, Berechiah's own great great-grandson, the man-boy. Haggai was becoming a Keeper of the Word. There may be the despised skins with stories, but the memory of Haggai, it was as living as was the Word. The Word was spoken! The Word was heard! How did Berechiah know to pick Haggai? He knew. Just as in others' abodes, there were ones being chosen and instructed. The Living Word, the Living Memory, the Living Story! One to the next to the next to the next, for generations, for centuries, as long as was the memory of his people!

Berechiah had heard others speak of rumors of other Keepers still in Israel and Judah. Others he did not know of, but no one spoke of these things lest the stones heard. There were more rumors: The Word had been written down, and it had been changed! Haggai had to survive. How could the Word be written?! It was alive! As Adonai spoke, Dirt was created! He Who Is spoke, and breath entered Adam. The One of Israel spoke, and his people became His! Together we hear the Word! Together we speak the Word! What will be forgotten when the Word is no longer spoken?! Who will remember who we are? Who will remember our Story?

There would be only a few more nights of worship for Berechiah, this he knew as well as he knew the roads to Jerusalem. Berechiah glanced over at the man-boy. His grandson had learned his lessons well: fear and caution! "Fear of the Lord, the beginning of Wisdom" had often been guiding words. Fear created humility. From fear one was driven to the warmth of Adonai! One knew! One did not have to see to know. One simply knew. In fear we sought! In love we stayed!

For Berechiah, fear now was only for tasks incomplete. Fear was for disease. Fear was for those who had turned their backs on their creator. Fear was not for death. Death was almost longed for—the ultimate peace. Courage was for the young, for the overcoming of fear enough to act.

Berechiah was beyond courage. It was faith. It was duty. It was responsibility. It was choice. It was necessity. It was imperative. It was his life. He did what he did because he had no being apart from what he did. He was righteous. He was faithful—not sinless, but righteous. They came to him because of his righteousness, to find righteousness.

"Prepare to leave the House of the Lord!" Berechiah, Nagid of the Zadikite, spoke.

It would be done. Leaving Jerusalem would be a dangerous act. Staying would be more dangerous.

Berechiah was deliberate in his movement. Thoughts moved through his mind. One last prayer!

Grandson! No . . . not grandson! Haggai, son of my grandson! Tears appeared at the edge of his eye.

He spoke in a whisper to himself:

"The precious sons of Zion
    Worth their weight in refined gold . . . "

"Ancient One!" The mature voice—the commander, called Uncle by Haggai—true grandson of Berechiah.

He was Shemaiah, son of Mikaiahu, son of Berechiah; someday possibly Nagid of the Zadikite, if found worthy. He was young, vibrant, powerful, a man worthy to be called a warrior in the service of He Who Is. He, too, had shed blood, not for Judah his people, but only for his clan and family.

"Ancient One!" Shemaiah was impatient.

"Quiet! We die soon enough. I must speak to the Almighty alone!"

As the others had stepped out of the Temple, Berechiah's strong hand snatched Haggai, the man-boy, off his chosen path and pushed him back to the prayer area, the only place where broken stone was not on top of broken stone.

"Adonai! Hear Thy servant amongst these stones,
    Once Thy footstool!

This boy, Thy son, I dedicate to thee!

May he remember Thy Covenant!
    May he remember Thy hand upon us,
        As upon my father's father,
            And his father's father.

Touch this Thy son, and the son of my grandson!
    I touch his eyes
        May he see Thy works;
    I touch his hands,
        May he be Thy servant;
    I touch his ears,
        May he divine Thy Word;

BERECHIAH

I touch his lips,
        May he speak Thy Word;
I touch his heart,
        May he love Thy Will;
I touch his breast,
        May he remember and defend our Story!
I touch his head,
        Grant him Thy wisdom!

The Possessor is in Thy hand!
        Keep safe Thy Keeper of the Word!

May it be Thy pleasure to keep him alive!"

    The *qadesh* was complete!
    Berechiah turned, leaving the man-boy to gather his wits. There was time for Haggai to wonder, later. Berechiah heard the command, "Now we leave. Now!"
    There was no contradiction.

※ ※ ※ ※ ※

Shemaiah the Zadikite, the commander, readied his men. All were relatives either by blood, marriage, or adoption. Even the Egyptian ate from the bowl provided by Berechiah. He ate, he worked, and he bled. Shemaiah knew eyes were everywhere for sure by now: traitors, thieves, mercenaries, marauders, by any name, enemies, and murderers. No one would be sleeping now. Their reputation and the sword would be their only safety.
    Light caused gray shadows to appear on broken pillars—shattered pillars, shattered dreams, yet unshattered faith! All thought the same, almost in unison, the result of training and Story and life experience. Prayer was life. Life was faith. The Lord would provide!
    The man-boy Haggai was overwhelmed. His mind demanded: Prepare for battle; his heart: the words of the Ancient One. He had always known a special burden. He had always had to learn things from travelers, and remember words spoken. Days he would learn; days he would repeat. He now could speak word and Word for three days straight with only a break for food and sleep! And there was always someone else coming to the cave as they used to do at their house—someone with a new message, or a new story. Some left bundles never opened, bundles despised by the Ancient One.
    What had the Ancient One meant? What did He Who Is expect of him? Remember the Words. Remember the Word. Always the Ancient One was

saying the same: Remember the Words. He would, he surely would! The meaning? That he would worry about later. He adjusted his sword; he rearranged his daggers.

Haggai leaned back into the shadows as he heard horses coming: muffled hoofs—they were theirs. It was "Uncle" Shemaiah, third son of Mikaiahu, fourth son of Berechiah. He had ordered their approach. Cousin Nathan, Shemaiah's first born, three years Haggai's senior, slipped off his horse, struggling to keep his and Haggai's horses from tearing off the rags covering their hooves. Their snorts added to the morning mist.

Haggai recognized his own breath, and his mind raced back to the words of his father, dead now eight years: "Think of the morning mist as the breath of Adonai, sign of the completion of all His mighty tasks. Remember how close is our Holy One!" Rizpah, Berechiah's wife, called him 'The Breath.' Why? He guessed it was his size! He was skinny as his father Hanamel, as was his father Jesse, as was his father Jehoshua, second son of Berechiah. Breath—how many things it meant!

Haggai took the reins from Nathan, offered with relief, and slipped onto the short, stout back. It was easier to control the horse astride rather than aside.

"Ride!" Nathan looked to his father Shemaiah and mounted his own horse. "Haggai! Out of my way!" And with pleasure he kicked into the back of Haggai.

"Pray you keep that foot this day," spoke Haggai. "Nathan, son of Shemaiah, son of Mikaiahu…" And in his mind: "Fourth son of Berechiah, first son of Obadiah, first son of Amoz, first child of Hezekiah, first of Johanan, first of Nathan… "

"Ride!"

"…and ten generations to the father of the clan." Haggai's mind forced him to refocus: *Prepare for battle; escape from Jerusalem alive!*

It had been eight years ago to the day that Haggai, then a boy, held his dying father in his arms, trying to hold in his father's blood spilled by the enemy marauders. His father's last words rang continually in his mind: "Be thou the servant of our Holy One of Israel!" His tears sealed the pledge. He never washed the blood off his hands. He would never forget. Nor would he forget Jonathan, firstborn of Elisha, grandson of Jehoshua, second son of Berechiah; or Amoz, his younger brother; or his grandfather Jesse, first son of Jehoshua. And Hosea, Jeshua, and Cushi, sons of Mikaiahu—all Zadikite—and others! Slain in a trap; condemned by a friend. It took years before he understood the impact of that one day.

But the wrath of He Who Is descended upon those marauders! Oh Adonai! Did not the Claw wail that day?! And did not the Claw roll the heads of all the slain to the gate of the governor at Mizpah?! For a month no one dared leave or enter Mizpah or Jerusalem! The governor could not and would not have begged assistance from his king. It would have meant death. Could he not handle beggars and thieves? But Berechiah was no simple brigand! Nor was he a thief. Nor was he a beggar.

The army could not find their enemy; they did not want to find the enemy. Most marauders were slaughtered or had abandoned the country. It took one Egyptian to approach the Gate at Mizpah. The message was clear! There had been no further frontal betrayals. From that time they had moved from the hills and farms outside En-Gannim to En-Gedi, to the caves.

But now the memories of the evil ones, the Nokri among them, had faded. A new greedy generation had turned to manhood. The marauders returned. Families have memories; the wicked and faithless soon forget.

The horse shivered. Nathan grasped more tightly as they moved through the Temple approach. As they rode, they were rejoined by their sentries. Shemaiah chose their escape well that day. Only the squeaks of rats upon being disturbed were heard, as well as the muffled hooves of fifteen Zadikite men and boys on twelve horses, and the dark Egyptian. Sixteen men had entered the gate; now sixteen were leaving the gate behind. Four boys rode with their fathers. The others were men able to do battle. The Egyptian was the finest warrior of Pharaoh.

And eyes followed, but no one was seen.

Shemaiah was relieved. Leading the procession was an honor and duty. The Ancient One had charged him, and he had fulfilled his charge. There had been no trap laid for them this day where they were most vulnerable. The humbled populace either had forgotten the days of celebration, forgotten Berechiah's will to worship, had never learned his pattern, or feared their number by reputation. If they had known, those who seemed to survive on stone and dust, they would have at least tried to kill a horse; an arrow in the dark would have been enough. Of course, unless....

The thought chilled Shemaiah. *Not in the City? Would they be on the road? The way home would be changed. One night, two days; no fire, little food. Holy One be with us! The caves of En-Gedi awaited...well, at least, near En-Gedi.*

Jerusalem!

Shemaiah turned to see the walls. Destroyed, burned, in some places crushed, yet still defensible. He had never seen the Jerusalem of old. He had only heard of her through the Ancient One. But his grandfather's love had become his love. *Jerusalem! A parent, a child, a whore, a wife—all with love and pain. How could I leave my child? How could anyone abandon Jerusalem?!*

Now Shemaiah would lead the Claw and Word Protector; he would lead him out of Jerusalem. He would die to protect him. He would protect the One of the Word. The first task was alignment. He drew up his horse. The procession stopped; no one questioned.

With the Dung Gate behind them, Shemaiah ordered the removal of the hoof rags. He formed his group in three ranks of three to lead. Berechiah rode alone followed by two threes. Shemaiah rode the center of the first line. The elder, more experienced warriors, rode the rear. The Egyptian rode where he willed, *dagal* of Pharaoh flying.

In order to enter the valley of Hinnom, whose slope rose to the walls of Jerusalem, the company had to pass beyond the head of the valley and the remains of En-Rogel. Shemaiah had learned his lesson wel. Within minutes, without order, the two on his sides rode up the edges and dropped their charges—Zadikite boys—at the top, returning halfway down the edge. The boys ran hard while the horses rode the valley below.

They ran to see; they ran to uncover the enemy.

There was nothing cruel. It was survival, and the boy was never sacrificed. No one dared touch a son of Berechiah or surely death would be his portion.

Two boys ran the edge of the valley. A long run it would be, but it was expected and done without complaint.

Shemaiah prayed and spoke aloud: "May the Almighty be with you!" Haggai prayed and remembered the days when that was his task. Keziah, second son of Jeshua, brother of Shemaiah, second son of Mikaiahu, was the twelve-year-old boy on the left. Obadiah, Haggai's youngest brother, age eight, was behind, but down the far side so his eyes could see Shemaiah.

"Our Elohim! No, He would not...." Shemaiah shuddered. "Oh Adonai! Oh Adonai! The day is upon us!"

The shudder was well founded. His sense was right! There was a cry from Keziah! Two figures pulled him down. There was silence. All stopped. Shemaiah turned on his horse, looking back at Berechiah's drawn face. Shemaiah ordered the boy Obadiah back. His mind raced, almost in panic! *What to do? Attack? Attack who? Split up? Adonai! Calm my mind!*

Shemaiah broke out in front, thirty lengths of the horse. *A bold enemy to attack Berechiah! But why take only the little one?*

"Berechiah! Swine of Judah!" The voice echoed across the valley. A Nokri! While the language was heavily accented, the meaning was clear. The body of the voice was still unseen.

"Berechiah! Hold your ground or the blood of this piglet will join the hundreds I have already shed on this godforsaken dirt!"

Shemaiah looked back to the Ancient One. The sign was given...no advance.

One man, large, uniformed—or once a uniform of the foreigners' army—unclean, stood at the ridge, a blade at the throat of Keziah. Assured

BERECHIAH

that no advance was occurring by Berechiah, he pulled and dragged Keziah down the valley wall, a hundred paces in front of Shemaiah, leading his horse.

"Are you but one?" inquired Shemaiah. "Are you so willing to die for the blood of my son?" (The boy was actually his nephew, but the point was clear.)

The enemy warrior, clearly a warrior in spite of his dishonorable look, disheveled attire, and poor language, threw Keziah down, stepped on his back, and sheathed his dagger.

"No! But a dead boy today is one less warrior to worry about tomorrow, and there are too many Jehudi in this land! There are already too many of this clan! And as for being alone, look again! Let us celebrate, for this day I will become a wealthy man and you will see your god! See who we are who look forward to the shedding of your colorless blood on this land!"

With that, the brigand waved. In less than a moment, hooves were heard—five, maybe ten horses. There were also a few sword men on foot.

Shemaiah thought the odds not so bad. He was prepared. It was almost easy.

Berechiah prepared, shedding his cloak. The *hoshen* of the Claw of Judah shone in the morning beams of the sun.

"Berechiah!" The brigand recognized his target, his enemy. "Berechiah! I heard you were in Jerusalem! Why did you return to your god of the rubble? Why have you not abandoned this god of fools? Why do you now make it so easy for me, after all these years?"

Berechiah urged his horse forward, slowly, until even with Shemaiah. *Time. Take your time. Time will build the courage of the young and take away the sting of surprise.*

Encouraged by his presence, Shemaiah cried, "To whom do we speak? You know us by name; is it not proper for us to know by whom we are to die?"

"I have no name to give you so you may curse me as you cursed the Moabites!" came the reply. "And no name to tell the Egyptians! Do you think me so ignorant as to not know the curse placed on the once living by this Claw? Where are the Moabites?! No, my name will not be spoken this day!"

"No-Name," Berechiah addressed the brigand. "Have we ever met before, sword to sword?"

"My head escaped your wrath eight years ago, but your sword took my brothers' heads! You played with their heads as boys play with stones! But today! Today I begin to create a family as great as yours once was. Today I become wealthy beyond your dreams. Jerusalem will be mine!"

"Are you so confident to boast where I spilled double your numbers' blood so few days ago? That day I alone killed more than those gathered here!"

"Days! Swine! You cannot count! You cannot see! Old man, what honor I will have to wipe your blood from my sword! Fool! Look now what comes up behind you!" And with a wave, more hooves were heard behind the Jehudi. Yes, a trap. The enemy had now more than doubled in number, horsemen and footmen.

"Where are your chariots? Where are your bowmen? You have brought numbers, but they are fools! They have no honor! They are godless and smell the same!"

"You can anger me no more, old pig. The slaughter begins. And know that in the month before the new moon comes, I will find your caves and spill all the blood of your clan. Know this as you die!"

"No-Name!" Berechiah spoke. "No-Name! You bring shame upon yourself! By your number we shall surely die! I do ask one favor of you before you take this *hoshen* and *dagal*. Let this my servant under your foot die at my side with me, if it is to be so told! Will the blood of a piglet honor the name of No-Name? Let him die within the reach of his father! Let a walker kill a boy! Let a warrior kill a warrior!"

Before the marauder responded—and during the response—Berechiah instructed Shemaiah: "To the wall. Go back, tell the others, as I reach down to pick up Keziah, charge the wall. Set archers in front, six of them. At one hundred paces, shoot the horses; at fifty paces the riders; at twenty-five, the footmen. The dogs remaining on horse, leave to our horsemen; they ride at once, all, if I am not there. Then let the bowmen draw their swords. Split the middle in the charge. I will deal with No-Name and the boy. May Adonai be with us!"

Shemaiah slowly withdrew...and instructed.

"....and let him suckle from his father's teats!" The brigand had completed his insults, removed his foot and kicked Keziah to his feet. Stumbling, ashamed, Keziah drew near to Berechiah. Tears were in his eyes, for he considered he had shamed himself. He stumbled, fell, got up and continued closer. At fifteen paces from Berechiah, Berechiah shouted, "Now!" He charged the boy, grabbing him by the only thing he could grab, the hair, and swung him up to the front of the horse, turned himself, and charged the wall.

"Courage my son! You did your job well! Adonai is with us and with you this day!"

He squeezed the love back into Keziah and rode. Keziah could not fear. He would soon have to use his arrows and shoot straight. This was no time to be ashamed.

Shemaiah's force had moved quickly. They were fifty yards ahead of Berechiah.

No-Name was livid. He had been startled by the maneuver completed before his eyes. He issued the fatal command: "Kill them! All of them!" He mounted his provided horse and watched the charge. Facing an awkward angle, the horsemen mingled with the foot soldiers, depleting the force of the attack. Few were bowmen; they were not prepared to meet the arrows.

As Berechiah reached within fifteen paces of the broken wall, he split the archers, all set. They let fly one arrow, two, and a third each. Berechiah heard the orders: "Now the riders!" He knew where the horsemen were, and dropped the boy at the wall. "String your bow, boy, and defend yourself and your family!" Then Berechiah turned his horse to charge.

At the turn, Shemaiah ordered: "Remember us, O Holy One of Israel! Now! Adonai lives!" And the charge began. Already distraught by the blows of the arrows, the charge was sure to complete the defeat.

"Adonai lives!" Berechiah followed the charge down the slope, scattering and slashing footmen, heading straight to No-Name. The advantage was theirs! *Adonai is with us!*

No-Name, no fool, yanked his horse right, heading parallel to the wall. As Berechiah pulled his steed up, with time wasting, pulling left, screams came from behind the wall. *My Elohim! No-Name was incredible! A superb trap!* Berechiah glanced up the hill to see a score of men, warriors, swords drawn, cloaks now drawn back revealing breastplates that shone in the sun, all descending upon his children! All was lost! Nothing to do but to die this day! *Lord! Keep my arm strong until I am dead!* And with ferociousness he swung his sword left, then right, then left, thrust and swing! They had heard of the Claw; now they believed! He struck terror!

No-Name threw his sword, piercing the throat of Berechiah's horse, who reared, and fell. The impact on the old man was immediate. The leg snapped; the shoulder dislocated. He was helpless, caught under the weight of the horse, with no arm to defend himself.

His descent had been so far from the wall that he had no way to hear the words of those that he thought had closed the trap. To him their screams were wounds. But to his sons, the cry "Adonai lives!" had immediately identified them as friend. The family began its slaughter. Revenge and a lesson to be taught. The defeated would be chased to the last.

But Berechiah for a moment saw No-Name's eyes, a drawn dagger, a throw; and Berechiah jerked, saving his life. The blade entered his side, under the *hoshen*. He knew the cost. It was only a matter of time—maybe hours, maybe days. The time for Abaddon was near.

There was more pain than finding the Ancient One wounded. Shemaiah, worn, with wounded leg and cheek, now knew the real pain would begin. Half the Jehudi continued the pursuit. "Kill No-Name!"

The boy Obadiah could not be found. Berechiah and the others were bound. The archer Johanan, firstborn of Elisha, third son of Nathan, firstborn of Berechiah, was dead. He died facing his enemy.

Then Obadiah had been found, and now would be buried with his father. Haggai was inconsolable. His tears flowed. His brother, dead, in his arms just as his father. "Oh Lord! How long, Oh Lord! Is life a gift? Who can say life is a gift but the privileged? The safe! Take my years and give them to Shemaiah! I want to be with my father and my brother!" Haggai was left to weep.

The score was not ever a concern. There were thirty dead, and more dying, including two Zadikites. Would ten score for two be good? No, there is no equal in loss. The Egyptian had not yet returned; he had killed as befitting a warrior.

Berechiah was alive, unconscious now; alive, but for how long? Would they make it to the caves? Shemaiah made preparations; orders were given. Protect the horses; bind the wounds; find foodstuffs; claim the booty of the field. By noon he figured they had to be on their way.

And these strangers—who were they? It was time to greet the believers.

"The great grandson of Obadiah the Zadikite, the Claw of Israel, greets you!" was the solemn greeting by Shemaiah.

"May Adonai continue to protect you as He has this day!" was the return.

"Stranger, we have little to offer, but what we have you may take. Clean the field!" The Zadikites cleaned the field except for the bodies of the *nokri*.

"We accept, but what is ours is yours also."

Shemaiah was amazed at the response. He was used to being the generous one. He was the commander! He was—would it be someday?—Nagid of the Zadikites.

"And your name?"

"We are brothers." The accent was of the North. And with that, he dropped his cloak, revealing not only the *hoshen*, but two armlets, identical to the ones on Shemaiah's arms. The shock on Shemaiah's face pleased the warrior, and he continued: "The great grandson of the Claw of Judah greets you! Zadikite! Brother! See now the blood on my *dagal* and know who I am!"

Shemaiah smiled, even in pain, for now he knew to whom he talked.

"Later we talk! Now, to the mountains. We head the opposite way, down toward the Salt Sea to a gorge of safety."

It was done—one half day's march to the gorge hideaway.

Pain of body and pain of heart. How would Shemaiah tell Johanan's mother? How would he tell the Ancient One's wife? How would he love Haggai? He could protect his body, but how would he protect Haggai's spirit? *Adonai be with me! Adonai be my strength! What would Berechiah do?*

Berechiah

First he would send for the *zaqen*. The *zaqen* would need to decide and approve. He would send for the friends of the Zadikites, to the Rechabites, and ask for a counselor! *How many years had Berechiah, Nagid of the Zadikites, had a counselor? Yes.* Shemaiah settled.

He would burn fires that night! Who would dare attack after the victory of that day?!

And the Story! The Story would need to be retold.

Chapter Two

✳ ✳ ✳ ✳ ✳

Encampment

By high sun the day was hot—too hot. Shemaiah had pushed the clan to the limit; now he ordered a halt and camp to be prepared. Berechiah was still unconscious; he had been so since the stop at En-Rogel. Cold reality dictated the thought that first, the Ancient One was holding back the family, and therefore placing the clan in jeopardy, and second, the likelihood of his surviving, even surviving until the family reached the caves, was very small.

Wounds were constantly cared for by all. Rizpah had taught the family and the clan well. Then there were those with special talent. But there was little to do for Berechiah, Nagid of the Zadikites. The wound had, no doubt, entered the stomach. There was just time, a short amount of time. And then the name that had lead the clan since the death of Josiah the King would be dead. What was to come? Shemaiah had to prepare himself. The *zaqen* would have to decide. But who else was there?

With that, Shemaiah's thoughts turned to his new-found brothers and their families. They had survived. Berechiah had thought maybe they had fled to Egypt or had been carried off. But they were alive! Tonight! Tonight would be glorious! It would be brother meeting brother! And, from the looks of some, there might be brother meeting sister! How Berechiah would be pleased! If only he would awaken and see the children of the children of his sister Deborah. They were family. They were clan. They were obviously of the faith! *Adonai! Praise Be Unto You!* Soon proper introductions would occur. And maybe, soon, there might even be a marriage!

But tonight stories! Yes stories would be told this night. Haggai would be busy, but who would not enjoy this night?

BERECHIAH

Never did an important occasion occur without Story. Stories were the foundation of who Shemaiah was, who Berechiah was, who the unborn would be. Family. Clan. Tribe! The Chosen of He Who Is! The One whose name could never be spoken! Praise be to the Holy One of Israel! Yes, tonight the Storytellers would repeat words that had been said before Moses, to Joseph, to Israel, to Abraham, and Ishmael. Some even had Word from before Abraham.

It was the courage of his family that gave Shemaiah courage. It was the Story, and stories, that gave Shemaiah direction. If one did not have stories, who would they be? How would they know Adonai? Where would they find strength? How would they know how to live? Story brought faith! Story brought responsibility. Story! Stories brought life.

Others might deny their hope, but never the Zadikites, and never the Rechabite.

Story, and prayer, and verse, and hymn. Shemaiah once counted and thought he himself knew about two hundred prayers, and a hundred hymns, and a hundred verses. He knew also, he figured, about four hundred stories, not word for word, but he knew when mistakes were made. Not Story, but clan stories. As for Story, Shemaiah knew Story—and Word—almost as well as Haggai, now his charge.

Berechiah's groan broke the silence. The groan broke Shemaiah's thoughts, and he snapped the head of his horse back and waited as Berechiah's litter approached. Berechiah's right arm reached up as he passed Shemaiah. Shemaiah knew the order and ordered a halt. *Adonai be with our Berechiah! And Adonai be with all of us, the living!* Shemaiah was deeply troubled. *When would Berechiah die? Was there a chance he would live? How should he die? Should he be abandoned temporarily to quickly move the family to safety? Should he simply be abandoned? Never!* The thought caused a shudder. Shemaiah would die before that would occur.

The thoughts had been mulled over and over in Shemaiah's mind and he had arrived at the conclusion that he would simply push on with all. If the Ancient One shut his eyes forever along the way, so be it. If he made it home, Adonai be praised! He would see his beloved Rizpah one last time.

Berechiah signaled Shemaiah to attend to him. Shemaiah dismounted and approached him with a sense of awe, respect, honor, and love. Berechiah was not only his grandfather, he was his father, his counselor, his protector, and his captain. He was his love. And it was easy to love such a man. Born to tragedy, born to greatness, born to lead, born to faith; he had claimed it all and had been as righteous as a man could be.

"My son." The pain was evident. "My son, we return to Jerusalem."

Shemaiah was stunned. *Jerusalem?*

"My son, take me back to Jerusalem! I will die tomorrow morning at the gate."

"But Rizpah?" Shemaiah's exasperation was evident! "Do you not want to see her one last time?" Shemaiah was then shamed, as he had stated the truth, that Berechiah was going to die. It was accepted. It was to happen. They both knew it.

"You know I will not make it home, my son! Wipe my tears from my eyes, for I know I will not see my gift from Adonai again. You will hold her, and you will caress her, and you will tell her of my love for her! For now, we camp. Tomorrow you and I and...we will return to Jerusalem, and the rest, you send home under Shaphan. And there, at the gate, Abaddon may take me."

It was quiet. Both reflected on the words. They were good words. Shaphan, son of Hilkiah of the Rechabites, was worthy. Elohim was with him. He was a warrior. He did not know fear! But he knew when to run from Abaddon!

"Who are these others?"

"According to their *hoshen*, armlets and *dagal*, and their words, it must be offspring of your sister, Deborah, and the honored Lemuel of Tirzah."

"Tell me they are not Masoretes!" Berechiah was distressed. Could his family be among those writing down Scripture? It was not only the writing down that distressed Berechiah, it was always the changes that occurred! An evil king, a prince, a priest, a family of ill repute—all had adjustable memories. Berechiah had heard of the changes up in Samaria. The words of Berechiah even disturbed Shemaiah.

"No, they are not. He showed himself with the *thum'mim* on his *hoshen* given to your father by Hilkiah the Chief Priest. He was also proud of his *dagal*!" *And*, thought Shemaiah, *he wore the Claw*. There was no doubt where these men stood. But Berechiah still worried. Where did his sister's family stand? Had they remained faithful to the ways of the Zadikite? Were they still of the Holy One of Israel?

"Did he wear the *urim*? Or was he without it? Tell me his words!" demanded Berechiah.

"I do not know, righteous one. And we cannot stop now to know!" Shemaiah touched his own small bag of stones, rings, bone, and one twig with a word. One pebble was from the Temple, a ring from his grandfather Berechiah's grandfather, Amoz, a righteous man, a claw from a lion given to Obadiah by King Josiah, dust the prophet Jeremiah was said to have brought into their home, and a twig with four unspeakable letters on it.

"What of the colors? What *dagal* do they wear?"

"My father! They are Zadikite. They all wear the *dagal* of the Zadikite, the gold color with seven slivers of silver and eight of red. Do not fret! I will find them out! It is not for you to worry. You must sleep."

BERECHIAH

For a moment it was quiet. There was struggle for life going on.

"My son. Cut my *urim* and tie it to my thumb. Let me hold it through these coming hours."

Shemaiah did as he was asked.

"Let there be no doubt, my son. I have seen wounds like these before. Abaddon will have come for me by noon tomorrow. Who else has died?"

Shemaiah was slow to respond. Should he respond? Should he tell the truth?

As if he could read his mind, the Ancient One said: "Why do you fear telling me? Will I not know tomorrow anyway? Is it not better to grieve here than to shed tears after my eyes are closed? Then there was panic, "Was it Haggai?"

"No!" Shemaiah understood the panic. "It was Haggai's brother, Obadiah, the boy. He is dead."

Berechiah sighed. Tears began to form.

"And Johanan, firstborn of Elisha, second son of Nathan your firstborn." Shemaiah paused. The old man seemed to fade even at the moment the words were being said. He wiped the tears from his eyes. *Oh, Ancient One!*

"What sacrifice do we pay to worship our Only One? Our Elohim?" There was no answer Shemaiah was able to give. Was there an answer?

Berechiah continued, "Would it not be easier for me to go down to Topheth to worship? How many have I sacrificed of my own to worship in Jerusalem! How many have I sacrificed to keep our faith! Age is not a blessing! Age is a curse! Would that I had dishonored my father and mother that my days would have been short in the land! Oh Elohim! Teach me Thy way! Tell me what I am to do, even in these last hours! Where are my enemies?"

There was no answer to be given. Shemaiah remained quiet.

"Shemaiah. I have two enemies I have fought all my life, like the two horns of Ba'al. Remember the horns of Ba'al!"

Berechiah was quiet and reflective now. The pain must have subsided momentarily.

"The horns of Ba'al! One horn is 'chaos,' a ferocious evil with an innumerable following; and the other horn is 'order,' just as dangerous, more so, as we all want to participate: We want no fear. We create a king to be like other nations, to battle chaos, yet we wallow in chaos! And the king glories in our fear of chaos. He will always want more order! Order becomes authority. But to whose advantage? No. The righteous man need avoid the horns of Ba'al. When we are drawn to one, we are impaled by the other. Both are my enemies! And soon they will take these bones as they took my son's this day. Which evil is worse? No. They are the same!"

Many were struggling to hear the Ancient One.

"Tonight, my son, tell me how many sons and daughters I have lost! Bring Haggai to me and let us hear our stories one last time together. And let me dream of Jerusalem!"

"Yes, Ancient One."

Shemaiah could tell he needed to say more and waited.

"Will Jerusalem ever be a Holy City? Will we always fear going to Jerusalem? What enemies will always remain in Jerusalem?" The Nagid yearned for his people.

"I do not know, Ancient One. Tell me."

"The Horns of Ba'al!"

The Ancient One groaned in pain. Then he spoke, "I should rather have fought ten Pharaohs and two score No-Names than bend my knee to one unfaithful priest. One has to watch one's back with the unfaithful servant, the professor of faith who professes nothing but lies! As a young man I once found one—a traitor. I killed him. But you cannot always tell who they are. They use your own words to hide themselves. They take from you to measure themselves. First watch the king, then watch the priest!"

Who did not know the story of the traitor?! thought Shemaiah.

"Ancient One. We have no time to talk now."

"To Camp. Camp. Quickly. You are right. You will do fine, my son!"

"Yes, Ancient One. We will set camp. Soon."

The camp was set as the experienced raised tents and the guards watched. After Berechiah's orders, they had moved on for safety through what would have been their noon meal. Instead of following the Jerusalem road farther south after the skirmish, they had turned off and had followed the river. While the river had many eyes, they were solitary, usually, and friends. Berechiah had protected many in his years, and had provided much, and the faithful of Judah did not forget a service. If a troop followed, they would hear soon enough. These stones had ears that were friendly; not like Jerusalem.

They had followed a *nachal*, choosing well, so there would be only one point of attack. There would be plenty of time to place archers as well as those with swords.

The *nokri* would have to have one hundred men, and there was no such troop willing to travel outside of Jerusalem, except for Bab'el's own army. An army was slow. There would have been word. There had been no army for almost two score years. There had been the Moabites. But Berechiah, Nagid of the Zadikites had delivered the fatal blow to that people. He had conquered the armies, and embarrassed Nebuchadnezzar to complete the final blow. That was part of the Story.

Shemaiah paused to count exactly. By his understanding it was thirty-seven years ago that the Moabites had struck into shattered Judah. It was not an army, but an army of men: four armies. There was chaos, and Judah bled further.

Berechiah had not been at his lands and home at the time the Moabites had disregarded the *dagal* of Pharaoh at the gate of Berechiah, and had killed many of the family. That was now a story of Haggai. Who would remember? The Zadikites would remember, and the Rechabites would remember.

Upon remembering, Shemaiah glanced around and found the Egyptian. He was guarding his charge. Thirty-six years ago, the Egyptian, a different Egyptian, saw the destruction and then returned to Egypt, gained a small detachment, and returned. The Moabites paid for their indiscretion. Not only that, but Pharaoh had discharged a messenger to Bab'el, reminding the King of Bab'el that it was his responsibility to manage his subjects. The insult was felt deeply. Horona'im, Kiriatha'im, Nebo, and Dibon were destroyed, as were many other smaller towns. It may have taken almost five years, it had been five years, but the curse was true and final. Who now was a Moabite? Had not Jeremiah the prophet announced it to be before it was?

And then, twenty years later, eight years ago, there was another attack by marauders—by the brother of No-Name. They had paid swiftly. But again, the family had lost ones who were loved and needed. Shemaiah had been a score and three. He briefly smiled at the thoughts of his wanting Zilpah, now his wife of sixteen years. He still wanted her, and he cared for seven children that showed his love for his Zilpah.

Shemaiah snapped his head. He thought to himself, *Shemaiah, you are getting soft. You cannot remember now. You cannot do anything but think defense. It is now on you. You now have to replace Berechiah. You are the guardian of the family, the Zaqen of Zaqen of the Zadikite.* Tomorrow. Berechiah was right, he would be no more, and Shemaiah would be the Nagid of the family. On him would fall the protection of the family, the protection of the Keeper of the Word, and protector of the righteous.

Tomorrow. But he could not think of those things now. He had to protect and defend. He now would be the teacher. Who would be his student? He would have to pick, and pick quickly.

It would be Keziah, thought Shemaiah. *Almost a man. Had he not been afraid at the hands of No-Name? But had he not done his task as assigned? And as Berechiah had retreated to the wall, had not Keziah taken a bow and shot it true —as true as when Berechiah at fourteen in the tent of Pharaoh Necho had pierced the neck of the priest Tibni? Is he not quick of eye and mind? Does he not see into the eye? Yes. Keziah.*

The *qadesh*. It would be done this night on Keziah, son of Jeshua, Shemaiah's brother, son of Mikaiahu, fifth child of Berechiah. Would his own sons be disappointed? Maybe, but he had no choice. One knew these things. Adonai led one's thoughts, and opened one's eyes to see what was within the child. "As Eli saw Samuel," the Ancient One stated. For a moment Shemaiah wondered what the Ancient One had seen in him. He had been chosen, too, above Berechiah's own sons—even his own father.

He would take Keziah to Jerusalem with Berechiah tomorrow. And as Berechiah had pronounced the *qadesh* on Haggai for his task, Shemaiah would do for Keziah. He would be dedicated to Adonai as protector of the family. Protector. Shemaiah returned to his responsibilities for the present. *Would there be time? Maybe the qadesh should wait. We shall see,* he thought.

"Father...." It was Nathan, his son. "Father...!"

"Yes, my son."

"Father! When will we divide the booty from the evil *nokri*? I want to see what we have!"

"Nathan. Are your first words to me about trinkets and gold? Go attend to the Ancient One and see his needs are met."

Character. Yes, thought Shemaiah, his firstborn was a warrior worthy of Hezekiah, father of Amoz, father of Obadiah, father of Berechiah, father of Mikaiahu, his father. He was going to be a good father, when that was arranged, soon, very soon. But he had too much the merchant's interest in gold, gold to have and hold and deem as a reflection of character, but as much a part of character as a painted face.

Maybe this was not a flaw in Mikaiahu, though Shemaiah tried desperately to minimize it, but as sons read their father, one of Mikaiahu's children would bring the seed to life, and Adonai forgive him! And what would be of his children? Or her children? Unto the fourth or fifth generation! Were there these seeds of evil in all of us? Good seeds were planted; were there weed seeds also planted?

Seeds of character. Shemaiah liked that. The character of a field was reaped from the seeds planted. But sometimes the field was never planted! Or it was planted by a lazy parent who could not tell the difference between seeds of grain and seeds of briars. Or maybe someone else got into the field and planted things. Or maybe Adonai planted the seeds and we alone chose which ones would grow. Maybe the seeds were gifts, And certain families kept certain gifts!

Did he not see in Haggai and Keziah character similar to Berechiah? Was Berechiah not a gift himself? Are persons gifts? Shemaiah immediately thought of his own wife! *Truly a gift! Was the gift given before life? Or was the gift seen by my father?* Shemaiah laughed with that! *Not likely! My mother!*

And what do we do with our gifts from Adonai? Some men beat them. Some men deny them. Shemaiah said to himself: "If I were given a gift from He Who Is, I would cherish it and protect it and care for it." And that he did. And again he spoke out loud: "Gold is not a gift. At best it

BERECHIAH

is a tool as simple as a scythe. At worst it separates us from our faith. Nathan needs instruction in this area."

Shemaiah thought, *There has been so little gold, due to the times. Is it not natural to want more?; To want gold? There will be time for the clan to regroup. It will be then that the wealth of the past family will be put to advantage. Then, and not before.*

"Talking to yourself again, Father?" It was Nathan.

"No, my son, I was actually talking to you."

"I am not sure I want to hear what you say to me when I am not before you. If you do as I, I temper my tongue and thoughts when I talk to you! You do tell me what you think, do you not, my father?"

"Not always, my son. And that is not fair to you."

"It might not be fair, but let us let it be! I do not need to know all your thoughts this day."

"I will tell you this, my son. I am hungry. Prepare the meal. It is time we eat, and we must be done before dark."

"Yes, my father. You see, gold is good. It is what buys us what we cannot raise ourselves. It will buy us fish. It will buy us sheep. It can buy us a field. It can buy us materials to build a home..."

"And it can buy you a pretty wife! But it might buy you your neighbor's wife because she sees what you have and is dissatisfied with what she has."

Nathan heard, but ignored, the intended lesson. "Will this gold buy me a pretty wife, Father? Do you promise? When, Father? When we return home?"

"We will discuss it after you tell your Great Grandmother Rizpah of our loss this day. Can you do that, my son?"

"No, Father, I cannot. Would it not be for you to do?" And then, "Father, what is this of Jerusalem? Are we returning to Jerusalem? Why? Must we?"

Shemaiah was quick to see the issues involved in the question. Should he protect his son? Should he place him in danger? Would his presence at the gate be a benefit? Would he learn anything? Would the family gain anything by his return to the caves?

"Yes, I will take the Ancient One back to Jerusalem. It is his desire."

Few will go back. Who? Maybe just the Egyptian and me, thought Shemaiah.

"Go, have the meal prepared. Tell me how many we are, and tell me the names of our guests."

"The last I will do first, Father. It is twenty-seven in all, but seven fighting men and six like me, soon to be wed. It is Hoshea, son of Jedidiah, son of Abnon, second son of Lemuel who married Deborah, sister of

Berechiah, the Ancient One. Hoshea cannot believe that Berechiah is still alive. He had heard the tales but figured they were lies.

"Hoshea's wife is dead, but he brings his sons Jehoshua and his wife, Amoriah, and his daughter, Rachel, and Nathan his youngest, who wants a woman as bad as I. I think Jehoshua has two children with him. They are babies. And then there are cousins, and relatives of wives. The family of the firstborn of Lemuel remains at Tirzah, even though Tirzah is mostly destroyed now. Hoshea said Samarians raided their town, you know, people of the capitol.

"He said something I do not understand, Father. He said that he has even burned the Samarian's Written Word. He said the words were not the same! What is this Written Word, Father? That means they are not Masoretes, is that not right, Father?"

"Speak more slowly, my son!" Shemaiah struggled with the names. "I do not think so, my son. Do they have someone like Haggai with them?"

"Yes, Father. But I have some trouble understanding them. Their accent is difficult, so we have not said much. How do we know a Masorete?"

"A Masorete is one who has written down the Word! It is as Baruch was, in a way, to Jeremiah. But Baruch was faithful to Jeremiah! Who are these that dare write down our Word from the Holy One of Israel? They take our Word and our Story and our stories! And we become lazy and cannot remember and we forget who we are! And they change our words to their own advantage! For ten generations! Cursed! Self-appointed favor-seekers of kings! For what purpose? Why is this done?! 'And He Who Is spoke all these Words saying!' It is not: 'Elohim wrote all these words!' No! 'Spoke!' Let us speak the Word!"

"Father!"

"Yes." And a pause of anguish led to, "Thank you, my son, for your information. Now go, we are all hungry and need our food as soon as possible. Remember to set fires through the nachal. Many fires! If an enemy is near, the fires may confuse him. And find out from the Egyptian what he will need tomorrow. Upon the death of the Ancient One, he must return to the service of his Pharaoh. I think it was Pharaoh Hophra who sent him here twenty years ago. We will soon send him on his way. Find out what he wants to do."

The shock on Nathan's face was a surprise to Shemaiah. His son's mood changed immediately, and tears swelled in the young man's eyes. He had not understood why they were to return to Jerusalem. Now he did.

"Oh Father! No! Not the Ancient One, too!" And the young man grabbed his father ferociously and wept. "Obadiah, and Grandfather, and Johanan!"

The young man gathered his wits, and pushed his father away. "I will serve you well tomorrow." Then he walked away to commit his assignments.

BERECHIAH

Quietly Shemaiah muttered: "Go, my son. Maybe you will forget your need for trinkets of gold after all."

✻ ✻ ✻ ✻ ✻

The meal had been good: fish, mutton, bread, wine, and water. Shifts were changed as the guardians, too, needed to eat. The Egyptian remained at the side of Berechiah, attending to his needs.

Joining the family were several strangers known only to Berechiah. They paid homage to the Nagid of the Zadikites. They ate well, probably for the first time in years. Word must have spread quickly. By dark, many travelers and wandering families had taken shelter with the camp.

The booty was brought forward. The pain of the day was put aside and the dreams of tomorrow became possibilities.

It fell on Shemaiah to divide the valued. The Egyptian was rewarded, then triple to the men with wives and children, double shares to the men with wives, single shares to those wanting a wife, and weapons to the boys.

Shemaiah took all the rings—a few he thought he recognized—and presented them to the women of the families which Hoshea led. For this wise action he was honored. Then some of the single women began to dance to soft singing and beating. Even Shaphan the Rechabite, husband of Abigail, who was firstborn daughter of Hananaiah, firstborn son of Nathan, firstborn of Berechiah, even began to dance.

When one of Hoshea commented on his dance, wondering if it were not aided by the wine, he was firmly informed of Shaphan's commitment not to drink wine, as he was a Rechabite. The stranger, not wanting to offend, did not ask any further questions. He had heard of the Rechabites, and knew of their strange but straight path.

Upon completion of the dancing, it was Shemaiah who invited all to hear Haggai. It was a night for Haggai to tell Story and stories. Shemaiah chose the Story of Samuel and Haggai told the Story. At the end, one of Hoshea's men, Amoriah, his son, stood and repeated the next Story almost word for word. All rejoiced. Two in one place! Shemaiah was extremely agitated. Haggai would have to travel with him to Jerusalem tomorrow. Amoriah would travel to the caves.

Then Shemaiah instructed the guests to state their lineage and relatives, and they did.

Shemaiah instructed Haggai to instruct the visitors of the offspring of Berechiah, which he did.

All was quiet, as Amoriah remembered the Word and spoke it, and as Haggai remembered the Word and spoke it.

Shemaiah asked of his family and guests: "My friends and sons, would you want to hear the story of Berechiah, Nagid of the Zadikites? Here he is, the Ancient One, a chosen one, a mighty warrior of Israel. Would you want to hear his story?"

Though customs were different in how approval was given, it was apparent that all were of one mind. Approval was given.

Hearts would be moved this night! Clan would reunite with family. Strangers would become family. The story of Berechiah would be told, and told in the presence of Berechiah, Nagid of the Zadikites for the last time.

"Come, my friends, hear our Story! Come, know who we are by our words and our deeds which we now tell you! Let us tell you the names of our own!"

And it was done.

BOOK *T*wo

✳ ✳ ✳ ✳ ✳

These are the words of the Storyteller Haggai. He recounts the story of Berechiah the Zadikite, which begins with a meeting during the eighteenth year of the reign of Josiah, king of Judah, ca. 623 B.C., in which Berechiah's birth is fortold. The participants in the meeting are: Obadiah, Nagid of the Zadikites and Berechiah, Nagid of the Rechabites. Berechiah the Rechabite informs Obadiah he will have a son. Upon the birth, Obadiah will name his son Berechiah after his old friend, *zaqen,* and mentor.

Chapter Three

✻ ✻ ✻ ✻ ✻

Rechabite and Zadikite

There was in Israel a clan called apart by the Word of their father, to righteousness and witness, by worship, faith, and service. They were known by their tents in an age of cities and stone dwellings. They were known by their refusal to eat or drink the fruit of the vine. They were known by their unwillingness to purchase land. They gained fame for their industriousness, their trade, and their herding. They spoke truth. They feared no man nor king, but only the Almighty, the Holy One of Israel. Their word and deeds were as if they waited upon He Who Is each hour of each day. This clan moved amongst all nations, to all people who knew them for their righteousness and word. And their *dagal*, black with a streak of red running through it, was recognized by the people of the sea to the North, and by the people to the South and south of the land of Pharaoh, to the East, and to the seas to the south of the East. And why is it we are not as one of these, known as the Clan Rechabite? Does not the Almighty One still remember their names?

And this clan loved the Clan Zadikite. They honored and protected the honorable, and in return the Zadikite Clan honored and protected the Rechabite. The wisdom of the Rechabite was known to all the people. There was one Rechabite to remember: Berechiah. Was there a king that did not know of Berechiah, Nagid of the Rechabite? King Manasseh knew Berechiah, once regretted it, but then loved him. His son Amon hated Berechiah. Berechiah, Nagid of the Rechabite, knew and loved Obadiah, Nagid of the Zadikite. He loved him as a man loves his son.

BERECHIAH

In the seventeenth year of the reign of Josiah, King of Judah, Berechiah the Rechabite, son of Uriah and father of Habaziniah the Rechabite, who was father of Jeremiah the Rechabite who was father of Jaazaniah who was father of Shaphan, who married Abigail, first child of Hananaiah, first son of Nathan, first son of Berechiah, son of Obadiah, came to the lands of En-Gannim of Judah, to meet, as was the custom of the Rechabites and the clan of Obadiah, seven times, once every two score years. The Nagid of each family would, on the appointed day, the same day, meet to renew the ties of righteous men.

Within the faith, they both were *nazir*, as had been Samuel. The old Rechabite was carried to the appointed *mizbeach* of Abraham by four great grandsons! Berechiah the Rechabite met Obadiah the Zadikite. Berechiah was four score years, while Obadiah was one score and ten years of age. Berechiah was tired of body, but he remained strong. His wisdom was apparent. There were none, not even the king, who refuted his wisdom, though some hearts were hardened against him. Obadiah was young, a soldier, captain of the king's whole army, and righteous in the eyes of the living, particularly his wife. He had been with his wife fourteen years, without child and without complaint. Obadiah was one who measured other men and perceived their hearts. He was blessed with many brothers and sisters and their children were many, with cousins and cousins' cousins. And he was also faithful. Chosen by Amoz, his father from all others, Obadiah served his clan as Nagid as Berechiah served the Rechabites or Neriah served the Perizzites.

Words of greeting were formal and Berechiah appointed the next time the Nagid of each tribe would meet. Obadiah was respectful—particularly respectful—not out of requirement but genuine love and admiration. There was no doubt there still were righteous men in Israel!

"My brother, Obadiah, would that my bones could wander Judah another forty years, that I could see the joy of your face as you look upon your great grandchildren as I now do, and that I could hear the names of those of your family that will be righteous. Hear the Word to you, faithful friend: You will have two children, a male child and a female child; even now they stir. Our Holy One requests that I tell you this thing that you may love your wife and your faithfulness be honored by all. Hear these words and plan for the children. And when your son comes here two score years from now to meet with my assigned one, may he remember these days and the words we speak which we are about to enjoy together. Who have you brought to remember?"

"Righteous friend, friend of my father whom I knew but nine years, and friend of my father's father, I will remember. And there is one with me still learning. Is this not satisfactory? Good. Now, do you remember my great grandfather? Were you the one who met with him in the thirty-second year of the reign of Manasseh, king of Judah?"

"My son, stop! Of course it was I. But you sow discord already! King of Judah? Why do you count years from the reigns of kings? Who are these men that we should count the years of our lives by their affairs? Let us count years from the time of Moses, or Abraham, or Noah! Who are these kings? Yes, it was I who knew your great grandfather. He was to me as I am to you—a friend, a brother, different, but the same. But tell me, did you not hear my Word to you? Did you not hear that your wife will bear you a son and a daughter?"

"I did hear, but as Samuel did not know what to say when our Elohim spoke to him until Eli instructed, I am dumbfounded and I am confused. Believe this, Ancient One, if I seed this son…"

"If? Do you doubt my word?" Berechiah smiled a deep smile of joy. He knew what this Word meant to Obadiah.

"When I rejoice at the birth of my son, I will name him Berechiah, for surely Adonai has blessed us. I will consecrate him to the service of our One, and he will be even before his birth a Nazirite. No, I do not doubt your word; my joy is too much for me to bear. And my wife? You have warmed my bed!"

"Yes. We have been blessed. And you will have time to consider this further! But, come now, to my tent, and we talk of things that have already passed, and things to be. This high sun we have been asked to sit with the *zaqen* at the gates of En-Gannim and judge this people. Let us now eat and drink and sleep in preparation for that task."

Obadiah said, "I am not a *zaqen* of this city, though I live nearby. There are many here who hate me. Why have we been asked?"

"I was asked. There are few able to judge these days, and I agreed as long as you sit by my side and say your word freely," spoke Berechiah.

"And they agreed? Do they not remember my retribution for their unrighteousness?" asked Obadiah.

"Yes, and there are those who thought it right. Here, now, the unrighteous are no longer with us or fear to be in the open with their ways."

"Would that I could make it that way in this whole nation!" said Obadiah.

"Ah, another point of difference! I—as was Joshua—am only concerned with those gathered in my tent! Yes, we are a people, not a nation. I love my people as Elohim loves us, but I am not the One appointed to cause righteousness in the land. There is none but the Almighty One to do that. You may attempt, but you will never succeed! There is but One. No, I have a difficult enough task within my own tent. I will show the way of fairness and righteousness, but I will not force compliance; I cannot force compliance. Let the story of our people speak for itself! Let the story of my life speak for itself. We, in this tent will serve the Holy One whose Name we dare not say!"

"Well, my friend," Obadiah chuckled, "if you allowed yourself to live in a house, you might be concerned with a little bit more than those of your tent! Will you Rechabites ever abandon the tent?"

"You begin! Come, let us eat and drink before our tongues are quick and sharp!"

"Yes, I begin...with more to come! And what is it we drink this day? Will it be warm water?" Obadiah questioned with a smile.

"Yes only warm water! Would you not have your clan drink warm water if that were the foundation of your righteousness? We, too, are pulled by the whims of this day and the sins of Sodom and Gomorrah. The issue is where you stop the fall. Your humor knows our public foibles, but do you know our heart?

"We Rechabites drink no wine, we own no land, we grow no seed, we recognize no man as Lord or king, for our Holy One is the only King of Israel. We live by a path few have chosen and many ridicule. Our path is straight and pure as the water which cleanses us and renews us. And this I beg of you: If our clan disappears in the night you will not allow us to be forgotten! Let no generation forget who we are or what we do! Remember my wisdom and my heart. Remember our righteousness and bear witness to it by your own life! Remember me, Berechiah, Nagid of the Rechabite!"

"This, Ancient One, I swear. As for your wisdom and faithfulness and righteousness, I have heard and seen and will find out even more as you, too, discern my own heart. But please, do not condemn me for ignorance!"

And there was a feast provided for Obadiah, Nagid of the Zadikite, in the tent of Berechiah. Obadiah had never known of the flavors, brought from the South and East and West and North, that caused such joy in eating. And his stomach, too, was surprised and let such be known.

"Ancient One, how is it that you have food never prepared even in the king's own house? Are you so wealthy?"

"Do you think that because we live in tents we are fools? Our caravans travel to the ends of the desert to the West and to the South and to the East. Some of my grandsons I have not seen for ten springs! No, Obadiah, Elohim has blessed us! Our tents are a reminder of who we are. How do you remind yourself who you are? How do you remember Moses, who lived in a tent, or Abraham, who lived in a tent?

"When you remove the dust from your bed, you will forget your Lord and create your own gods. When you remove the stars from your sight you will soon forget how insignificant you are and what a gift it is to have an agreement with the One Who chose us. We were chosen. We were made free from the bondage of Pharaoh, and what then did we do? We have created our own Pharaohs in our own land!

"Listen, Obadiah. When you barricade the door of your house, not only is the thief barricaded out, but you are barricaded in, away from your appointed task. As for me, in less time than it took to prepare this meal we would have been gone and you would not know we were ever here, nor where we would be tomorrow."

"And who protects you? Is it not the king?" asked Obadiah, Nagid of the Zadikite, captain in the king's army.

"No. It is the One Whose Name we do not speak, the One Who Is. For He can make and unmake kings. He can make and unmake peace. He can make and unmake cities. He can make and unmake peoples."

"But did I not hear of one of your camps seeking shelter at Beth Jesimoth? How many times have you sought shelter within our cities?"

The Ancient One, Nagid of the Rechabite, responded, "If I am camped at Machpelah and a storm arises, would you find fault for me for hiding in the caves until the storm is passed? And what do I owe the mountain? I give thanks to the One that it was there in the time of my need, but that does not mean I continue living within the caves, nor do I owe the cave anything. We will protect our people, not the king. In poverty or wealth, in peace or turmoil, in life or death, it is the Holy One of Israel who is with us, not the king."

"But is it not the king who protects all of us in war? If we were all as you, who would protect our people when there is war?"

And Berechiah replied, "Are there not two kinds of war? There is war of kings. This king wants that king's land and goods and women. Or that king wants to be a god. Are not all kings the same, no matter their name? Then there is war to protect the righteous. That is our One's war. Tell me when it last was that the One Whose Name we dare not speak was with the army of the king? Are we blind to the acts of those who consider themselves kings in this land? Are we not a divided people because of the kings of this land? What wrong has occurred that has torn our family apart? Where are the sons of Israel? Was it not Rechab who saw the work of the king and his son Jehonadab, servant of the king, who slaughtered the false men of Israel? And what came of it? The king himself did evil.

"No. We will not do war for a king anymore, for Elohim is our king. We will cause righteousness to happen when unrighteousness is put upon us. We hold men to their word, just as our One holds us to our Covenant. Can I fathom the righteousness of the Almighty One? No. But if you steal the wife of a son of mine, I know that the One finds that intolerable and so do I. If you sneak into my tent, you will pay the price, particularly since you could call at its entrance for mercy and be brought in as a brother no matter who you are! In my tent no one dies at our hands and no one need fear until unrighteousness occurs. Then we all need to fear!

"No, there is no more war of kings for the Rechabite," Berechiah affirmed. "But I will die seeking righteousness in my tent and in the land given to the twelve brothers. No more. No less. If I am not in this land, I seek righteousness only within my tent. I will defend our tents only when we know we must witness to our faith and only if we have been righteous. If unrighteousness be done, let us cast it out and accept those whom our Holy One uses to chastise us. If we do not cast it out, will we all not be chastised and suffer? Who will I defend? Only the righteous.

"How many clan remain in Judah? Not as many as there once were! How many know their own tribe? The king is ever jealous of the clan and tribe and he is jealous of the righteous! Serve a king? Never! Especially on the word of the king, for by these kings we have suffered and because of them we have suffered. Do you not hear Isaiah? Have you not heard the new Word of Jeremiah the prophet? No. We are a divided and conquered people who are losing their memory because of the kings—all the sons of David! And who really was David, that he should have sons who bring us such shame?"

And there was quiet. Obadiah was taken back. He then said, "But an eye for an eye. Is that not righteous? And is that not the purpose of the king—to perform righteousness, to protect the weak and innocent, and to protect the righteous?"

But Berechiah the Rechabite argued, "My brother, let us look at this land and remember our Story. How much righteousness do you remember from any king? You must remember, before the Masoretes adjust our common memory, that Samuel anointed Saul under protest; and did not our One object? Remember the Words of our Story! Does it not say:

> "Then all the *zaqen* gathered themselves together and came to Samuel at Ramah and said to him, 'Behold, you are old and your sons do not walk in your ways. Now make us a king to judge us like all the other nations.'
>
> "And Samuel prayed to He Who Is, and He Who Is said unto Samuel, 'Hear the voice of the people in all that they say unto you, for they have not rejected you, but they have rejected Me! They want that I should not reign over them, according to all the evil which they have done since the day that I brought them up out of Egypt even to this day. Now they have forsaken Me and serve other gods, so now they also forsake you. Therefore hearken unto their

voice. Still protest vehemently to them, and tell them the manner of the king that shall reign over them.'

"And Samuel spoke all the Words of He Who Is unto the people that asked of him a king, and he said, 'This will be the manner of the king that shall reign over you: He will take your sons and use them for his own pleasure, for his chariots and his horsemen, and some will run before his chariots. And he will appoint for them captains over thousands, and captains over fifties, and he will have them sow and reap his harvest, and to make weapons of war and instruments of his chariots. And he will take your daughters to spice his food and be his cooks and bake. And he will take your fields and your vineyards and olive orchards, always the best, and provide them for his own servants. And he will take the tenth of your seed and your vineyards, and give to his officers and servants. And the king will take your men-servants and maid-servants and the best young men and use them for his own desires. He will take a tenth of your sheep and you will be his servant. And you will cry out in that day because of the king you have chosen yourselves, and He Who Is will not hear you in that day.' Nevertheless the people refused to obey the words of Samuel.

"Remember!" said Berechiah the Rechabite. "Fear the Masoretes that they take these Words from us! When you write the Word down, we forget how it lives; then those who wish to destroy the Word will use the Word and twist the Word and change the Word. While we may argue and speak our heart, let us swear never to tolerate those who change the Word! I hear that Omri ordered this and more deleted from his scratches, and how many Keepers of the Word died? You will suffer the same fate if you let it be known who you are! Possessors of the Word, beware! You are being hunted!

"But! Take the point! He Who Is, the Holy One, is jealous! He is king! Who is king? He is king! There can be no earthly king to determine the righteousness of the faithful. Who was Abraham's king? Isaac's king? Jacob's king? Who was Moses' king? How dare you place over me one who would be the Almighty One! Yes, our father once erred, and we supported David the king, but we learned and have returned to our Adonai. It is hard enough to complete the Covenant of Adonai, let alone comply with the fickleness of a king or even a people."

Reacting to the pain of these words, Obadiah said, "You are close to insulting me, my brother, in your own tent! I have supported this king,

Josiah, and find him righteous. Has he not chased out those of Ba'al? Has he not brought back proper worship in Jerusalem? Has he not ordered me to search out false gods and destroy them? Was this not done in all Judah? Was this not done here in En-Gannim? Is there an idol in Jerusalem?"

"My son, yes, there are idols in Jerusalem! Ask the king's own sons! But why should I worry about Jerusalem? Is this not simply the throne of kings? To whose glory is the city? Come now, let us go to Jerusalem, and see if Ba'al is out of Jerusalem, or lies out of the Genizah. Do not women still whore for priests and princes in their chamber room by your Sacred of Sacreds? For as Samuel had Benebelija'al, so has Josiah!

"Yes, I have heard of righteous men in Jerusalem." Berechiah tried to be fair. "I have heard of Hilkiah the Chief Priest, who found the written Word! But why did he need that? I could have had five, yes, five, repeat the Story as you know it should be repeated. Why does his finding words on skins somehow make it worthy? Is not the Living Word more reliable? Who remembers the written words of Pharaoh? But a people remembers their Story! I hear of Merari, of Tikvath, and of Jeremiah. I believe Isaiah a prophet; the One was with him, but where is he now?

"For each righteous man, or Huldah the prophetess, there are twenty in Jerusalem who sneak and pilfer and plot and despise the Word, or use the Word to their own advantage. How many thousand Teraphim would you find in Jerusalem? Yes! Unrighteousness. How long will our Adonai tolerate this insult within any tent placed on the land promised to Israel, let alone in your sacred Jerusalem? Idols are but one commandment. There are nine more! As for me, I think that a Mizbeach of ten uncut stone used by a righteous man will be more pleasing to our Holy One than ten thousand sacrifices by the unrighteous on an altar of gold and silver."

"Ancient One, you take advantage of me and my ignorance, and you take advantage of my courtesy to not address each of your points by interrupting you as you speak. Yes, there is unrighteousness found in Jerusalem, but is there none in this tent? Where there are more people, there will be more evil compounded, which must cause the righteous to be doubly careful. How will we root out this evil if we do not have the authority of the king? Who will rule tens of thousands and thousands? Yes, you may lead your people and flee evil in the night, but what of those of us who cannot flee? What of the poor who need to be protected?"

"Does the king think of the poor when his whores come to him at night?"

"Who is the king's whore?" asked Obadiah.

"Open your eyes! Go ask Josiah! But, let us begin count with David. I do not understand why you glorify a man who stole his neighbor's wife! And where was the correction? Who paid for this evil? David's son? And his other sons? Where is the righteousness in this? How many sons did he take into battle to their death for his own glory? Why does the king try to take our sons into his army when they are but little ones? Even though of the age of account, they are not able to reason. They only dream of being mighty men loved by the people, particularly young women. Being mighty men of the Almighty is not important. For this they are willing to die before they understand life. What is the difference between Josiah taking a young son into battle or the Philistines taking a child to Topheth and sacrificing it to Molech? Send old men to war. Why not? Old men are too clever. They know the foolishness of dying for a king.

"But whores? What is a concubine? What is a harem? No. How many women did our One create for Adam? How many ribs did he take from Adam? He took one. Let us take the same to ourselves. It is hard enough loving one! As for me, I would not die so that a king could whore with whomever he pleased or his sons watch my daughters dance."

"And what would you die for, my friend Berechiah?"

"I take this dirt, and I die for it. I take this tent, and I die for it. I take my family, and I die for it. My clan, I die for it. We are called to serve our He Who Is. This I will do. Abaddon is not afar off for me, my friend. And I fear for you! I know who you are! You are Josiah's right arm. You are his trusted servant. You are the Claw reborn. And how will you die, friend Obadiah?"

"I will die at the side of my king. It is my duty. Good or bad, righteous or not, I will honor him even as I die at his side. I will be faithful to him, for Josiah is good. And he is good for this people. He is my king."

"Do you not hear yourself? You talk of this man as if he is the Holy One. You even use terms we use in our faith: faithful, 'good for this people,' good! What is 'good?'" asked Berechiah.

"In some ways, yes, I do. Because in some ways my responsibility is sacred, as is the king's responsibility. The king may be unfaithful and irresponsible, but does that negate my responsibilities and my duty? Is this how one brings honor to one's family and to oneself? Is it not in doing the Will of Elohim that one is found righteous?"

"Absolutely. But our difference is in how we determine what is expected of us. What is the Almighty's Will? 'Righteous?' Righteous is doing what He Who Is wants us to do, what we were created for, why we were chosen. Elohim did not call out a kingdom. He called out a people, be it a stiff-necked people! There is no covenant with a kingdom. There is a Covenant with a people. What does the Almighty want of us? Does He change His mind? Is He constant? Does He give you a Covenant and me a Covenant and they are different? And how, with all the different words spoken in this land, do I find the Word? For indeed there is a Word!"

BERECHIAH

"Ancient One! I may rub my *urim* from now until I die, and I still will question whether the word I hear is the word of my groin or the Word of our Adonai. In fact, I have never heard the Word from my rubbing! I can only think that some of us are chosen to provide the Word, and some of us are appointed to do the Word, and I am apparently a doer, not a hearer. When I depend upon others to direct my path, am I an unfaithful servant of He Who Is? And if my path be false, will Adonai be so angry as to destroy me and my family, or will He Who Is find my confusion at least honorable? I have known but one king, and he is good. He tries to find the Will of He Who Is, and is righteous by even your standard. Do you not have mercy even for him?"

Berechiah said, "Again, what is 'good?' How can there be mercy for the authority of men? How can there be righteousness found within corruption? Is an ass an ass only some of the time? How is faithfulness found with kings? Can you not tell an animal by its dung? What have our kings left behind for us?!"

"Now you think things beyond my thoughts. I must consider things I do not know. But tell me, am I counted as unrighteous if I am righteous in my private life and serve an unrighteous king?" asked Obadiah.

"That I do not know! I cannot ease your concerns nor make you angry. I do not know. I do know I serve according to the tradition of the Word passed from one to another to another to another, from Moses to us! Hear O Israel! The Almighty is One! We are one people."

"But how can you go one path and I another?" asked Obadiah.

"Obadiah. That is why when you ask entry into this tent, you are found to be a brother! How do I know a righteous man? Dare I turn a righteous man away from my tent? If I find one wanting in terms of my thoughts, but still pursuing righteousness, dare I turn him away? Has not every prophet found welcome in our tents? How many prophets did we know as prophets only after they passed from us? Have we not protected even the enemies of the kings of Israel and Judah? Not one of them asked a cup of wine from our hand. If one of us enters Jerusalem, dare you turn him away because he is Rechabite? Are we not tested again and again? Will we be found to be righteous?"

"Yes, we are all tested. There will always be a time when we choose a path from which we cannot back away. You have your path. Your people are witnesses to righteousness. You are a yardstick by which we measure ourselves. Kings have lain awake worrying how they will deal with you, for they know that if one does not obey, their authority is limited. But do you take pride in this?" asked Obadiah.

"The question we must answer first is, 'Who will you obey?' The second is, 'Why?'"

"That is simple. I obey the king, because he has been appointed and anointed to rule over Judah, and if he could, over all Israel."

And Berechiah questioned, "First, who said he was appointed king over all Israel? And second, if he does not do the Will of Adonai, is he still king?"

"I do not know the answer to either of your questions. But he is king!" answered Obadiah.

"You must know the answer, your life and the lives of your clan and this people depend upon it! If he is an ass, will you follow the ass? If he is a worshiper of idols, will you worship idols? If he says, 'Go to this place and do this thing' and you know it is not the Will of the Almighty, will you do it? You must decide! And you must decide these things before they happen or you will do evil and later claim ignorance! But it is not ignorance, it is carelessness of mind and therefore defiance."

"I would not do one thing that I know is unrighteous!" protested Obadiah.

"If I do not do what the king orders, tell me, Obadiah, am I sinning? If I disobey a king, will Adonai find fault with me?"

"It depends upon what the order is. Is the order righteous? If it is and you do not do it, yes, you sin. If it is not righteous, and you do not do it, it is not sin."

"Then tell me, Obadiah, how do you know if it is righteous or not righteous? Do you know? And does the king know you will judge his command? Have you now not made him less than king?"

Obadiah replied thoughtfully, "I must consider these things."

Berechiah said, "This means you must consider what you know of Adonai and His Will and His Word, and compare it to the order of the king, and if it is not right, you do not do it. If it is right, you do it. Is that not what you have said?"

"Yes, Ancient One. That is what I am thinking at this time."

"But, if you know what is right already, why are you not doing it already? Why do you need a king to tell you what to do? Or why do you need a king to tell you what not to do? If Adonai will hold me accountable for what I do and what I say, then I will bear no one else to have authority over me. I am accountable. I will determine what I do and do not do. If I do wrong, I deserve punishment; if it is really wrong, I deserve a great deal of punishment; but even within the punishment, I know Adonai is with me. And if Abaddon comes upon me due to the unrighteousness I have done, or my bones are too old to carry on, will not Adonai hold me accountable? If I do wrong because the king told me to do wrong, will Adonai not still hold me accountable? Or will He hold the king and me accountable? Or will He just hold the king accountable?"

"He will hold the king accountable. He will hold the king doubly accountable. But He will also hold you accountable, I think, friend Berechiah."

"Then, if you know that, and all men know that, what man, knowing our He Who Is, would dare raise himself up above other men and dare to be king? Either the man is a liar or he has no fear of He Who Is! Who would be king? Who would be king! If I know gold will jeopardize my relationship with He Who Is, dare I hold gold? If I know whoring will jeopardize my relationship with He Who Is, dare I go whoring? If I know that what I order might jeopardize the relationship of my subject with He Who Is, such fear would grip me that I would never utter another word!"

Berechiah shook his head. "In your Jerusalem, men and women plot for the throne! They kill for the throne! Priests vie for favors and vie to create kings! Evil. This kind of authority is evil. I would say that if an evil one states, 'do this,' I should not do it! After generation upon generation, I would say that the Word which came to us by Samuel is indeed the Word! Did not those things that did occur not sound like covetousness? Is therefore the king taking from me not the result of his covetousness, which is a breaking of the Covenant?"

"But do you not have the same authority over your people, as Nagid of the Rechabite? Do you not say, 'Go here' and one will go?" asked Obadiah?

"You confuse the kind of authority I possess as compared to the authority of the king. I say to one of age, 'Go here,' to my son, to my son's son, and to my son's son's son, and to my son's son's son's son. Yes. I have the authority of parent that passes generations. But each one, upon the age of accountability, has a choice. He may do or he may not do! They may stay or not stay in my tent. They may stay or not stay in this land. They may stay in my tent while my tent is in the land of Sheba, but they are mine by their choice. I am theirs by their choice. That is family. That is clan.

"But, Obadiah, what would the king say if I said to the king, 'Today I choose not to do as you say?' Would not my life be taken from me? But I say to my son, 'Son, it would please me if you went to this field and reaped for me.' And my son may say, 'Yes, father, I will go,' or 'No, father, have you not heard that I must be in Jericho tomorrow?' Or he may say, 'Father, that is contrary to the Word of Adonai. Please think about what you are doing.'

"Yes, I have authority in my family. But it is for those who submit to it. My sons and daughters bring honor upon themselves by this relationship. I honor them, and they honor me. As the Word says, 'Honor your father and your mother'—and may Adonai care for my father and my mother and my wife—'that your days may be long in this land which I have given you.' Now, sometimes I think that having long days is a punishment, but I have honored my parents, and I am honored. In this there is unbelievable joy. My heart bursts with pride at seeing my righteous son, Nathan or Shaphan or my daughter, Judith. What we have is incomparable. Gold and fields are worthless without family. That feeling and interaction is the foundation of our beginning to realize the Covenant we have with He Who Is. Is it not the same in your household, Obadiah? Is this the same authority as that of a king?"

"No, but also yes! But there are no children of my own…today," said Obadiah.

"There will be! But do you not understand what I say? He Who Is comes first; family and clan are second; my neighbors are third, be they of this people or not; and this dirt below our feet is fourth. Each of the last three I must care for as I care for the first. If I do the first, if I am righteous, the outcome of the following three is honorable no matter the pain inflicted upon us by others. We, I, we, have done as He Who Is Wills. Done. There is no room for a king.

"Then I do not need to worry, 'Is this king righteous?' or, 'Is this king not righteous?' They have no authority over me and mine. There is no question to be asked. I give to a king, any king, the same service I would give to anyone, from the poorest to the richest, from the humblest to the most powerful. We serve kings only as we serve anyone. We honor kings only as we honor anyone. Are we not known for our service?" asked Berechiah, Nagid of the Rechabites.

"It is easy for you in this tent to speak this way. But I was born in a house; I am nailed to a way of life that is in one place. The king knows where I am, and he will come and take me or mine." Obadiah still struggled to understand.

"Now you talk of fear! Is it fear that causes you to serve the king?" asked Berechiah.

"Just as much as you fear Adonai and do His Will."

"Dare you consider the fear and love I have of Adonai comparable to the fear you have of the king? When I feel the Shadow of Abaddon on my arms, will I think of my king? You, again, want to grant the king characteristics of a god! 'He creates fear in me as I fear Adonai.' Never! The king is a tool of evil ones. The king can be used by evil ones. Yes, I fear evil. Yes, I fear Adonai. But he is the messenger and do I fear the messenger? Never!

"Here we think completely differently. This is why at times we do not communicate well together. You think differently than I. If one comes in here and puts a knife to my throat, yes, I will be afraid, and, yes, I may even plead for my life, but I do not fear that man as I fear the One, unless that man can somehow separate me from the Almighty One." Berechiah struggled to be clear.

BERECHIAH

"There is emotion fear and there is being fearful. This king does not bring even the emotion of fear to my being. Nor did Manasseh, the once evil one, or Amon, the evil one. We are Israel. We are sons of Abraham, Isaac, and Jacob. We are of Moses and Joshua. How can you say, 'I am servant of Amon,' or, 'I am servant of Josiah?' Israel is beyond these petty men.

"Forgive me, I insult your king. I do not mean to insult your king, but I do mean to insult his authority. I do hear he is righteous. I hear of his prayers, even in private. I hear he spends time with prophets. But he must be careful which prophets he spends time with! Some will put ideas in his head, ideas for their own gain! You know that!"

"Yes, Ancient One. I see that. I heard the words of Ahijah and Isaiah and now this Jeremiah. And I fear He Who Is! Oh friend Berechiah! I humble myself before you! Pray that I do righteously! Would that I were your son and could do as you request! Would that I had your path assigned to me! But I can do no other than I am assigned, the best that He Who Is will allow me! And if I am wrong, let He Who Is still love me, for I will die trying to be righteous. And surely you have heard that I am righteous! If you have not, I fear for my being and my clan, for then maybe He Who Is has not heard! Ancient One! Comfort me in my distress!"

"I cannot comfort you, my friend Obadiah. But I have heard of your righteousness. I have heard of your fairness to the king and to his sons, to the Priests—though they do not deserve it—and that you treat even the beggar as fairly as you treat the king. For this righteousness, for doing right, you find favor with our One and therefore you must heed my words, as I once heeded the words of your great grandfather, and obeyed my father's father. Are you willing to hear my command to you?"

"Yes, I am your servant."

"First, hear and know the names and places of my five who remember the Word, the ones you call Possessors of the Word. Never repeat them but to the one you charge to know. And when you find a lad to be a worthy one to repeat the Stories, assign one to each of the five, and to their five do the same. Whenever possible never let one of the five be in the same place at the same time with another of the five, unless it is with you. All these are of my people. And with your own clan, there are but two? One is in your house but you do not know him. There is another in Tirzah, but he may now be dead. We have not been able to find him now for ten years. We know there were ones in Tirzah murdered by Omri as he wrote the Samarian Law. We must destroy that creature. If you find it, destroy it without a question. Yes, it was the Word, but it is written and there is error. If the sons of Joshua remembered through stories, so will we do. We will not agree to written words for the Sacred! It is too easy to change the words to fit the needs of priests and kings. Fear these men, for they will change righteousness to fit their own needs of the day. And others will follow as it will be to their advantage."

"You have no pity for priests and kings?"

"Obadiah, are you not able to be a priest? Are you not able to create an altar, prepare a sacrifice, and offer it unto Adonai? Why do you need a priest? We who worship, are we not all able to be priests? And are you not able to be a king? Can you not? How long have the true sons of Aaron been gone from us? Who now is a Levite? A dog could claim to be a Levite and who would know better or care? Soon there will be no Levite at all. Soon we will forget we are of Judah! Where are the twelve? We have lost our people, we are losing our tribe, and soon we will lose our clan, and will it not be soon we will even forget our family?!"

"May He Who Is forbid it! But to your question: Yes, I could be a priest and I could be king."

"First, why are you not? And secondly, what makes you different from them?" asked Berechiah.

"I am not, because I am not; I choose not to be a priest and do not want to be king. I differ, I swear, in that I cannot do as they."

"If you, a righteous man, know that you could not be a priest in the temple, and know you cannot be a king because you could not do as a king, how much more He Who Is who sees all and knows the hearts of all must reject those that are false! Is it only the prophet that is faithful? No. We who are simple tent dwellers are also faithful. We are not only faithful, but we are righteous, as righteous as we know. If we do not know, we cannot change to that which we should be. If there is something we should know, may Adonai Who has been with us, tell us, and we will do."

"Are you saying Josiah is false?" There was a touch of anger in Obadiah's voice.

"No. But I say that it is very unlikely that a king can be righteous. And it is more unlikely that he who has been a prince first can be a righteous king. If no one humbles or chastises or corrects me, will I not think of myself as a god? And once I have the ultimate prize, will I not be a god? Who will say otherwise? Of the kings, how many were righteous? David? He may have been beloved, but he was not righteous. If that is not remembered, the Masoretes will have done their work well."

"But his words, are not they good words? And his hymns, do not they disclose his heart?" asked Obadiah.

"When one says, this is a psalm of David, do you think David wrote it? I do not think so. He adopted them for his own, yes. Just as I take the words of Moses to heart, I take the words of David, but that does not mean I made the poetry. If you whisper something to Josiah and he orders it, is it not Josiah's order? If David sings a hymn, is it then not David's hymn? But that does not mean David created it. Again, you want to make gods—all-knowing and all-thinking and all-powerful and all-creative—out of men who are 'chosen,' maybe, but, surely, as simple as you and I.

"I may be creative today and think great thoughts and great wonders, but do not make a god of me! I may have wisdom, but I also may be a clever person, wise enough to repeat the words of others, but nothing more. When you hear, 'David said this, therefore it is true,' be careful. For how many men thought they were prophets but were liars? How many have told us that knew they were doing the Will of the One, but were simply selfish and mean of spirit? Do not confuse the Will of He Who Is with the will of men."

"How can it be that one charged by Nazir calling and by oath to protect the Word, can speak the way you speak of David or of priests?" asked Obadiah.

"Because I know this people. And I know how men will change our story to use others to their own advantage. I love David. But I do not love what others have made of David. I do not love the expectations that came from memories of David that really are not memories at all," spoke Berechiah.

"The Word is the same today, tomorrow, and yesterday. Yes. But the spoken Word never changes, and there is reason for your fear about the written Word. Do you, too, want the Word written?! Cannot both be changed?" asked Obadiah.

The Ancient One responded quickly, "Never written! Never! Yes, it can be written, but if you remove the Word from our memory, how our lives will change! I want the Word spoken, just as it has been received! When the Word is spoken, it is alive! Just as the breath of He Who Is created, our breath brings us to faith and righteousness. It becomes part of us. It becomes us! To write is to deceive. A lie today is truth tomorrow! But our Keepers of the Word, they dare not change their Word. They could not do so."

"The words you speak are true and are my thoughts. But there are others who think differently. And they are righteous men. I must consider all points. As you know, I will die protecting my Word Possessors! It is one of my reasons for being," said Obadiah.

"Think on it. And let my Rememberer speak it back to you when you will. Promise me you will think on it," spoke Berechiah.

"Does our faith depend upon this?"

"No, my friend, our faith never depends upon only one of us. If all the Chosen died at once, would not He Who Is call out of the earth those who are Chosen, and would they, too, not hear the Will of He Who Is? No. Do not think too much of yourself, nor do not think too little of yourself! You are. You are called of the One. Treat all persons as you would have He Who

Is treat you. None are special; all are special. None are gods; all are creations of Adonai. That is why you cannot kill wantonly in battle! That is why you cannot do as a king orders, because by doing as a king orders, you remove yourself from being righteous, or having to judge righteousness in another. Would you kill a righteous man?"

"No, I would not," stated Obadiah.

"How do you know that the man you meet in battle is not righteous?" asked Berechiah.

"I do not."

"And when you order your guard to kill, do you know whom you have taken it upon yourself to slaughter?"

"I do not know," stated Obadiah.

"Friend. Obadiah. Why do you have a guard with you? Why are there fifty guards with you this day, beyond your family, dressed in clothes of the king?"

"It was the king's wish. I think he fears what you will do this day. It is not my concern! I begged him not to send my corps."

"But do you fear me? Do you not know that when invited into my tent you are treated as a son? Why would I kill even an unrighteous son, let alone a righteous son? Your king insults me even from a distance."

"No, I do not fear you! I know who you are! But we all seem to do things we do not understand; we simply must do them. This was done. I could not change it," said Obadiah.

"But Obadiah, I am pledged to you; you are pledged to me. Was it just the will of the king?"

"Yes. But more, Ancient One. Let us say you are righteous and Adonai says, 'Come, meet with me, Berechiah, and let me see who you are!' Would you not be afraid? While in all you do and all you think you try to be righteous, would you not still fear? While I love Adonai, I would fear such a meeting! And so, while I tried not to fear you and knew I should not fear you, I fear you, and I think the king knew my fear when he asked of me my task for this fortnight. He ordered me, and I accepted."

"I see. And if I had you killed here, what good would your corps be?" wondered Berechiah.

"None. But they would avenge me."

"My Obadiah, my son who would be righteous, we are far from He Who Is. We of faith, will we ever be able to accept the faith of the righteous whom we do not understand? You make me sad. I fear that you may enjoy the authority of a king, for you enjoy saying to one, 'Do this,' and to another, 'Do that.' I see it in the pleasure even of the uniform. 'I am the king's own. I can order these men as the king orders others.' You may take pleasure in authority! This makes me sad."

Berechiah

Obadiah's response was swift, "I am always sad, though I love Adonai with all my heart, my soul, and my mind. I have killed many for defense of you and the Chosen of Israel. I am not able to be happy about what I do, but I am the best in doing it. I know that sometimes I do not make sense. I have been given authority; therefore I must use it. It is authority given to me by the king, who was given authority by Elohim. Who would cause righteousness in the land if there were no king? This I do not understand! Is there ever anything that does not make sense to you?"

"To answer your first question: He who Is would cause righteousness to be in the land, that is who! And secondly, yes, there are things that do not make sense to me. We are ones in tents and tend flocks and trade. We do not own fields though we use fields and meadows and mountains. We will not tend vines for grapes nor drink wine. But we will eat bread. We will eat good things of the ground. Some of our people will eat grapes and drink fresh juice, but they will not, and we will not, drink wine. I do not understand sometimes why we do as we do, but it was done by my father and his father and back to those who wandered in tents in the wilderness. Bread was provided by He Who Is. We, His people, did not prepare it. Therefore the Rechabites will not prepare it, but we will eat it. So, yes, there are things I do that I do not understand why I must do them. We are Rechabite. Therefore we do these things and do not do those things."

"Why do you not drink wine? Is it not good for you? Does it not aid in your eating and in how you feel? Yes, yes. I know there are those who drink and are fools, but anything to excess is wrong, no matter how good it is to begin with. The sun is good, but I shade myself from it; sleeping is good, but I know when to awaken and to rise. Wine is good, when I know when to stop," said Obadiah.

"I think we do not drink wine, not because it is possibly dangerous to some, but because it is a symbol of being in one place. I must have vines, I must protect those vines, I must protect my skins that I prepare; I must protect the land that grows the vine. No, I cannot do that. For while I firmly believe this land was given to us by He Who Is, I must be willing to sacrifice all—just let it go—because He Who Is Wills such! A king will not let me do that. The rich will not let me alone; they will take my sons to protect what they have. If I have vines, along with my sons, one day we will approve of the authority of the king and his way of life. While I firmly believe this land was given to us by the Holy One of Israel, the Holy One may take it away. How am I to know what is the Will of our Holy One?

"But Obadiah, I can remove the total condemnation of this people by not participating in its kingdom's activities. I must care for mine and my clan and a remnant will survive. Will I die in defense of what the Holy One wants to take away? Never. What He takes this day, He may return in a generation.

Does He take from those who are faithful? Yes. They are in the midst of the unfaithful. What is different? The difference is in the result of their suffering. If we all are faithful, will He take from all of us? No, but will we all be faithful? No. Look around you. If we return to our Adonai, after being chastised, will He provide once again? Yes. Where? Anywhere He sees fit.

"That is why Jerusalem is nothing," said Berechiah. "He Who Is can make us ten Jerusalems! Have not the prophets spoken of the doom of Jerusalem? Have you not heard the Word of Isaiah? Or this new Jeremiah? Does Jeremiah not say the same thing? Keep your eye on what is important. What is important is righteousness and faithfulness. A righteous man is worth ten kings. Where anyone bows down to the Almighty in earnestness is worth ten Jerusalems. The vine is not important; its fruit is a trap against the righteous."

"But, Berechiah, Nagid of the Rechabite, how can He Who Is give to us and take from us and give to us and take from us?"

"Just as you claim to be faithful and fail, and are faithful and fail! Return to our Holy One! Each act of each day should remind you to return! In spite of the chastisement and because of the chastisement, we return to the Holy One. It is within the Covenant that we find who we are and find our comfort."

"Is there hope as a kingdom?" asked Obadiah.

"Hope as a kingdom? No. Hope as a people? Yes. We are called to be a righteous people, person by person, Family by family, Clan by clan, and Tribe by tribe. We as a people do not need to place stone upon stone to prove who we are. We do not need a king to tell us what to do. A king did not choose us. We are because we are 'chosen' by the Almighty. We are, because we believe. We are, because we have a covenant with the Almighty One. And that always is, whether I am here in this tent at this Mizbeach near the gates of En-Gannim, or at Hazazon, or at Sumaria, or drinking at Kidron.

"I believe, friend Obadiah, that if a prophet says, 'This will happen when this comes to pass,' there is a ripple. The ripple is that that prophecy is not only true for that time the Word is first spoken but that Word will ripple as a stone causes a ripple in the water, from generation to generation. Is it not our prophets who remind us of who we are?

"Jerusalem! It will fall again and again, just as we make kings again and again and they fall in their own blood. Both detract from who we are. When we consider Jerusalem, we forget to consider our Elohim. We sacrifice for Jerusalem; do we sacrifice for the Almighty? It is easier to dream of Jerusalem than it is to dream of righteousness! When your desire is for a city, you will lose that city. But when you desire a faithful people, the Holy One of Israel will be with you! Wherever you go will be your city! The dirt where you sleep becomes your home.

Berechiah

Berechiah further affirmed, "For the faithful will be righteous. Righteousness flows from ourselves to our family, to our clan, to our neighbors, to our tribe, to our people, to all within our lands. Do not call upon Elohim and not be righteous. Do not call upon Adonai and mistreat your family or steal or cheat or kill your neighbor. Then you lie and you break the covenant. Do you think you can deceive or cheat the Holy One? Do you think you can hide evil, or be as the jackal with our Elohim? You will steal nothing from the Holy One! You will steal no blessing. You cannot pilfer love.

"When you buy a field for a piece of gold and sell it for five, you have cheated and lied. And there is a curse on the field and on the land. When you say, come and be my servant, and the man comes and serves you and you mistreat him, or treat him differently than a son or daughter, have you not brought shame upon yourself? Was not Jacob a servant fourteen years to gain the wife he desired? Treat your servant as you would have treated Jacob. Or Joseph, was he not a servant to a servant of Pharaoh? If you put a whip into the hand of your own overseer, do not be surprised when he uses it! So treat your servant as you would have had Pharaoh treat Joseph. And would you do less for your wife or a child?

"Obadiah, let us say this generation suddenly becomes righteous and Jerusalem is saved. I tell you the sons of this generation will forget and cause wickedness because this generation does not know how to teach righteousness to a child. If you struggle with your own righteousness, how will you teach a child? If you struggle with doing what you must do, how will you teach the child to do what he must do? Each generation must learn again and again the requirement by Covenant that we are not our own. Each generation must learn how to be obedient, each must learn how to be righteous, independent of their parent, but it is the parent that gives them the way to do this task. Each generation must hear its own calling and hear the call to return to our Holy One of Israel.

"Friend Obadiah, we must feel that we have been released from bondage and brought out of Egypt. Yes, there is no other land than this land. This is our land. If, by our behavior, we deny our Adonai, and our land is taken from us, and we have to repossess it, and we lose it again and regain it again and lose it again, how long will it be before we commit murder to take back that which was taken from us? We then take back not because the Holy One is with us, but because of what we want. Jerusalem becomes a sign for the takers. And takers forget who they are. If I hear Isaiah, there may be a Covenant with all of Elohim's creation. There can be no other land designated as our land. We cannot take and give and take and give. The day will come when we will have to murder to take. Fear that day, for our Holy One will know what we do.

"And that day I fear, for as righteousness has its joy, sin has its day of judgment. Jerusalem is ripe to be judged. What reason is it that our Prophets speak from Jerusalem? Is it that it is a holy place? Or is it that it is where evil is most identifiable? As long as we find Jerusalem to be our salvation, we will consider ourselves too important to fail. Just as we choose kings that lead us to our ruin, Jerusalem will be the city in which we vainly wait for salvation that will never come.

"Salvation does not come to a city." Berechiah shook his head. "Salvation comes to a people. Celebrate in Jerusalem? Yes. But no more than here, at these unhewn rocks, my son. For glorious things have happened here, and we, you and I, worship here. This unhewn rock is, then, just as valuable a place as any hewn rock in Jerusalem! This tent is as valued as any palace of the king. It is the Word of the Holy One of Israel, that is what is life! Not the word or desire of a king. It is this holy land under my foot that I value! Not a building that causes others to covet."

"You say many things I fear, Ancient One. No wonder kings wish to remove you from the land!"

"Do you bring me warning? Shall I move my tents this night?"

"No, my friend. But there are persons in the Temple and in the king's house who would not mind removing you from the land, you and your clan. There may be a day that I warn you."

"Thank you, Obadiah. And I will continue doing for you. Even doing for you when you do not know I am doing for you! But now, come, we have work to do at the City gate. The time approaches that we will act together as *zaqen*."

Chapter Four

✼ ✼ ✼ ✼ ✼

The Gates of En-Gannim

Berechiah the Rechabite and Obadiah the Zadikite, son of Amoz, were at the Gate of the Forgetful in the City of En-Gannim, they and their entourage, which included Berechiah's bearers, one who Remembers, called Word Possessor only by Berechiah, six servants bearing arms, and Obadiah's fifty of the king. At the Gate of the Forgetful there were waiting a spokesman of the city, the *zaqen* of the city, and a throng of two thousand, excited to see the Rechabite, known throughout the land, and the warrior, Obadiah, servant of the king, known as the Claw. The heat of the day had somewhat passed, but Berechiah was shaded by a small tent covering, placed high so that all could see him and hear.

"May the Holy One of Abraham, Isaac, and Jacob, the One who brought us to this land, be with you, Berechiah, *zaqen* of all Israel, sent to this land of Judah to judge us this day." It was Jeriah, the spokesman of the city. "We have anticipated your coming and have prepared for you. Have drink before we begin." And water was provided for all.

"We thank you, Jeriah, spokesman of En-Gannim, son of Pelatiah, who fought with Amoz against the Moabites. I present to you Obadiah, son of Amoz, warrior for Judah's King Josiah. He is here as I asked of him."

"Yes, we know Obadiah, who was once quick to destroy worshipers of Ba'al upon the king's orders. He has visited this place before and is feared, but we hear he is righteous, and your bringing him here this day causes us to welcome him as a *zaqen* of this city and Judah, one able to judge this people."

"Will it be, then, the three of us to judge?" asked Berechiah.

"No, Ancient One, it will be five of us, certainly a good number, so that where decisions are determined, no one can complain."

And Berechiah turned and whispered to Obadiah, who was sitting in the sun, far enough away so that more than Obadiah heard the comment, "And a good number so that if they do not agree with our wisdom, they may overrule us without our being able to take offense."

"Are your words for all the people, friend Berechiah?" asked the eldest *zaqen* of the city.

"No, my words are chosen here for few, but now that we begin, my words will be for all. Am I to be the one who speaks judgment?"

"Yes, it is you who will speak first. And if one *zaqen* objects, he will speak. Let us begin." And turning to the crowd, the spokesman said, "Who is to be first, or shall I appoint the case?"

There was absolute silence.

"There are those who fear righteousness and judgment, particularly from you, our guests," said Jeriah, *zaqen* of the city, to Berechiah and Obadiah. "Then I will choose: Bring forth Jachan and his son, Jehiel, and the mother of Jehiel, the woman called Avvah."

And out came a man of less than two score, throwing a young man at the feet of Obadiah. The boy, timid and slight, cowered before his father and the *zaqen*. The woman followed fearfully, wanting to pick up the son, yet fearing her husband's wrath.

"And what is it you seek, Jachan?" asked Berechiah.

"I want the law enforced this day, for this, my son, is worthless. He is a liar. He does not do as he is told. He defies me when I order him to do my will. And this woman encourages his defiance and dishonor by protecting him. The law is that if a son is defiant, he is to be stoned at the gate. This I demand."

"And is there more you will demand of us this day?" questioned Berechiah.

"I may, for this wife displeases me."

"Why is it that you come to us this day? Are you a Jehudi, son of Abraham, son of Judah? And is your wife Jehudijah?"

"This I am, and she."

"And do you follow in the path of righteousness as demanded of us by He Who Is?"

"I do."

"And do you have any other gods before Elohim?"

"But why do you ask these things, Berechiah? Is his not being of this city and a man amongst this people enough?" spoke Jeriah, the *zaqen*.

"We must determine if this man, who wants righteousness done according to the Law, is, in fact, one who is dependent upon the Law and fears and loves He Who Is, as did our great forefathers. Otherwise, we will do righteousness to an unbeliever. One cannot claim righteousness be done, and not be dependent upon that righteousness. I cannot allow one who comes for judgment today from us who represent He Who Is, and tomorrow find he seeks benefits from Ba'al or Astarte. If our judgment is of He Who Is, it is for that One's people. Would you expect me to judge an Egyptian, one of Asshur, or one from Bab'el?"

"No, Ancient One," admitted Jeriah. "Continue your questions."

"Again, Jachan of En-Gannim, are you of He Who Is?"

"I am. This I swear."

And Berechiah leaned to Obadiah and whispered, "I doubt his word. Look at his belt. Is that not the horns of Ba'al? Send a few soldiers to this man's house and have them search for Teraphim." And Obadiah ordered it to be done.

"And now, Jachan, speak to me and bear witness to the sins of your son," said Berechiah, Nagid of the Rechabite.

"He is defiant. If I send him to the fields I own, he will work but half a day and I must hire others to work the fields with him. When I say, 'Get me this,' he is defiant and will not get it. When I send him to purchase food in the market, he pays too much, and wastes my money. When he sleeps, he sleeps outside to shame me. Do I not provide a warm house for him? Why would he shame me by sleeping outside? And he lies to me. And he has raised his hand against me. For this I now demand his blood."

"Let us deal with each of these. Bring me one who has worked the fields with this young man. Is there a man here that has worked the fields with Jehiel?"

And in an aside, Jeriah said to Berechiah, "I regret there may not be, for few would work for this man, and if they did, they might fear swearing as to what has happened."

"Is there no one who has worked the fields of Jachan?" called out Berechiah.

"Yes, I am one who worked too many days in his fields," spoke a farm worker.

"And did this boy do a day's labor for his father?" asked Berechiah.

"He worked as hard as a boy could work. When the sun was coming up, we were in the fields. When the sun went down, we were in the fields."

"But did he work all day?" shouted Jachan.

"No, he did not work all day, for when the sun was high, we rested and ate and he did the same. When we needed water, he went and got it for us. When we believers left the field and left the remnant for the poor, Jachan ordered the field be cleared completely, and the son refused, saying, 'This is not the way we were taught.' And for this defiance, Jehiel was beaten— beaten until he could not rise."

"He defied my order!" said Jachan, the boy's father.

"Is this true?" asked Berechiah, and from the crowd came many: "We so witness."

"And whose order should a son obey? His father or the Will of the Holy One of Israel?" asked Berechiah.

"His father, for that is the Law," stated Jachan. "If I sin in my command, I will be punished by Adonai, will I not? It is not for my son to decide."

"That depends upon whether the son is a man, and whether or not the son knows if what he is assigned to do is sin," said Berechiah.

"And when will a son know that? When can a son judge the words of his father?" asked Jachan.

Berechiah became pointed, "When the son is able to see what is done is sin, then he cannot do as the father orders. If he does, the sin is then also upon him. If not, could not a son wallow in sin as a pig in mud and fear no guilt, as he did as his father ordered? Do we think we can fool our Almighty One?"

"What you then do is to set the son over the father!" Jachan was angry.

"If the son is righteous, the son may choose not to do the father's command. That does not mean the son is over the father. If I say to my servant, 'Go, sell this land and cheat this man by selling the land at an unfair price,' and my servant refuses, is the servant disobedient? He is not disobedient; he is a faithful servant. Does he become my master by refusing my command? No. What he does is call me to account. That is why we are family; that is why we are clan and tribe and people of the Holy One. Dare I beat such a servant when he reminds me of who I am? He is not disobedient; he is faithful. He is faithful, as he causes me to be righteous, and that alone is our first task. And from your anger let us see what toll you have exacted from your son for his faithfulness. Tear the rags from the boy's back."

Jachan tore the rags from the back of his son, throwing him down before Berechiah.

Berechiah ordered his servant to pick up the young man and showed the scars and open wounds on the back and the legs of the young man to the gathered crowd. And the crowd groaned.

And to the people, Berechiah the Rechabite said, "If I am one Chosen by the Holy One of Israel, is not my son also Chosen? And how shall I treat one Chosen by our Elohim? If I beat my son, will he not turn from me? Then on whose head is his sin? Will my son not turn against the Holy One? Is this not on my head? Treat your son as you would care for your own faith! Do not be a liar to your child. Do not lie about our He Who Is! Are we to fear our parents when we do righteousness? Would we fear the Holy

One when we do righteousness? We might fear others, but never would we fear the Holy One! Why should a son doing righteousness fear his father? This is not righteousness in this home, but evil."

To the servant he said, "Take the woman and remove the cloth from her back."

The servant did as he was told. The woman was not ashamed but stood. Her back still bled from the beating of the day.

So Berechiah said to the woman, "Why has this been done to you?"

The woman was afraid and said, "I must be quiet this day. I cannot speak against my husband. Do not ask me to."

And Berechiah thought on these things.

Then he asked, "What fields do you own, Jachan?"

"I own four fields of grain one may see from the wall, and two groves of fruit and one of grapes. You will not hold this against me, Rechabite?"

"Do not play me for the fool. Because I do not choose your path does not mean that I do not understand your path. But how is it that you own these fields?"

"They were provided to me upon the death of my wife's father."

"Therefore it is this woman who has brought you wealth and brought you honor in this community, and yet you dishonor her, her family, and her father. Did you beat her like this before the death of her father?"

There was no response.

"If he were here, would you beat her? What would he say if he saw this, his daughter, with these wounds? What would his honor require of him? Daughter of Israel, did he beat you like this when your father was alive?"

There was no response.

At this time, the soldiers of Obadiah returned with a sack, Berechiah knew what was in the sack, and ordered them strewn before the *zaqen*.

Then Jachan was afraid. He knew the things to be idols of Ba'al taken from his own house.

And Berechiah ordered, "Bind him."

Then Berechiah the Rechabite said, "There is great unrighteousness in this house of En-Gannim. First, Jachan lied as to who he was. He wanted righteousness—a judgment against his son, for the law states that a disobedient son may be stoned to death. He wanted the righteousness of He Who Is, but he is not of He Who Is. If you are of the Holy One of Israel, you may ask for the righteousness of He Who Is. But if you are not righteous, what right do you have? You are a liar and blow wind. Your own words and actions condemn you."

Berechiah's voice hardened, "This man asks for righteous judgment, and yet he is a liar and a thief, for has he not stolen what belongs to He Who Is? If I am to leave a grain in the field for the poor, that grain is not my grain nor the grain of the poor, but the grain of He Who Is, Who commanded it be left in the field. You cannot pick and choose when you will be righteous and by whose word you will have others be judged, and not be judged yourself! If you are to receive honor from your son, is it not true that you also must honor your son?

"There even is honor in disciplining. Does not this disciplining begin at birth? When a child turns away, does not all Israel weep, and more so the mother and father of that child? The parent had better be humble as he points to the guilt of his child! For does he not point the finger at himself also? If you create a righteous son with the Holy One's help, does not that son bring you honor? The blessing we have this day is that while the father was not righteous, the son was righteous. And where did that righteousness come from? Where was it learned? Surely not from this father who has his idols. No." Berechiah shook his head.

"Come, sister. Take my *dagal*. Has not this *dagal* seen much honor? Has it not seen many lands? Do not all who see it know who owns it? Take this *dagal* and find relief. You are now protected by it. Where was righteousness learned? Was it not from the heart of this woman, the very woman who through the work of her father brought wealth to this family?"

And Berechiah the Rechabite leaned forward and said to the *zaqen*, "Hear my judgment and stop my words if you find fault."

Berechiah said to all the people gathered at the gate, "Hear, my people, the judgment of the *zaqen* before this city wall, according to the traditions of Israel. First, this father will not have his request fulfilled by the Law of He Who Is, for he is not of He Who Is. But in this land given to us by He Who Is, this boy is now a man, free from the command of his father and he cannot be bound over to service to another. He is free to choose his path.

"Secondly, this man Jachan found fault with this woman and if judgment had been reached against his son, is there a doubt he would not also have divorced this woman and claimed all that is hers? So, he is hereby granted a bill of divorce, and he is free of her. Not only is he free of her, but he is also free of the responsibility of caring for the fields of grain and groves of fruit and grapes that came to him from her father. These are to remain with the woman as given by her father, who would want his fields cared for by a righteous man. Is there a widower here? Is there a righteous man here this day?" asked Berechiah.

There was quiet. The people were afraid. "Is there not a widower able to care for this woman and this young man while they learn a new life together? If there be such, let him speak now."

There stepped forward one who was crippled, and he said, "I am Jemuel, servant of Josiah, in battle wounded for my king. I have nothing but my word and honor which have never been found wanting. I have a small shelter a half-day's walk from here. I am not Rechabite, nor Kohathite nor Prathonite nor Zadikite nor of any clan, but I consider myself righteous before the Holy One of Israel. I have known Obadiah the Zadikite, for I fought with him and protected him."

Berechiah turned to Obadiah the Zadikite and asked, "Do you know this man?"

And Obadiah said, "Come forth, Jemuel, friend of Josiah and friend of my father! Why have you not come to me? Are you afraid of the Zadikites?"

Jemuel came forth slowly, as his legs were worthless.

Obadiah said, "Yes, this is a man who is worthy. I attest to his righteousness."

When Jemuel came forth Berechiah instructed him as to how he was to deal with the woman and her son, and Jemuel accepted the charge. Berechiah ordered Jemuel to leave with the woman and the young man.

After the three left the people at the gate, Berechiah said, "As for this man Jachan, he is to be removed from this land and his name will now be Jehiel, for 'He Who Is snatches away,' for righteousness was expected and deceit was found. Take him bound to Dibon in the land of the Moabites, and give him to them, him and his idols. Take the house and the belongings in the house and sell them and give him this money, that he may not curse us saying, 'They took from me what was rightfully mine.' There is nothing in this land which is now rightfully his. Take him away."

There were two thousand quiet, as were the *zaqen*. And Berechiah let it be quiet.

Then there came forward a man whose age was two score, but he was in poor health. And he said, "Honored *zaqen*, your word this day has been hard, but your judgment shows wisdom. I, too, come to you for righteous judgment. I come fearful, for while I try to be righteous, who knows what the Holy One of Israel will find fault with in my heart! I, too, come for righteous judgment against my son who dishonors me."

"What is your name and where is your son?" asked Berechiah.

"My name is Malchiel, although most poke fun at me and call me Qaton. My son refused to come here with me. He is a big boy, and I am unable to cause him to do as I say. I cannot even beat him, for he would take the rod from my hand."

"We will hear you. Obadiah, send three to get this boy. Have them take one who knows the boy with them."

So the boy was brought to Berechiah the Rechabite and the *zaqen*. As Malchiel said, the boy was large for his twelve years—strong, unruly, and rude.

Then Berechiah said, "Come here, boy, that I may see your face."

The boy replied, "Why? Who are you that I would care?"

Berechiah said to the boy, "Because I told you to do so, and I am your *zaqen*. What I say is reasonable and I have been respectful of you and your father."

"I do not care about what you think of me or of my father. So I will stay where I am."

And Berechiah signaled his servant by eye, who immediately knew what to do, and he took the boy by the scruff of the neck and placed him, kneeling, in front of Berechiah.

The boy remained disrespectful and said, "Curse you and him!"

The boy's language brought shame to the father, and the father wept.

And Berechiah said, "Adonai listens only to the curses of righteous men." He signaled his servant, who adjusted the boy's attitude.

The boy cried out, "Stop him! That hurts!"

Then the servant raised the boy up in front of Berechiah and Berechiah said to him, "Do you wish to strike me as you have your father?"

And the father wept bitterly as he knew the cost of these words.

The unruly boy lunged forward to strike Berechiah, but the servant snatched him in mid-air and caused pain so that the boy began to cry.

"Do you need a rod to train you? Blessed is the child who learns without the rod. Is it only a rod that will correct your behavior? Why cannot it be simply your thoughts that change your behavior? If it is only the rod, let it be the rod."

The servant caused the boy to hurt and he quieted and cried.

"Here we have a child who thinks himself a god, able to do as he wishes, be an adult, curse as an adult, and yet not suffer as an adult. He has clothes on his back which are fine, and it is obvious he is well-fed, yet he is not gracious and thankful. He is defiant and seems to have no fear of authority and clearly no fear of his father nor of these *zaqen*. Why has no one corrected this boy?"

A *zaqen* near to Berechiah said, "Because we love his father and respect him, we did not want to bring shame upon him."

"But now you have hurt him even more as he has a son who will become unrighteous and disrespectful as an adult. Have you honored Malchiel or dishonored Malchiel by your inaction against his son?" asked Berechiah.

He turned to the boy and asked, "Do you only correct your behavior when you are in pain? If that is so, we will provide one for you who will cause you pain, who will remind you of your limits on a daily basis. You will learn your place and learn how to treat others with respect. How much more righteous and fair is the son who, seeing the weakness of the father, still honors him and does as he is asked. If you do not fear your father, how will you ever respect him? Fear does not only mean fear of punishment, but also fear of disfavor. Fear of the One Who Is is the beginning of wisdom.

Berechiah

"How does a little one learn to fear the Almighty? First, he must learn limits within his own home, within his family; then within his town and clan, and then his tribe. He is then able to seek our Holy One of Israel. If I have no limits, why do I need a god? I am a god! And if I am a god, I will do as I wish and who is there to judge me? One who knows his limits will be of service to his people. One who thinks he can do what he wants when he wants is first a dishonor to his family and then to his people. If you do not put a child on the path to righteousness, you do damage to your people and hurt yourself," Berechiah instructed the people.

"On the one hand, always treat the child fairly and righteously for goodness' sake, particularly the poor child, as they teach us who we really are. But on the other hand, treat the child fairly and righteously within discipline, for from discipline comes the backbone of the child, which becomes the backbone of the people. If there is no discipline, there is no righteousness nor will. Boy, I know you do not understand all of this, but you do understand my right hand."

"You can stick your hand up your own ass."

Berechiah moved his right hand in a circular fashion and the boy was moved in a circular fashion and held high. The boy cried as he began to learn shame and began to learn fear.

Berechiah said, "Hear my judgment and stop my words when you find fault."

And the father fell on his knees and wept, for he feared for his son whom he loved.

Berechiah said, "Here is a boy who deserves the rod, if any child ever deserved the rod. I find fault with the community that they saw but did not help the father. I find fault with the father that he did not ask for help from the *zaqen*, or even a righteous neighbor. I find fault with the son.

"While he will soon be of age, his manhood will now not occur for two years. During that time I provide this faithful servant of mine, a man who has served me well, to protect this family. I now place him on loan to the father to enforce the will of the father. This servant will report to me. The servant may need to discipline, and the father will accept the discipline of this worthy servant. Upon the end of two years, the father and the son and the servant will appear before these *zaqen* of this city and the *zaqen* will determine whether or not the boy is to be given manhood.

"If and when he is found worthy, such will be done, and this, my servant, will be free to go as he wills. Until that time I will care for my servant's family. Upon completion of this task, the *zaqen* of this city will buy two fields and a tent and give it to my servant. The father will also purchase a field and give it to my servant to do with as he wishes. And for two years this boy will be the servant of my servant, and upon completion of the two years, this boy will return to his father's house. May he then understand the love of his father, and respect his father, and love this our people and respect this our people."

There was quiet.

"Be there a challenge to this judgment?" asked Jeriah the *zaqen*. And there was no word.

The servant stood before Berechiah, bowed, and took his hand and kissed it. The blackness of his hand shone from the tears that fell.

Berechiah said, "Go, faithful servant, and teach this boy to be a man. You will then care for yourself and your family in this land you now love. May the Holy One of Israel go with you! Go!"

Then the father and the servant, carrying the boy by the scruff of the neck, left the presence of the people. And the crowd was silent.

Then there were brought to the *zaqen* thirty cases looking for righteous judgment, for the people found the judgment of the *zaqen* to be righteous, and all gave thanks to the Holy One of Israel.

And there was brought to Berechiah one accused of putting his manly thing into ewes, and accused of other acts of sodomy. The man feared for his life.

Berechiah asked of him, "Are you one of us, of the House of Israel?"

The man said, "I am not." And he showed that he was not circumcised.

Berechiah asked, "Does not your people find evil in this act, or at least, is it not considered perverse? Is there a people that finds this acceptable?"

"Even here there are those who take what they want and do what they want. Is that not true? Is not only the act different? I do not steal from others and I do no harm to others. What harm is there then in what I enjoy?" asked the man.

"Nokri, do you justify what you do only by comparison to another? Will there not always be a more base man in your own eyes than the sin you commit? Does that lessen your shame or lessen the evil you commit?"

The man stated, "It is only my affair what I do. Did I hurt you? Even if there is shame, how have I brought shame upon you? Why, then, is my behavior a concern of yours?"

"It is because we as a people are called apart by our Holy One, and this land, simple though it be, was given to us on condition, and in this place we hold ourselves not to our own standard, but the standard of the Holy One who called us out. To do one is to deny the other," said Berechiah. "The sin of one affects all of us as a people."

"With respect to you, Ancient One, there is none but myself. I decide what I will do. There is no god that will make me do anything. What is a god that I should be mindful?" asked the Nokri.

BERECHIAH

"But what of women, or children, or the weak? What stops another from taking from you? Or doing what he wills? When you are the biggest and strongest, I can understand your words, but otherwise I would live in constant fear in your house and in your land."

"Is that why you create a god?" asked the *nokri*. "To assure protection of the weak?"

"Ah! That is the issue! Is our Holy One a god of wood or stone or our own will of the moment, or truly the One?! Can I tell you of our Adonai's hand?! But you would not believe, because you do not want a limit on who you are or what you are able to do. Yet you take advantage of our civility and generosity and protection. You would have it both ways, just as the child of Malchiel. You would take without giving. You would find shelter without responsibility. You would be protected by our own restraint, but remain unrestrained. You sneak and pilfer from the first fruits from our own painfully learned and tried righteousness. You not only sin, but you have no honor. You are as true as your word. You take what you want when you want it."

"As you have said it," said the *nokri*.

"In this land, as one of our people, you would surely die. But, as you are not of our people and not of this land, you will be thrown out of this land to the land of Bab'el and abandoned there. You will take what is yours. Four soldiers will accompany you to the border and my *dagal* will protect you until Bab'el. At Bab'el, you will find the tents of my people and return my *dagal*. If it is not returned, you will surely die."

"I honor you for your word. I will return the *dagal*," said the *nokri*.

"I do not do you a favor as you think, but your blood and dishonor will not be on our hands."

At this there was murmuring, for there were many who would have stoned the *nokri*.

Upon completion of all the complaints, Berechiah, Nagid of the Rechabite, and Obadiah, Nagid of the Zadikite, withdrew from the city and the Gate of the Forgetful. The wisdom of Berechiah the Rechabite was honored. And Obadiah drew strength from the wisdom of his friend, and was seen as wise. They withdrew to the tents of Berechiah, and it was approaching evening time.

Chapter Five

✳ ✳ ✳ ✳ ✳

Visitation

Then Berechiah, Nagid of the Rechabite, with Obadiah, servant of the king and Nagid of the Zadikite, departed from En-Gannim with the family of Berechiah, and the servants of Obadiah and several soldiers of the king.

And Berechiah said to Obadiah, "Let us take a side road to visit two friends of years past. I would like you to examine our people, and determine the righteousness and faithfulness of our Chosen. Let us leave our friends behind. Pick me the strongest of your men and let them carry me on a litter of less dignity, for you and I and they will be poor travelers in this land for the rest of this evening. Let the others follow farther behind."

"You have my life in your hands!" said Obadiah.

"For a lot longer than you have ever known," replied Berechiah.

"Am I to understand that your right arm has been stretched out over my life without my knowing it?" asked Obadiah.

"Yes." replied Berechiah. "I have been completing a vow I took many years ago to your fathers, before you were born, before your father was born, and when your grandfather was a boy. I was a young man, and for services rendered to me, I was designated to serve and protect you, the third one I have so protected. I soon will have completed my vow, only by my death, Elohim willing."

"And, in return, there will be a response expected on my part, will there not?" asked Obadiah.

"As you say, it will be." The Ancient One grinned. "Come, let me be carried, and you walk by my side. At times, you could provide rest for one of your soldiers. Please, remove their *dagals*. Where we go, I do not want anyone to know who we are. They may keep their weapons."

They walked so far that when they were atop a hill, they could not see the city. While Obadiah knew of the fields, he was not familiar with the men of the area. Darkness added to his apprehension.

"At this house we are approaching, let us stop, and at the gate, let me call out to the family therein."

"As you wish," said Obadiah.

When at the gate to the house and outbuildings, Berechiah called out, "Jehudi! Hear the word of a stranger wandering through this land! We need water and shelter for the night for an old man and his sons."

There was no response.

Again Berechiah said, "Friend of a traveler, come to the door, as we seek shelter! At least come and look us in the eye! We only request water and shelter for the night!"

And from the house came a voice, "Who is it so foolish to travel at evening time? Who would come to my door and threaten my family at this time? What is your name?"

"I am a Jehudi, with my sons; I am a Rechabite. Do you not have water to provide to us? And are we not able to lie this night in your stable?" asked Berechiah.

"Who are you that I should provide my water for you? And who are you that I should open a door for you this night? No, traveler, you need to continue to wander away from this house and away from what is mine. What I have made, I keep, and what I own will remain mine. If you want something, you may pay for it, as I have paid all of my life. If you want shelter, earn it!"

And Berechiah said, "But we have traveled a long way. Do you not have mercy on us? Even a drink? Are you so indifferent to others that you cannot remember a time when you were in need and a friend helped you and your father?"

"What is my business is my business, and has nothing to do with your request. Who I owe, I owe, and it is not your business. If you want water, there is a *wadi* up the road. Satisfy yourselves there and sleep under the stars as your foolishness deserves. And, no, there has been no one. Now be off. It is dark now, and you will need to make yourself a shelter."

"There has been no one to help you?" Berechiah was disbelieving. "If this is true, what would you deem an appropriate compensation by our One?"

The voice said, "Why do you mention He Who Is in this? My righteousness is not a concern of yours. Who are you to examine who I am? You are nobody, an old, dirty man soon to die. Go, do not burden me with your questions. If I lie, may I lose all that I have before my death, and may my sons be without a place to lay their heads—like you!"

"May it be as you say," spoke Berechiah.

And they departed from that house. As they proceeded, Berechiah spoke to Obadiah, saying, "Here is a man whose father was a servant in my house. He chose to be a servant as the poverty of his situation was beyond compare. He had seven children who were starving and we sheltered all of them and his wife. This one was the eldest boy. The father worked hard for me for seven years, and I rewarded his service not only with granting his freedom at the time of Jubilee, but I provided the gold necessary to purchase the four fields surrounding this home. He borrowed to build, interest free, as righteousness requires and is our custom for the poor.

"Some of the children became soldiers, and some were married to righteous men, but this eldest son inherited his father's lands and the home. Now the father is forgotten, his brothers and sisters are forgotten, and who he is is forgotten and He Who Is is forgotten. You heard his words; he condemns himself, and what is worse, he condemns his sons. Here he is, far from the city, and who is there? No one. For while he can speak of sons, his sons treat him as he treated his father. There may be fire in the hearth of this house, but it is a cold place. Come, let us move on, and let me rest until we get there."

Over two hills lay another house, simple of construct, with few outbuildings and no light. At the gate, Berechiah called out, "Hear me, servant of the One Who Is, and provide to me and my servants a cup of water!"

There was no response. Berechiah called out again, "Hear me! Is there no one home? Hear me! For we are weary travelers needing water and a place to lie the night. Is there no one in this place?"

From inside the house came the words, "Stranger! I hear your voice, but give me time to dress. I and mine are already sleeping this night, for tomorrow comes early and there is work to be done! But please! Wait a moment and water is yours, for you and your servants!"

"He Who Is will be with you!" said Berechiah.

"Your blessing is important to this house, stranger. My sons are faster than I, at my age. There is one coming to you now with water. Drink your fill, for tonight I will treat you as I treat my sons. Was not Moses taken in by Jethro? And can I do less, for maybe you or yours will be another Moses!" And water was presented by a young man.

"Thank you, friend. The water does refresh," said Berechiah.

"Here comes a second son with bread!" And it was provided by another young man. "How many are you?" asked the owner.

"There are six of us; do you not want to know who we are?" asked Berechiah.

BERECHIAH

"There will be time for that. You are hungry and you thirst. Let me provide for you, and then we will talk and you will let me know who you are and where you are going."

"He Who Is must be with this home," said Berechiah.

"We are simple people, persons of faith, who do not know much about the Law, but what we do know, we do!"

And the homeowner, somewhat deformed in the legs, came to the door and continued by saying, "Do not be fearful of how I look. I was hurt many years ago. But I do well, particularly given my age of two score! Here, have my youngest sons provided your fill? Do you need more before you bed for the night?"

"No, we have plenty, thank you. But a place in your barn, that would be pleasing."

And the farmer said, "You are kind to call it a barn! But here, come close. I think I remember your voice. Let me see your face! You will surely lie down in this house this night, you and your servants. Let me come and greet you! Son, blow for my eldest, Letushim, that he may help me. Stay, traveler! My eldest son—who by his name reminds me of my suffering and yet great joy—will come and provide a lamb for us and for you!"

"No, friend, stay where you are. We deserve no lamb. Bread and water is plenty!"

"Berechiah! It is you! If you are alive, Moses crossed the Jordan! Berechiah!"

The farmer fell to the ground in front of his sons, and wept, and crawled to the cot of Berechiah. He took Berechiah's hand and his tears fell on his hand. Obadiah was moved by the love the farmer showed Berechiah.

"Blow the yobel, my son. Blow for Lettie. Oh Berechiah, how is it you come to me this night? How is it I have to guess it is you? Why do you not have trumpets play and soldiers dance and petals be strewn when you come to my home? Come, let us erect a Mizbeach, a high place, and celebrate and give thanks to our One Who Is, that you have come to my home wanting water, and I have been found worthy to offer bread and water to my friend and guide! May our Adonai be praised that you have come to me and I am able to serve you!"

"Yes, my lost brother! I have come in the night! And you have shown your faithfulness beyond compare. But it is not for you to serve me this night! Let me blow my yobel and let me bring my tents to surround this house. Let us celebrate together. Let me serve you from our blessings provided by our One Who Is. I give thanks this night! Let me show it by providing for you! And where is your wife?"

The farmer was quiet. Then he said, "She has been dead nineteen years. She died in childbirth with this, my youngest."

"And you have not had a woman warm your bed nor comfort you? Have you not been able to find love again?" asked Berechiah.

"I do not want love again. I loved my wife forever. I will continue to honor her as I did while she was alive. This I learned from you! Yes, I am lonely at night, and during the day. But I have my sons, and they now have children! Oh Berechiah! I am getting old. Not as old as you must be! I have told my children of you—and my grandchildren! You must be at least four score and more!"

"Yes, old friend. I am old, but I still remember!"

"And is that not who we are? We are ones who remember!" said the farmer.

"Yes, so let us blow our yobels and let us celebrate! Let us light fires and remember!"

And it was done, and there came a time in the evening that Berechiah and Obadiah spoke with each other.

"You have heard the story of this man, Obadiah. Poor unto death, and we brought him in and helped him recover from his wounds. In return he served us well for ten years. He took a wife while with us and they left our tents for this land which we provided for him. He worked hard to pay us for this land, and he developed a herd of sheep and goats, and now he has ten fields and a thousand sheep and a hundred goats and twenty ass and a horse. If a stranger comes by, he is welcomed into his home, be he of this land or not, be he poor or rich, all are treated the same and welcomed the same. Tell me, Obadiah, tonight you saw two men, both were provided with the same from within the same tent, and yet they chose different paths in life. Who is it that is righteous? Who is it that He Who Is will remember?"

Obadiah said, "Truly this man is beyond compare! Before he knew who you were, he offered you his water, his bread, and a place to sleep. He treated you as he would a relative, if not a son. And he would have washed your hands with his tears, in demonstration of his love."

"And the other?"

"He has chosen his path. Not only does he not follow the Law, he is not faithful nor righteous, nor is he a friend. He does not remember, and condemns himself in his ignorance. He condemns his sons by not telling them his story nor the story of this people."

"You speak well and right, Obadiah. Hear and remember these things I have learned. Family is those whom you have chosen and who have your blood or carry in their veins who you are, out of your seed. I sit here because my father made it possible, and his father, and his father, and his! Good or evil, right or wrong, they are behind me. I must choose what is right and good, what is righteous and faithful, what is the Word, and determine if what was taught to me stands the test of the One's Word. If it does, it must remain a part of me. If it does not, I must place it aside. How can I condemn my father? I cannot. But I must change what he did if it was not righteous. Upon that foundation I then move amidst neighbors and travelers and city dwellers. And I must serve. Be I poor or rich, I must serve.

"Wealth condemns all too easily! Wealth must be limited, Obadiah, or it turns one's head away from He Who Is, for who needs the One when gold and silver and cold stone walls protect? With the child of a concubine, protected and honored in comparison to most, food is provided; there are walls to protect. What does this child know of suffering? What does this child know of righteousness or despair or illness or death or deformity? In such a cocoon there is life but no need for faith; there is breath but no need for understanding. And the sons of kings and priests, are they not in a cocoon? What do they know of what is righteous and what is evil? 'Good' is what they want! 'Good' is what they demand. But this is not our 'good.' Who will stop them from their self-destruction?

"Now I have some understanding for those whose fathers' greed binds and blinds their children, but what of one who has experienced mercy? Is not his sin doubled by his not remembering? If one forgets, will there be forgiveness still? How? I do not know. But I do know this man, this simple farmer, is blessed beyond measure, for he knows who he is, knows who the Almighty is, and knows what is important in life and in death! We must honor those who are like this man! We must honor their sons so that their sons do not forget! It is not that this man remembers what I did for him. No. He knows why I did what I did for him, and that is what matters. That is what changes this situation from my personal glory, to glory for He Who Is. I open my tent to all, even the thief, for that is what He Who Is expects of me, and of you.

"Here, Obadiah, the chain of gold which holds a family together is created anew by this man. Where is it the child feels the safest? Where is it the child learns his place in the world? It is in a family, not simply the husband and the wife, but the grandfathers and grandmothers, and great grandfathers and great grandmothers, and sisters and brothers and cousins and uncles and aunts. This is family. This places a child in a net of safety beyond compare. Even the Chamber of Princes in the Temple cannot protect the prince. For there are those who lie and cheat to create kings. But here in these tents there is peace, because we make peace. Even in war there is peace.

"Choose your path very carefully, Obadiah. Where you take your family will determine their character! And you cannot think only of your sons and daughters, but you must think of their sons and daughters and their sons and daughters. When you think in terms of generations past and generations to come, your behavior changes, for it places in perspective who you are and what is expected. Can the righteous turn away the poor wanting a drink of water? No, and do not think that just because you place yourself in a situation where no one comes to your door for a drink of water or piece of bread that your word has not already said, 'No! I will not give you water or bread!' Just because you do not see the poor does not mean you are not responsible for their care and particularly the care of their children. If I build a wall, do the poor disappear? If I build a temple, will unfaithfulness disappear and righteousness flourish? No. We must watch and see all things."

"Berechiah, you speak too much too quickly! Let me think on these things!"

"There is no time! I do as I do as it was directed by my fathers to do and I find what is being done to be righteous. I will not change my path, nor will I change what I teach to mine, or have taught to mine! What are you teaching your family? Judge righteously. Search the heart of those you serve, because their evil will be compounded, or their good seen in your children. Do not say, 'I do this because my father said this,' or 'I do this because my king said to do this.' Say, 'I do this because I think it is right, because I think it is the Will of the Almighty, and I must do it.' Today you saw a child able to choose that his father was not doing right, and he paid a cost beyond what any child should pay! What cost will you and yours pay for the evil a king will do or ask of you for his own sake?" asked Berechiah.

"What king? Do you think Josiah is evil? Is what he is doing wrong? Has he not cleansed the Temple and defeated towns where Ba'al is worshiped? Has he not killed priests of Ba'al and Astarte and Molech? Has he not tried to divine what it is He Who Is wants of him and his people?"

And Berechiah replied: "Is the Temple cleansed? Are his priests pure? I do not believe it. As for what you ask, I am not sure. But do you not remember the prophet Ahijah? These kings will not be with us long. Why do you think that is?"

"I do not know. I do know there are faithful and righteous Prophets in Jerusalem at this time and in cities around Jerusalem. Shemaiah of Kiriathjearim or Huldah or the Kohathites or Buzi of the Zodokite clan. Is not Hilkiah the chief priest worthy? Or Shaphan the scribe? Are not good teachers found in Jerusalem teaching at our school? Yes, there are serious problems with princes and priests and false prophets, but that does not mean He Who Is has abandoned the sons of David! I have chosen to serve the king, as did my father, as did his father, just as you have chosen your path! Yes, your words about family are true, but as regards the kingdom, I cannot turn to your path!

"Obadiah, you are choosing a mistress that knows no god. The kingdom is nothing. It is not to be loved or hated or pitied or healed. It is nothing. It is the people that are 'Chosen,' not the kingdom. The kingdom creates itself. The king will claim your whole being. He will know your needs and use them to his own advantage. You speak of the kingdom as you speak of a friend, a love, a wife. You see your own identity in how you serve the king. You think the king is the people. He is not. If the princes disappear, so does the kingdom. What is left? The people, the land. Why do you organize yourself into a kingdom? Is it for the glory of He Who Is? Do you think He Who Is needs Jerusalem as a point of pride? Or a king's crown as a glorious treasure? Never!

"What is cherished by He Who Is? It is faithfulness and righteousness. Can a king be faithful? No. Can a kingdom be righteous? No. You will never find a righteous or faithful kingdom. It cannot be. If you think so, Obadiah, you do not understand the evil of this people or any people. And any god they create, be it of gold or what is called a kingdom, is just that, an idol. It is here that I stand, in the midst of friends, family, and clan. Faithful, righteous men and women and children. There are others like us—clans and families of similar interest and obedience. It is these I serve, not a king who cannot hear the Word because of what he wants to be.

"There are those who want him to think as they, for their own gain, and they will lead him astray. There are those who are righteous and faithful, and he will not be able to hear them. Why? Because the Word is often painful. And there is no king who can accept the hard way for long. How do we know this? Look at his children. Look even at David and Solomon. Look now honestly at Josiah! See his sons! Are they any different than Omri or Amon? Look how they tried to destroy the Word! Even in your school there is turmoil. What Word is to be written down? Is what is at Tirzah or Samaria the Word? Is it as the Masoretes write or as Isaiah spoke?" Berechiah was unrelenting.

"You cause me pain," said Obadiah. "You question what I think and who I serve, and I cannot change this night. But this I promise: I will consider what you say."

"There is one more warning, my friend."

"I fear to ask what it would be!" said Obadiah.

"You know the Word on the gifts which we bring to the One. 'For Cain and Abel brought their First Fruit to the Creator...' But even more so, the words we repeat:

> 'A wandering Aramean was my father, and he fled into
> Egypt and sojourned there, as a small clan, and there we
> became a people, great, mighty, and populous. But the
> Egyptians treated us harshly and tormented us. And we
> cried to He Who Is, the Holy One of our fathers, and He

heard our voice and saw our torment and our toil and our oppression. And He Who Is took us out of Egypt with a mighty hand and an outstretched arm, with great terror and with signs and wonders. And He Who Is brought us into this place and gave us this land, a land flowing with milk and honey. So now, behold, I present to you the first fruits of the land which Thou, our Holy One, has given us.'

"Here is our responsibility to present to He Who Is a portion of what we were able to gain through the year. The issue is to whom this should be presented. There may have been times when it was appropriate to present it to the priests, and we have provided, and continue to provide even for Prophets in times of trouble. But now? Where is it that we are able to present our gifts that they will be used in accordance with the Law? I might travel to Anathoth, but even there I fear the misuse of our gifts. What is the solution?"

"Are you not to provide to a Levite? Is there not a Levite city nearby?"

"And in that city is there not evil? Do not the Levites behave as those of other nations? Do they not take what is given to He Who Is and keep it for themselves for their own pleasure? Is my gift to our Holy One meant to enable sin? Do they not accept gifts so that they need not work?"

"In this we disagree again. For I will give, no matter, and he who accepts is blessed or cursed by what he does with the gift. It is not for me to judge the veracity of the priest, for if that were the case, there would be those who would not give, not for righteousness' sake, but to keep what they have," said Obadiah.

"For this thought of yours, I will present to you this night, my First Fruits of this year. And this treasure you will take and transport and provide to the true Prophets in Jerusalem at the School of the Prophets. There will come a time when they will need to escape from Jerusalem. This you must provide for their care. There are those of us who have prepared to go to the South these many years. If you are trusted, send them to where I designate. For if we cannot be a people in our own land, then we will need to be a people in all lands. Do not, under any circumstances, provide this good to the priests, for then there will lie a curse upon it. He who steals from this First Fruit will not see his grandchildren, but will see his children die."

"Will you cause this to happen?" asked Obadiah. "I have heard much is caused at court by your hand."

"I am sure it is only evil that is accounted to me?!"

"Yes, but no bother. No hand dares to raise against you!" said Obadiah.

"That news means little to me now, but the care of my First Fruits for this year! You will take them?"

"This I swear."

"Then let us move back to this mountain and see our fruits."

And Obadiah was amazed and moved by the wealth of the Rechabites. Their First Fruits were wealth beyond measure! Five asses would be needed to carry it all to Jerusalem!

"We are seven thousand seven hundred thirty-two, with two thousand able to draw a sword this day, all of whom can be on horse if need be. There may be fifty expecting birth this month, and may Abaddon be kept from our tents. Within Samaria and Judah, in all of what was once Israel, there are only five thousand. The others are sent on trading tasks which must be completed. Others move flocks from here to there to our advantage. Still others maintain flocks under the protection of princes unknown to you, Obadiah. As we trade and provide livestock, our services are appreciated.

"We move from the land of the Sabaean to the sons of Asshur and sons of Bab'el and to the sons of Sidon who sail to the North. We do not hold fields or mountains, but we move from place to place as did Abraham. We are known in Egypt and welcomed in the court of Pharaoh. If we are harmed, we ask protection of the prince or protect ourselves; if righteousness is found, we continue; but if there is deceit, we exact fair due ourselves. As you say, 'You must feed your ass to ride to Jerusalem.' We have many friends by our open tents. We are protected and sought out in all lands but our own! We go to lands you have not yet heard of. We have great increase."

"Are you feared in Egypt as here?" asked Obadiah.

"Why should Pharaoh fear us? No. It is our reputation! We hide nothing. We earn a fair living, no more and no less. We are honest. We do not cheat or lie. We serve unto death. One may travel now from En-Gannim to the coasts of the Sabaean and sleep each night in a tent of the Rechab. In Sheba, alone, a tenth of our people live. Among the Sukkiim is there not a clan of the Jehudi from the time before Solomon? It is there I met the Prophet Isaiah. This people do not forget."

"And still you look as if you do not have enough gold to take a day's travel. Why do you not show your wealth?"

Berechiah responded, "There are many kinds of wealth. You think only of gold and silver. I think about the protection of our clan and battling the evils of chaos and order. When I wrap my blanket around me, I wrap myself in Story, in faith, in my people, in our reputation, under the protection of He Who Is. Does not my *dagal* speak this Story? Why do I need gold when I have family and clan? Why do I need silver for men to honor me?

"If I be righteous, I am to be honored, and that is enough for any man, be he poor, or of no clan or no family. I would, to this moment, be a servant in the home of a righteous man. For where there is righteousness there is all that He Who Is wants for us and we want of Him. If I dress in gold and silver, who will come to my door? Will not the thief want to kiss my hand? Let me disguise my gold and let him who kisses my hand do so out of love, as Jacob loved Joseph or Joseph loved his brothers. Will He Who Is evaluate me by the gold I possess? Is not He Who Is able to make gold out of water? Why am I needed to make gold? If his true Prophets need gold, will He not provide?

"When gaining wealth becomes the task, Obadiah, we make little kings of ourselves, and our sons become princes, and see what that means! Does not our One abhor sexual dishonesty? Does he not abhor dishonesty? Does He not abhor unrighteousness? Do not fool yourself into unrighteousness by denying what is sin! If I stick my thing where I will and if I convince myself it is not sin, in my mind I make myself worthy before Adonai, and then I can feel good. If I can cheat and lie and take the belongings of others and believe it is not sin, then I can see myself as worthy before Adonai and I am able to feel good. If I can lead others to do the same, so that we do as we will and tell each other it is no sin, we all can feel good! But does that make it not sin? Of course not! Is our Holy One a fool?

"Who determines what is sin, Obadiah? We do not determine what is sin. We do not determine what is good. I have determined what the Word speaks and have lived accordingly and have taught my family accordingly. You must do the same. But think of your responsibility if what you teach as something to be done is in fact sin—what burden do you bear, and you do not even know you bear it! But you should know! That is your task by being 'Chosen!' That is your task by bearing a child. If you do not know your burden, why do you wonder why life is painful? Do not ask unless you are righteous! It is at this point we become humble. And if we be humble before our One, how can I not but be humble before others? If I am to be humble, how dare I show the wealth of this clan?"

"Are you humble before the king?"

"You misunderstand the difference between humility and obedience. I am humble before Josiah, but that does not mean I will do as he orders. Before He Who Is, I am both humble and obedient. Before my father and my *zaqen*, I am humble and obedient. And there are times that even with my sons, I am humble and obedient. Is there a man or woman anywhere that cannot learn from their children?" stated Berechiah.

"Does He Who Is learn from us?" asked Obadiah.

"I think he has learned how unfaithful we are as a people, yes. He learns as He must respond to our disobedient ways."

"Does He Who Is change?"

Berechiah

"When I was born I heard the words of my grandfather and uncles and aunts and cousins and brothers and sisters. When I chose a wife and had a son I spoke to him as I had learned. With all my children I did the best I could to meet their needs and correct them and praise them. And then I did for my grandchildren, and then for my great grandchildren, and now I see and hear my great great grandchildren. Does my great great grandchild hear me as did my children? Is what I say different? Let us say not. So I have not changed, but how things are heard changes. What needs to be said changes. Once I said, 'Do not go to Egypt,' but today I said 'Go to Egypt.' Have I changed? I said 'Do not go' because I did not want harm to come to my family. Now I say 'Go' because I do not want harm to come to my family. Have I changed? It depends upon what you are measuring, the 'Go' or 'Do not go,' or the love I have for my family.

"Is not the Word of the Holy One like that? To one grandson I can say, 'Go to Josiah for a fortnight and gain an answer to a question,' and he will go and not drink of wine. But there may be another grandson who is not so strong. Do I disallow all my grandsons from going to Josiah to protect the one grandson? Does not our He Who Is worry over us the same way? Does He Who Is change? Yes. Does He Who Is Change? No. The Word is a rock. But the Almighty's responses to us may change. We perceive this, maybe, as the Almighty changing."

"You speak of one thing and then of another. Berechiah, I must think on these things."

"Think, but you must decide. You will have a daughter and a son soon, and you will teach them."

"Friend Berechiah, I know you will not be long with us. Therefore, grant me one favor. Give me one as yourself to live in my home and teach my family and help us consider what is righteous. Do you have one who can do this that I ask?"

"I have, but I must ask if he is willing. He has a family; they will be in your care."

"Berechiah, I agree." There was a moment of reflection and Obadiah added, smiling, "Is there not time for you to have a good time? Are you glum and hard and thinking all the time?"

"Who can joke and laugh like the Rechab? Who can celebrate like the Rechab! We will stay here a day so that you can experience a Rechab feast and judge for yourself how glum we are!"

And so it was, and the third morning Berechiah went apart with Obadiah and spoke to his heart and spoke words of command.

"Remember, now, Obadiah, you are to take my grandson Malluch with you to Jerusalem to be your advisor and your children's instructor. You take with you a Word Possessor, and the title Word Protector remains with you.

Let no one know of the Zadikite Possessors! Take your charge seriously; nothing can separate you from your charge but death. You are the Nagid of the Zadikites; you are protector of the Rechabites. In return, the Rechabites will continue to protect you and yours and remain at your side and at the side of your charges until we are no more. Go, servant of Josiah, and remain righteous. You are a man of faith, as you have shown in these days! Go in peace, and He Who Is, is with you and yours."

So Obadiah, Nagid of the Zadikites, left the presence of Berechiah, Nagid of the Rechabites, knowing they would meet no more. And the words between the two were remembered.

Chapter Six

✳ ✳ ✳ ✳ ✳

Josiah and Obadiah

And Obadiah the Zadikite went to Jerusalem to the School of the Prophets as requested of him by Berechiah the Rechabite. He delivered to the School of the Prophets to Ahikam, son of Shaphan the scribe and advisor of Josiah the king, the five asses bearing gold. With him went the fifty soldiers of Josiah, Obadiah's guard, the servants of Obadiah, and Malluch the Rechabite, son of Elizur the Rechabite, son of Berechiah, Nagid of the Rechabite. The asses were driven into the House of the Prophets and Ahikam received the First Fruits of the Rechabites with thanksgiving. But Ahikam was fearful, for he knew the princes of the land had spies everywhere.

And Obadiah went to Josiah, King of Judah, as the king had ordered. The king asked Obadiah of all that had happened with Berechiah the Rechabite; this was done in the presence of Malluch the Rechabite, advisor to Obadiah. Josiah heard the counsel of Obadiah that day and Malluch the Word Possessor heard the word of Josiah and the word of Obadiah.

And Josiah asked Obadiah of the Rechabites, wondering, "Do they hate me that do not serve me yet call themselves servants of Elohim?"

Obadiah explained to Josiah: "They are servants of He Who Is; they are righteous in the sight of the Holy One of Israel. The word of Berechiah is wise and true. It is different from my word to you and my service to you, for he would not serve a king, as the Holy One of Israel is his king. But the king has nothing to fear of the Rechabite as long as the king is righteous toward his people and the Rechabite. The king must ask of the Rechabite, and he may serve and comply if the bidding is deemed righteous. This they would do for any man."

"Is a king a king if he tolerates this insubordination? If I am to be examined, am I king? Is a king the king if there be even one to judge the king? Where but in Judah would a king not be king? Someday kings will be kings! There will be no clan nor tribe!"

"My king, did not Nathan call upon our father David and judge him for his sin? And did not Elijah sit in judgment against the sons of David? Did not Elisha do the same? And would it not behoove a king to accept the Word from the Prophets and change his ways? Is not the Word a judgment upon us all? Is not the Word a judgment against the king as well as against the people? If I have taken the wife of my neighbor, should not a righteous man address that with me, whether poor man or king? You have been different than other kings because you have heard the Word and tried the Way. What other king is in covenant with his god? What other king is judged by how he deals with and protects the poor? It is this your forefathers failed to teach their sons. It is why this throne is in jeopardy as stated in the Word as delivered by Isaiah!"

The king said, "If this throne is in jeopardy, why do you remain?"

Obadiah responded, "I remain because I am your servant, because my clan has chosen to serve you, and because I swore to serve you through all things. I serve you in spite of the unrighteousness of your fathers or of your possible unrighteousness, for I consider that by serving you, I serve He Who Is, as long as what you ask of us is righteous. If you say, 'Defend my kingdom,' I will defend it to the death, not because of your kingdom, but because of the people, our people, Chosen of the Holy One of Israel. I will then say, 'I have defended the people of He Who Is,' as did my fathers before me. But if you say, 'Go, take the land of this farmer that I may be able to eat and drink my fill,' I will not go, for this is not righteous. One does not need to hear the Word of a Prophet to know this. But if our people are threatened, and you say, 'This Prophet says we are to defend this land because that is what He Who Is says it is what we are to do,' then I will do it. I and mine will stand by your side."

Then the king said to Obadiah the Zadikite, "And which prophet is it that you would have me listen to? Here in this building is my trusted Shaphan the scribe who brought to me the Word, written. He read it to me and told me it was Hilkiah who found the Word. And did it not burn my heart? And did I not go to the School of the Prophets to Huldah the prophetess, wife of Shallum the son of Tikvath, son of Hasrah, the one who dresses me and keeps my shield?"

"Yes, my king, you did. And you cleansed the Temple and have cleansed Judah as best you could."

"But now where is Huldah? I only have those I know who hate me because of what my fathers said and did. I know they sinned! But have I not done what is 'good?' Have I not done what is right? Why am I still hated by these Prophets? Why cannot they speak a good Word to me? I need a Word to know where to turn!"

And Obadiah replied: "The Word does not always have to foretell evil. Yet I fear there are remaining in Judah those who have turned away from He Who Is and are in rebellion against the Holy One, even here in Jerusalem. I hear rumors of those who would be king. I would fear more not those who sit in judgment against you and are found to be righteous, but those who praise your wisdom and encourage your path in a way that brings gold into your storerooms and into their own houses. Their poison is to be feared beyond the Word of the Prophets or Prophetesses, for their evil turns you against the Holy One of Israel. Both may cause death, but before He Who Is, I would choose confusion rather than open rebellion. You may ask me to stand with you in confusion, but you may never ask me to stand with you in open rebellion against our Adonai."

And the king said, "This I will never do, friend Obadiah! I am confused! I find it hard to know whether my will is the Will of the Holy One, or simply greed! I cannot always tell what the Word is and who to call before me for the Word. In this I need advice."

"That I will give, my king. But I may need to consult my Elohim and my friends for the wisdom to respond to you."

"Tell me, my friend Obadiah, are you a Prophet?"

"My king, I have had but one woman and to her I have been faithful, as my father was faithful to my mother and his father to his woman. But there are times when I see a pretty woman and my thoughts wander to things I should not think. Does a prophet think this way? I do not know. No. I do know. I am not a prophet. I know that I can be evil in my heart and in my deed. I do my best to not do evil. I do my best to be faithful. I am considered righteous. This is an honor. I do know I have not been called upon to deliver the Word. I do have a concern with the Word, but there is no new Word from my lips.

"I have only been called to be faithful to He Who Is, to be righteous in my dealings with He Who Is and in all I attempt. That task is difficult enough. There is no deceit in my heart, my king. There are those who are prophets within this city! Call upon them if you are in doubt. There is Jeremiah, son of Hilkiah the priest of Anathoth, who is to you and your sons as was Isaiah to your grandfather Manasseh. Jeremiah is young, but be there no doubt, the Word has come to him. I have heard him, and he strikes fear in my heart. He is at the School and with him are others who are worthy."

"And who are they, friend Obadiah?" asked the king.

"There is Maaseiah and his son Neriah and his young son Baruch, now at the School in this city. There is Shaphan the scribe and his sons and

Hilkiah. There are Maaseiah and Joah, son of Joahaz. There are Jahath and Obadiah the son of Merari. There are the priestly Kohathites of Hebron. There are the Hachmonites, Jachinites, Barhumites, Jerahmeelites, Pirathonites, Pelonites, Gileadites, Gershonites, Jezerites, Palluites, and Jashubites. Do not all these fear our Almighty One? Do they not all come to Jerusalem?"

"But do they serve me?"

"My king, should you not be king of all the land that He Who Is promised to Abraham? If there be no king in Samaria, are you not king as Solomon was king or David was king? If your word is not found in Samaria, who is pained by it? Are you pained or are not those who live in that land? You are king of all who are of He Who Is. There is no other. But where does your authority lie? You are king of those here, and those in Ethiopia and Sheba, those in the land of the Sabaean and the land of the Sukkiim, in the land of the Asshur, Egypt, Gracia, and in Bab'el. You are king of a land and a people. Because they do not do as you ask does not mean you are not their king.

"You must remember, my king! We are a people drawn out. We are a people Chosen by He Who Is. We are not Egyptians or Assyrians or of Bab'el. We are of He Who Is. With that there are obligations that you have that call you out to a special responsibility to be righteous, not only when it is easy, when the Word and Will of He Who Is runs with what you want, but when the Word and Will of He Who is runs contrary to your will. Are you the only judge of that?

"While there is greater honor, there is greater responsibility and greater condemnation, for what you do and what this people do may bring the wrath of He Who Is down on all of us who bow down and worship our One with our very bones. Can I change your will? No. Can I change the will of this people? No. I can only address my clan and I can tell you what I think and I can tell you where to find a true Prophet and I can die at your side. That is all I can do. That is the extent of my faithfulness to you. It is all you can ask of me."

"Let us pray you do not need to die for me, Obadiah, but live for me!" The king paused. "Your words concern me, however, for while you mention the righteous, you do not mention the unrighteous. I fear that by the omission there is pain in your heart. Tell me, be to me as close as David to Jonathan, and as righteous as Nathan with David. Whom should I fear? Where is there unrighteousness?"

"My king, I pray you, look to your sons. Was not Eli righteous and did not his sons dishonor him? And was not David somewhat righteous, and think of the pain his sons caused him! Did David not mourn over the evil of Amnon, who had loved Tamar, the sister of Absalom his brother?

BERECHIAH

Absalom hated Amnon, not only for his sin against his sister Tamar, but out of jealousy for what Amnon might take: the very throne. Why did Absalom rise up against Amnon and kill him? Was it only for his sister's honor? Who was it that plotted with Absalom? Was it not Jonadab, the one who plotted with Amnon? Why was it that David was relieved that not all his sons were killed by this one? Had not David loved Absalom? But could David's love turn away the evil in his sons' hearts? Hear my words, Josiah, from one who searches for the heart of He Who Is: learn from the death of Absalom; learn from the death of your father! For this court is no different! You may be righteous, but those near you are plotting!"

"What you say to me is that I have sons that are deceitful?! And their advisors are as was Jonadab?" The king was irate.

"Do not be angry with me, my king, but it is so. Do you not see? I do not need to be a Prophet to foretell the heartbreak to come! Look to your sons as you look to your own salvation! Cleanse this house as you tried to clean Judah!"

"Do you say that Jehoahaz, Eliakim, Zedekiah, and the others are unworthy?!"

And Obadiah pursued the King with his words: "If I am to provide counsel, do you wish me to tell you only what you want to hear? Has any person dared to tell you of the theft from your treasury? Has any one dared to tell you of the theft from the Temple? Do you wish me to only serve you with the cut of my sword, and not with the cut of my words? Is there honor and respect where there is deceit? I honor you with my eyes and ears and words and sword! Find deceit in any of these and I will die here before you by my own hand. Why do you push me with your words and then anger? If you are angry with me, how will you hear the prophet?

"Am I Ahijah, the one who spoke the Word of the end of the kingship? Or am I not Obadiah, the Claw, your right arm, son of Amoz, your grandfather's servant, despite Manasseh's evil, who was son of Hezekiah, who died in the service of Manasseh. Or am I not heir to Johanan, father of Hezekiah, who buried Hezekiah and still served Manasseh, and Nathan, father of Johanan, who served and died at the command of King Hezekiah, who also did evil in the sight of the Almighty One. Did not Nathan send his son Amariah to Tirzah to serve the king of Israel? Have they not served even those kings who turned away from He Who Is? No! In spite of the unrighteousness of the kings, of all Israel, the princely Zadikites serve the king! Do not be angry, my king, with this Zadikite, for this righteous clan serves the king as well as Jonathan served Saul! But dare not plot against the Zadikite! Does one honor those who bring dishonor?"

"You call me blind with my own sons!"

"Do you not know yourself, my king? If not, are you able to discern who is a Prophet?"

"I fear I cannot!"

"Are you able to discern the truth in the words and deeds of your sons?"

"From your word, no! Do you accuse?" There was bitterness in the voice of the king.

"You have heard me this day. And not only your sons, but the second priest of the Temple, and the third. They desire to be chief priest. They want the ear of the king, and they now prepare the ear that they wish to have hear them. And there are others."

"I need names! Give me names that I may watch and see and hear and consider!"

"My king, watch Immer and his son, Pashur. There is deceit in their hearts. They pursue gold as Elijah pursued Ahab. They pursue power as if they were gods. They spend more time in the Chamber of the Princes at the Temple than in worship. And, my king, your trouble with children is not unusual, for the chief priest Hilkiah is troubled by his own son, Aza, and his son, Seraiah, who has fathered the deceitful Jehozadak. Into whose hands will you give this people and this land?"

"You speak truly. I honor Hilkiah for he has been an honorable man and faithful and righteous. He has been righteous in word and deed. Is it not the age? Are we all not troubled by our sons? Was there ever a father who bore a son who was worthy?"

"Yes, my king! Your father! It is not a matter of all sons dishonoring their fathers! Far from it! It is in the work of the mother and father, and in the choice of the son! But if there is one thing that is destructive of our children, it is uncontrolled will. Princes and those who would be princes particularly have this illness, for who will chastise a prince? Does not the son see the subject bow to the king, and does the son understand that the bowing down is not to the man but to the anointing of the Almighty? The son considers this his due, and then wants more! The Almighty will not have us give more! We, the Zadikite, will serve the king! But who will be king? Are there not thousands of us with the blood of David in our veins? Ten thousand could be king, and more!"

"Thousands? How could there be thousands when I have but five sons by wives and seven by concubines—and more to come, I pray!"

"No, my king, the requirement is to have the blood of David in the veins. How many of us have the blood of kings in our veins? Does not all of Judah after these four hundred years?"

"How can that be?!"

"Have there not been thirteen generations or more since David? Did not Solomon have a hundred sons or more of his wives and concubines?

BERECHIAH

Would they not have had three hundred sons? Is not all of Judah now touched by David? Is there a clan not touched by David in all of Israel? Is there not somewhere someone more worthy than your father Amon? We should keep our generations by our women as with Ruth! Our blood would be clearer and our pride more tempered, for I think there are few that have escaped the curse of princely blood in their veins.

"Where were those concubines and wives of Solomon from? Were they not from Sabaea and Honadu and how many concubines were from the Queen of Sheba? How many from Egypt? It would be hard to find a Judean in any of them! What prince has been concerned with family as long as she whom he takes is beautiful? Have our princes taught us to value virginity or righteousness or faithfulness? Have not all the daughters of the earth moved through Israel and left their seed? Do not our people move through the earth and leave our seed? We cannot purify our blood! We cannot eliminate the blood of princes from our own blood! We can purify our relationship with He Who Called us. Our priests have been no better! Is it not our own Levites who claim the right to the rites of Ba'al?"

"You do not think much of princes or priests!" The king was almost amused, for he considered the priests he knew.

"Do you, my king?"

"No, but I must. You almost ask me if I love my sons!"

"No, my king, but you must understand who your sons are, who we are as a people, and how we are different! We are different. Even amongst our people there are differences you must accept."

"What are these differences that affect me?"

"First, there are those who want the king to have all power, and make his authority the only authority. Then there are those who willingly support the king if the king be righteous. Then there are those who will treat the king as they would any man. Then there are those who are deceivers, who will speak differently to different people and will only do right when it is convenient. To me, there are only two groups that are able to be righteous in relationship with He Who Is and with the king."

"I am tired of your words. They weary me. Have we more to address at this time?" The king paused. "Do you love your wife, Obadiah? Is she a comfort to you?"

"Yes, my king. And word is that I am to have a child. A messenger came to me today. You know, Berechiah the Rechabite foretold it and now I await to hear if it will be a girl or a boy."

"Your wife has loved you well. I pray she continues to love you. I am not sure if my wife loves me or loves to prepare her sons to eye the throne. A woman has more control over her sons than her husband; there is more authority for the mother of a king than the wife of a king. My bed is getting cold."

"All our beds are not as warm as they once were, my king. The passion of youth has been supplanted for me with an abiding peace. There is passion, but the love and peace in my bed is more important. For her whom I love there is no replacement. He Who Is blessed me! At the time of my wedding, I did not know this. From passion has come a peace I never knew was possible."

"My friend, I now need concubines. If I find my bed is cold, a concubine will at least warm my bones. I know nothing of the peace you speak, let alone love."

"That is your choice, my king. Or maybe they are not concubines but…Which came first, the loneliness or the abandonment of your wife's bed?"

"For once, Obadiah, do not present me with a choice for righteous behavior! Can it not be simply a 'yes' or a 'no?' Or, can it not be just, 'as you will it must be?' Would that I had been born a pharaoh! I would not have to put up with you Jehudi!" And the king smiled at his own thoughts.

So the king stood, and Obadiah knelt as the king left the courtroom, and Malluch stood at the side of Obadiah.

The King immediately returned to the courtroom and said to Malluch the Rechabite, "Is there no respect in Judah for her king?"

Malluch said to the king, "King Josiah, I only grovel to He Who Is. I find you a righteous king, as kings go, but you are not a god, let alone the One I bow down to!"

"And my sons want to be king of Judah! Will the king ever be rid of these wounds?" And Josiah departed from the courtroom.

When the king had departed, Malluch said to Obadiah, "The king's anger may rise against us who are Rechabite for standing against him, but what have you done this day? Do you not know how these walls have ears? Do you not know the penalty you will pay for your words this day? Is it not better to be silent?"

"How can I be silent with the king I love?" asked Obadiah.

"The difference between us is that I see a broken branch and want it burned; you see a broken branch and want to hold it up until it heals. Maybe we are both wrong. I do know that I once thought only the Rechabites worthy because of their righteous stand, but I can flee. You take a stand with a king who does not know who you are, and he accepts your kneeling down before him! Could not your courage be greater than mine?"

"I do not know, Malluch, nor is it a concern of mine at this time! I do know I am hungry. Do we go to my house in this city, or to your tent?"

"Let me enjoy the comfort of your house, Zadikite, as you have enjoyed our tents, but only as we eat. Maybe you intend to tempt the Rechabite? Bring on the temptation!"

Berechiah

So they departed from the Chamber of the King. And indeed, the walls had ears that day.

In the night there fell upon the School of the Prophets five men skilled with the sword, and they broke down the door of the school. They took the men at the school and bound them and beat them, they took the gold, the First Fruits of the Clan Rechab, and they left Jeremiah for dead. Neriah and his son Baruch were also beaten, as well as Jasiel, son of Shallum and Huldah the Prophetess. The Masoretes were also bound and beaten. The servant of Berechiah the Rechabite, seeing this, ran to the home of Obadiah the Zadikite and reported what he had seen. And he reported to Obadiah that the undergarments of one were purple and gold linen, the hilts flashed as gold, and their boots were those of soldiers of the king, but faces were wrapped as in the desert.

Obadiah went that same night to the School of the Prophets. He found many of the students and scribes injured, Jeremiah bound and beaten to death, and Neriah and his son Baruch in great pain. They found that the gold had been taken out of the school and Obadiah found that there were horses held nearby that carried the gold away.

Obadiah the Zadikite asked Neriah as to who did this thing. Neriah could not answer, as he had not seen a face, nor had anyone at the school seen the faces of the assailants. But Neriah knew they were skilled with the sword and whip, and one, with a cloak like a beggar's, expected his orders to be completed. They had been completed, and more so.

Then Obadiah sent the servant of Berechiah the Rechabite back to his tent to report what had happened to Malluch and to inform him of the Masoretes at the School of the Prophets. The servant returned to Malluch, who then sent a message to Berechiah, Nagid of the Rechabites. And Obadiah considered the foresight of Berechiah the Rechabite at placing his servant so as to see the door of the School of the Prophets.

It followed that the Masoretes asked those who considered themselves to be servants of the Almighty to remove themselves from the school as the school was in danger. And Jeremiah was carried away that night and was hidden within the city, as were Neriah and Baruch, his son. And Obadiah's servant followed the tracks of the horses of the thieves of that night through the city of Jerusalem up to the gate of the Temple.

Then Obadiah led his servants to the House of the king, and called out for the king. The king's servant heard Obadiah, and awakened the king, and the king brought Obadiah into the Chamber of the King and heard Obadiah. Malluch the Rechabite was with Obadiah as he entered the Chamber of the King.

And Obadiah said to the king, "Hear your faithful servant this night! There has been a grave injustice wrought! Hear, my king, that the injustice comes from this house!"

The King said quietly to his servant Obadiah, "Why have you come to accuse me in the night? Of this I know nothing. Do you not see I have been sleeping? What is it that I have done this night?"

"My king, this night the School of the Prophets was fallen upon by thieves, and the thieves not only stole what was not theirs, but bound and beat the prophets and scribes of this city!"

And the king responded, "Obadiah, your information is grave, but what is being said? What has this to do with me? Say it clearly that I may fully understand what is your word, that I may judge the value of your word and consider my response."

Obadiah said to the king, "Within two hours I was awakened by the servant of Berechiah the Rechabite, the young man Jaazaniah, son of Jeremiah, son of Habaziniah the Rechabite, and he told me of thieves in the School of the Prophets. I went straight to the School of the Prophets and found the Masoretes beaten, and Jeremiah bound and beaten and near death, as was Neriah and Baruch, his son, and others in their company. I found the five loads of gold given to the school for the care and well-being of the school, which I had brought this day and hidden within the house, to be stolen.

"When I asked Jaazaniah what he had seen, he said: 'I saw four men who appeared to be beggars but were soldiers, wearing footing which bound their legs as the soldiers of the king, break down the door of the school. A fifth wore undergarments of purple and gold linen and told them what to do and they did it. While I heard wailing and shouting, I saw bags like those our clan makes carried out and placed on horses.'"

"And where is this Jaazaniah the Rechabite now?" asked the king.

"I sent him to report to Malluch, and Malluch has sent him to the Ancient One, Berechiah, Nagid of the Rechabites. As we speak he rides."

"Have you done this thing so that I may be killed in my house?" The king was angry and fearful, for he knew immediately what was being said.

"Who would kill this king but his own? Surely not the Rechabites, for you have not stolen from the Rechabites, but from He Who Is!"

"Me!" The king went into a rage.

"You, my king! Who was missing money in the treasury? Who had taken money from the Temple? Was it I? Was it Hilkiah the chief priest? Why would he want gold? And why would I want this gold? No, it was you who needed gold. Either you or your sons! And if it were your sons, it is the same as if it were you!"

"How dare you talk to me this way! Who are you to accuse your king! I swear by He Who Is that I had naught to do with this thing! And if it were my sons? Can you control your own sons? No! You have no sons, so who are you to say what a father can and cannot do with his sons! Who are you to judge a prince of this land! You have no need to remain in my presence. Guards! Remove this man!"

"And what guard dares? What ten will heed your command? Hear this, my king! If you do not find that gold and return it, there is a curse that will burn your soul and the soul of the thief. I will tell you where you will find that gold! You will find it in your storeroom! And you will know the gold, for it comes from Parva'im, and not from Judah. And you will find it in the Temple! When you do, know that it was your son, if not all of your sons! Pray I live to see the day the curse is fulfilled! And my king, until you search out the truth and punish the guilty, I give you my sword and my *hoshen* and my armlets. Find in Israel a new champion. And tell me where in all of Israel will you find one who has served you more worthily than I? You know where I will be! Have he who has sinned come to me on his knees bearing these things when it is that the great Josiah, servant of He Who Is, has need of me."

"Tears of shame will flow from my face on that day! Out of my sight, thou unfaithful and disloyal servant! Out of Jerusalem!"

"You forget who I am servant of! I am servant to He Who Is! I am servant to the righteous king! I am Nagid of the Zadikites and Abaddon does not keep me out of Jerusalem! If you want me, you know where I am!"

"And if you ever find a righteous king in any land, serve him! Will there ever be a righteous king on the throne of Judah? What will satisfy you? A god in king's clothes? When is He Who Is satisfied? When are you satisfied! What do you want of me? Out! Out of my sight! Out of Jerusalem!" And the king's guards, now that they saw Obadiah without a sword, moved toward him, so that Malluch removed Obadiah from the sight of the king.

※ ※ ※ ※ ※

It was still night as Obadiah was returning to his house, and a messenger from Shaphan the scribe and administrator for the king came to Obadiah to request that they meet at the room named Genizah, a storeroom in the Temple. And Obadiah went to the room with Malluch, and there he found Shaphan the scribe, Hilkiah the chief priest, and Maaseiah, governor of Jerusalem.

"Are we all not Nazirite?" asked Hilkiah. "And if we are, can we not all speak frankly together?"

"As I am last to come, let me speak first," spoke Obadiah the Zadikite. "Yes, we are Nazirites and each one of us is known to be honest and righteous before He Who Is. But as you called me here, you must have already heard the words between the king and me. You must already know that I am expected to leave Jerusalem immediately. I have yet to decide if I will leave."

"Come, Obadiah, and see something through this space," said Maaseiah, governor of Jerusalem. "I want you to see what kind of king we have!"

Obadiah reluctantly climbed a ladder with Maaseiah and at a ledge peered through into the Temple, and there, in the outer chamber, was the king, prostrate on the stone. The king was praying aloud. There was no one in the Temple. Obadiah watched as oil burned dimly.

It was Hilkiah who spoke to break the silence, "He comes here every morning before dawn, year after year. Listen to his prayers. Listen to his humility and confusion before our Elohim. There was a time that our kings desecrated this Temple with false gods and false worship and crude and sinful behavior, even within the Holy of Holies! It even occurs now over our objection, but now it is in secret. Here we have a king who stays in the outer chamber out of fear of the Holy One of Israel!"

There was silence.

"Do you want something of me?" asked Obadiah.

"Yes, friend and brother in our faith," said Hilkiah. "Each one of us here has concerns about Josiah. Each one of us here still loves Josiah. And we not only want Josiah to remain king, but we do not want his sons not to be king. With your defiance this night, which by now is known throughout Jerusalem, the party of Prince Jehoahaz will grow in power. The sons of Jerusalem plot against the father. What you did not know was that the king had known the treasury had been robbed, and we knew there had been theft from the Temple. The king had spoken quietly to his sons. If the gold was not returned, they each would have been sent out of the land. We did not know how this would resolve itself; there was fear that the king would be killed by a uniting of the parties of the princes.

"But they heard of the gold you brought to Jerusalem, and a theft occurred which protected the princes and released the pressure on their parties. Many things were solved by the theft—and we do not make judgment as to who did this thing—but now two problems developed: your reaction and the damage to the School of the Prophets. You concern us the most this night. Your anger has hurt the king. He is weakened by you not being at his side. Your defiance enables others to do the same, but while your defiance may be righteous indignation, the defiance of others is the defiance of evil ones. The forces of chaos use your behavior to their advantage! Consider obedience! The king would then still be seen as strong. Would your honor be damaged?"

"Are you saying I was wrong and now need to go to the king and humble myself?"

There was silence. The three knew that anger was still with Obadiah the Zadikite.

"We need a compromise in order to maintain stability," suggested Maaseiah. "I do not doubt your righteousness, Obadiah, nor your honesty.

BERECHIAH

I do wonder if what is occurring because of what you have said, is what you want to happen. The throne is shaky, not only because of the princes and their squabbling, but also because of the priesthood. There are those who want us dead. There are those who would have great advantage if there were not righteousness in the Temple leadership. I fear after the death of Hilkiah. Who is there? And after Josiah? Who is there? Truly Ahijah's Prophecy is about to come true."

Obadiah stated, "I do not wish anyone to take advantage of my words to the king. I do not wish this man to fall from the throne. But the very problem I spoke to him about is the cause for your coming to me in the dark. When will we be able to do what is righteous and find blessing in that righteousness? Before I say more, I need to know: Whom am I to fear?"

Shaphan answered: "Forgive me, Hilkiah, my friend, but I mention Azariah, your son, and his son, Seraiah. Money and power are their desires. Azariah would be king! He already acts as if he is one."

Maaseiah said, "And Immer and his son, Pashur. And Irijah. And Hananiah, son of Azur, who thinks he is a prophet, and watch those who lap the wine from the table of the princes."

"You have spoken clearly." Obadiah's fears and thoughts had been confirmed.

"Forgive me, Obadiah!" Hilkiah wept. "Would that you were my son."

"What is it you want of me?" Obadiah was respectful of the chief priest. Who would not tremble for the parent of a wayward child?

"We need you to speak a word from the Temple gate, or let us repeat your words in court this day."

"What word would you have me speak."

"You need to say you still love the king, and your sword will slay anyone who would do harm to the king, be it friend or foe, and that out of respect for the king, you will withdraw from Jerusalem."

Again there was silence.

"Tell me, Hilkiah, as I think on this thing, tell me how it is that you happened to find the Torah written on skins in the walls of this city. Would it not have been easier to pull a copy of the Torah from the stacks in this room? Do you not know who I am? You know I would burn this room! Does not the king know of this room?"

"We did find the Torah written on skins in the wall. It was not a copy we had made, nor was it of the Masoretes. We have lost contact with any Word Possessors, so we could not tell how the words compared. Do you know of any Word Possessors?"

Malluch examined the eyes of Obadiah.

"Why would you want to know?" asked Obadiah. "To tell the king, so that his princes would know who to kill? Friend, I give you honor and respect, but you would do best to withdraw the question, for it is one I will not answer with truth or falsehood. Look what King Omri did! Look how the Torah now is written down and changed to please the King of Israel! And there is no King of Israel...or Samaria. But the words that he changed are still written down! And what do you say in the Temple? Do you say Words that are in the heart, or are they not words written down on the skin of pigs?"

"Why is it that you think only the Word Possessors know what is the Word? Are they not capable of changing a word here and there? And suddenly history is changed," asked Hilkiah.

"They would die first! It has never happened. But I can show you time and time again where your scribes have changed the Word to their own advantage! Give me ten Word Possessors and they could chant the Word together and never skip a letter; give me ten scribes and I will show you error upon error."

"Are there ten?" Hilkiah was amazed.

"There are more than ten! There are ten times ten! It is only our lack of trust of the sons of Jerusalem that causes us not to sing out the Word from the walls! The only thing that would occur, when it was realized what was being sung out, would be an arrow in the back!"

"Is there such distrust and hate of us?" Hilkiah was truly grieved.

"Yes. For have not the innocent died at the hands of the king and have not priests taken what is not theirs?"

"Not this king," spoke Hilkiah.

"But this king could be gone tomorrow! And then what would we do? Die?"

"We?" asked Maaseiah.

Obadiah was quiet, then he responded: "We, the righteous."

All pondered in silence the words that had passed between them.

And Obadiah spoke these words: "Repeat these words to the king in his courtroom this day: 'Obadiah, son of Amoz the Zadikite, known as the Right Arm of the King Josiah, humbles himself before the king and asks forgiveness for his words of anger. Let the enemies of Josiah know that if King Josiah calls in defense of the king or of Jerusalem, the Claw of Judah will slay the enemies of the king. Let all the people know that Obadiah the Zadikite withdraws from Jerusalem to En-Gannim to wait upon the call from the king to serve against the enemies of Judah. When will the king send for Obadiah?'"

"Your words cut as well as your sword." Shaphan knew his friend. Obadiah's words announced some and hid more.

"Be careful. There are those willing to have you die before your words are given to the king." Maaseiah was astute. Obadiah might not trust Maaseiah as he did Hilkiah or Shaphan, but his thoughts were accurate.

BERECHIAH

"I will give these words to the king this morning. And may He Who Is continue to protect you and your clan!"

Obadiah said, "If the clan were to pass, the authority of the king would have to take its place! Thank you for your blessing! Chaos and order—a friend of mine recently spoke to me about these two evils! You know the evil of chaos. But I had not spent much time considering the evil of order. The Horns of Ba'al! The wisdom of Berechiah the Rechabite is great. We must remember the Rechabites forever. Are they mentioned in the stories you have written, scribe?"

"No," answered Hilkiah for Shaphan the scribe. "They are not mentioned. Nor are the Zadikite." There was sorrow in his voice. Was this regret for the work of the Masoretes?

And Obadiah said, "Is that sorrow in your voice, Hilkiah? You sound like someone who lectured me several days past. He said, 'So you have the blood of kings in your veins, Obadiah. What does it mean? Can you feed me with your blood? Can you shelter me from the wrath of the Almighty One? No! Blood of kings is worthless as horse piss! You made these kings! You, the same ones needing idols. Idols and kings! Whores both! Chaos and order; the Horns of Ba'al. Both bring Abaddon to us and our children!' Someone needs to add the Levites to that list! Soon the Levites will be no more, just as the Prophet spoke of our kings being no more."

"I do not understand you, Obadiah! How can you speak this way and still love Josiah?" asked Maaseiah, Governor of Jerusalem.

"Two reasons: I consider that He Who Is did create a Covenant with our forefathers concerning David; and secondly, I am pledged as a Nazirite to He Who Is through service to the king. One is by thought and two is by pledge. Until the kingship is ended, I will serve the king. At the same time, I see there are limits to my obligation. An unrighteous king will gain my rebuke. There will be honor given if his word is straight."

"It is good to know where you stand, my friend, Obadiah," spoke Hilkiah warmly. "I find you intense and fascinating. You would make your father and grandfather proud."

"Let us who lead remain righteous. If I am to take the warning of Maaseiah as valid, I must leave now to protect you and the king. I take my leave from you as a brother."

Obadiah bowed, and four stood and bowed to each other.

"Be alert," warned Shaphan. "The enemies of the king abound. There is unrighteousness behind every door."

And the five left the Genizah.

So Obadiah left the City of Jerusalem with Malluch and his servants. The sun was rising above the hills. Obadiah stopped at the Dung Gate, looked back into Jerusalem, and he feared for Jerusalem.

As Obadiah the Zadikite proceeded down the Jordan to En-Gannim, there came to him a woman dressed as a Moabite. She appeared old. With her were two male babies—twins. She stood far off on a knoll.

And the woman called out to Obadiah, "Obadiah, Nagid of the Zadikites, *zaqen* of En-Gannim, known as a servant of Josiah the King and as a righteous man before He Who Is! Obadiah! Hear me and come to me!"

Obadiah turned to Malluch and asked, "Is there something to fear from this woman?"

Malluch responded, "I do not think so, my friend. Go to her, but remain alert. I will circle around and see if there is a problem to consider."

Obadiah spoke out, "You know of me! But what does that mean? The sons of the king know who I am, but do I do their bidding?"

"I am not a king, not even a servant of a king. I am a sinner, asking a word of a great and righteous man. Would you not come to me so that I may speak to you in private without the goats hearing our words?"

"You have a sharp and clever tongue," said Obadiah.

"Would that it had paid well, but it has brought little good. Do you come to me, or do I return to Dibon?"

"I recently was with one sent to Dibon."

"Yes. I know of him, as does all Dibon! By some your name is cursed, not quite as much as is the name Berechiah, but it is cursed. But for us who know righteousness, we wonder at Berechiah's wisdom. You are his friend and equal. From you I seek a righteous decision! I ask for forgiveness!"

Obadiah was intrigued. Who was this woman? She was bold! She knew of him. "I will come in a moment." Malluch returned and nodded that it was safe.

And Obadiah went to the mound and said, "Here I am. What is it that you would say to me?"

"You are Obadiah, son of Amoz, son of Hezekiah, son of Johanan, son of Nathan, all Zadikites of Judah, and beyond. Tell me the names of the children of Johanan; was there not a son named Azor, and did not Azor have a son Elizur?"

"Third son of Johanan was Azor, and the only son of Azor was Elizur. Yes."

"And, tell me, did not Elizur have four sons and a daughter, Jedidah?" the woman asked.

"It is spoken of Jedidah: 'And Jedidah left the house of her father Elizur with the *nokri* who had been granted refuge in his house, and they departed for the land of the Moabites, and Elizur heard of her no more. And Elizur wept for his daughter Jedidah, for there was no father who loved his daughter more. And Elizur spoke no more until the day he died, for his sorrow was great.'"

"It is I, Jedidah, the daughter of Elizur, who brought sorrow to the house of Johanan."

"Your father has been long dead, cousin Jedidah. But show me the birthmark on the back of your neck, and the scar on your right leg, and I will consider your plea."

"See my birthmark and see my scar. Is the memory of the Zadikite so long as they do not forget a birthmark?"

"Not only do we not forget a birthmark, but we do not forget a child, or a child's child. But which is more important?" asked Obadiah.

"A child is most important. And this is why I am here. When I fled from the house of my father after he denied me my request and the request of the man I chose and who chose me, we went to Dibon and there had a daughter. My husband left me and I raised my daughter alone as best I could. My daughter chose her own path and here are her two sons, twins as the Zadikites are known to have. Now my daughter is dead, and I am two score years. While loneliness burns my heart each day and I so regret the choices I have made in my life, I have but few years to live and I fear that if I die great harm will come to my grandsons. I am willing to bear the shame and indignation of our clan for the sake of my grandsons. They are great great grandsons of Johanan, and are they not therefore Zadikite? It is this that I ask: 'Will Obadiah the Nagid of all Zadikites allow the return of these who are innocent?'"

"I do not reject you, Jedidah, and I will speak to you. But I have many questions and things to say, and then I will decide what is to occur. I make no promises, but you must hear me as I now have heard you. Did Elizur shame you in your innocence?"

"No."

"Did he unjustly punish you and deride you?"

"No."

"Did he make you work too hard or in any way not treat you with respect?"

"No, he was a good father."

"And yet you chose a different path than the path of our people. Why?"

"I loved the man who became my husband, and I think he loved me when we were in this land."

"Could you not wait until you found a man in this country of this people? Did your father not beg you not to leave? Was he going to provide you with someone that you could not love?"

"Yes, my father begged me not to leave, not for his own sake, but for my sake. He asked me what his grandchildren would know of him. He asked me what of my faith in He Who Is. He asked me if I would not want to be nearby at the death of my mother. But these things I did not understand

and I willed that I be with the man I chose. So I defied the will of my father and I rejected my clan. I know what I did was my choice and only my choice."

Obadiah considered these things and said, "Now that the fruit of your choice is upon you, how is it that you choose to return?"

"I have lived in shame; I have denied my Elohim to please my husband. I have wept evening after evening and bore the fruit of my decision in a cold bed and with an empty stomach and heartache."

"And what if your stomach had been full? Would you be here now? What if your husband had completed his vow, would you be here now? Is it simply because you have pain and sorrow from ill treatment, and see the fruit of your pain and sorrow doubled by the babes, that now you pick and choose to do the will of the clan? When your clan needed you, or your father needed you, or your mother needed you, you were not here, because you chose not to be here. Now that you have needs, you return? Not only is your will bent against us, but it is dishonest! Is that not true?"

"I ask you to address not my will or my needs, but the needs of these babes. If you will, I will leave them here and depart to my death among the *nokri*, as I deserve. But do these babes deserve this? Are they not of this Clan Zadikite? If you found them on a hill, would you not take them in?"

"These babes deserve their inheritance, but what is their inheritance? Is not your defiance their inheritance? Is it not that which you chose? When you chose against your inheritance provided by your father and mother, did you not deny it not only for yourself, but for your children? If I have two sons and one says, 'I do not want that field,' and so I give my field to my other son, does the son of my first son come to me and say, 'I now want the field that my father did not want?' No. What the father gains as an inheritance, his son inherits. What the father loses, the son has also lost. What the father rejects, the son will not receive. And is it also not true that the weakness of the parent is multiplied in the child? If I beat my son twice, will he not beat his child tenfold? What I own, my children inherit; what I am, my children inherit; what I believe, I pray my children will believe."

"You speak true, as I have seen in my daughter. Is this not why I bow down and grovel before you for forgiveness? Do I not see my error and are you angry with me for wanting an inheritance for my grandsons? Does the Prophet not call us to return? Deny me mercy! But grant mercy to the innocent!"

"When a young girl, did your father and mother not explain these things to you? Did they not discuss the importance of what you were about to choose?"

"I was told, but I did not understand. I did not want to hear anything but what I wanted."

"And could you not be patient? Could you not trust what your father had to say? Had he lied to you before so that there was cause for you not to believe him?"

"He did not lie to me."

"Do you know what pain you caused him? You think you know pain. You do not know the pain of your father from your actions! Was he not a man of the Holy One of Israel? Did you know that he never spoke another word to his other children or to his wife or to anyone? He thought he had failed He Who Is. He thought he had failed you! You were his joy. You were his pride. And you denied all of who he was by what you did. And your mother wept. She, too, felt at fault."

"She was not at fault. She was a good woman, and she said she had learned to love my father deeply. This I remember."

"And still you chose a path which denied your parents."

"I chose a path that brought me joy, then sorrow, and brought my own child an early death and brings my grandsons to this dust on this road."

"What is a righteous path to choose? What discord will you bring with you? If you were to be able to return, at what cost would it be?"

"I am willing to not use my name! I am willing be a servant in the house of the lowest of your servants, my Nagid. All that I ask is that they be known as Zadikite, great great-grandsons of Johanan, and let them worship in this land and know He Who Is as their Elohim. I will bear the thorn of my father; I will not speak! Or, if you demand, I will turn away and leave the babes in your arms."

There was quiet. And Obadiah wondered what Johanan would expect of him.

Jedidah also said to Obadiah, "I did not know my father wept for me. My pain is beyond measure, for I did love my father. I simply did not understand life. I did not understand that there are no rules for the faithless. I did not understand that there is no right that restrains the wrong of the unrighteous. For today this is true and tomorrow that is true and generation forgets generation and there are none beyond self. There is no restraint on the will of authority and there is no demand that causes the unruly to fear. I long for the safety of a righteous home for my grandsons. Even the threat of death in a righteous home brings no fear like the fear found in the loneliness of an unrighteous house or the despair or hopelessness. There is no restraint but the care of the moment. The unrighteous will never understand the heart of the truly righteous."

Then Obadiah said to Jedidah, "The words of my father are the words of my grandfather and so my great great grandfather reaches out from beyond the grave and comforts me and guides me. The Word of He Who Is speaks to me through them and through the Word spoken to me. Your daughter did not hear the Word. Did her heart ever burn for comfort? Did she not ever wonder about the One of her grandfather? Did she ever ask of us?"

"She did not hear the Word. My daughter only wanted to hear the words of her own father, but there were no words that came from him that would have quenched her needs. She sought him and could not find him. She found a man who caused pleasure and she forgot even me, the one who could have helped her. And I found a new emptiness in my heart. She came home to me only to deliver these two babes. I have called one 'Chebel,' for there is 'sorrow' in my heart. And I call the other one 'Nehi,' for surely there is 'wailing' for those that are lost and do not know they are lost. I have buried my daughter, as she died in childbirth. Her love never came to her, nor to me. Now Chebel and Nehi are why I live."

"Did your daughter have any idea of what she was doing or what she refuted by her path?"

"She had no idea."

"And did you?"

"I thought all were as good and kind as my father and mother and family and clan. I did not know the difference. I did not understand evil and how our One's Covenant combats that evil. I only thank the Almighty One that He granted me remorse and has not kept my heart hard, that I may choose right, not for my own benefit, but for these who may be of service and are of your clan."

"But are they?"

"They will be if you guide them and be to them as a father, or at least an uncle."

"You ask too much of me."

"If I cannot ask forgiveness of you, how am I able to ask forgiveness of He Who Is? To whom has the greater offense been given? To whom can show my repentance? Who will forgive me? Am I able to be forgiven?!"

"Maybe it is too late," said Obadiah.

And Jedidah groaned and fell to her face.

"Was it ever too late for David? Would it ever be too late for your children?"

"I have no children," spoke Obadiah. And there was quiet.

Obadiah pondered his anger and the words of Jedidah and her pain. He pondered his faith and his family and his clan. Obadiah dismounted from his horse and knelt down to Jedidah and wept. He wept as did Elizur and as did Elizur's wife in their loneliness and pain and anger and blame.

And Jedidah wailed the wail of twenty-five years of loneliness. Then she went home with Obadiah and dwelt in the land outside of En-Gannim, and was known as Jedidah, daughter of Elizur, son of Azor, son of Johanan. And Chebel and Nehi learned of He Who Is and knew who they were.

Chapter Seven

✳ ✳ ✳ ✳ ✳

Megiddo

And there was joy in the land, for Hannah, wife of Obadiah, Nagid of the Zadikite, son of Amoz, delivered a son, and he was named Berechiah, son of Obadiah the Zadikite. Obadiah took Berechiah and swore an oath and Berechiah was known to be a Nazirite. Hannah, wife of Obadiah, also bore that same day a daughter who was named Deborah. Deborah was a beautiful child, and her father loved her, and she, too, was a Nazirite by the pledge of Obadiah.

And Berechiah, Nagid of the Rechabites, looked into the eyes of Berechiah the Zadikite. And Berechiah the Rechabite died in his tent with Malluch and all his sons at his side. Habaziniah took the *dagal* of the Rechabites and ordered a second line of red in the field of black and fringe of red, and said, "Is not Berechiah a righteous man as was our father? We the Rechab will remember both in all we do and wherever we go."

So Habaziniah became the Nagid of the Rechabites, and he was an old man. In the twenty-fourth year of the reign of Josiah, Habaziniah slept with his fathers, and his son Jeremiah became Nagid of the Rechabites. And Jeremiah, son of Habaziniah, was wise even in his youth. He had a son Jaazaniah who was also a worthy son. They were Nazirite. The Rechabites prospered and were faithful to He Who Is. They continued in the path of their fathers in spite of the king.

And Malluch the Rechabite remained with Obadiah and served him and taught Obadiah's son Berechiah and daughter Deborah. Both were worthy to be ones who spoke the Word, and they learned the Word and possessed It.

When it was time, Obadiah the Zadikite sent to the city of Tirzah to the family of Zephaniah the Zadikite, whose great great grandfather was Nathan, as he was for Obadiah, and asked of Zephaniah if there were any worthy sons eligible to find delight in his daughter Deborah, Zephaniah sent three sons. One, named Lemuel, found favor with Deborah and with Obadiah, and he returned to Tirzah in Israel to await the time for marriage, for there was war in the air. Obadiah sent word to Zephaniah that Lemuel be sent to provide service for Jeremiah, Nagid of the Rechabite. So Lemuel served his uncle as a *malak* between Jeremiah the Nagid of the Rechabite and Obadiah the Nagid of the Zadikite.

In the twelfth year of Berechiah, son of Obadiah, Jeremiah the Rechabite sent word to Obadiah the Zadikite that Pharaoh Necho of Egypt had requested purchase of sheep. A fair and good price had been agreed upon. Pharaoh Necho also had requested delivery of 5,000 sheep to the city of Ashkelon, and in one later moon, 5,000 sheep to the city of Samaria. And Obadiah considered these things. Jeremiah the Rechabite sent word to Obadiah that the king of the city of Bab'el had requested 20,000 sheep be delivered in preparation of a festival to their gods. Jeremiah the Rechabite reported that the Asshur feared the king of Bab'el and the king of the Asshur was fortifying his own city and requested assistance from Jeremiah, Nagid of the Rechabite, as famine was in his land.

Then Obadiah, Nagid of the Zadikite, called for the *zaqen* of the Zadikite to come to his land in the country of En-Gannim to advise them of the messages from Jeremiah the Rechabite. The Zadikites looked to Obadiah for counsel. Obadiah waited for word from Josiah. Josiah was confused, as the prophets of Jerusalem were many but their word to Josiah was one, except for Jeremiah, the son of Hilkiah of Anathoth. Josiah also knew that the people of Bab'el were moving against the city of Asshur, and that the Egyptians were moving to protect the city of Asshur as in treaty, for it was an advantage to Egypt to have a weak Asshur and a weak Bab'el.

Since Josiah desired to be king of all Israel, he considered in council that if Pharaoh Necho were to withdraw from his approach through the Valley of Jezreel, north of Jerusalem, Asshur and Bab'el would consume themselves and Josiah might become king of all Israel. Josiah considered this a good thing, as did his prophets and his sons. So Jehoahaz, with deceit in his heart and pretending knowledge, told the king, his father, that Pharaoh Necho planned to move two troops, one through northern Israel and one to proceed up the plain from Jordan from the Arabah. Josiah believed his son and prepared to meet the two armies of the pharaoh.

Then Josiah sent his son Jehoahaz to the land surrounding En-Gannim, to the house of Obadiah the Zadikite. And the Prince Jehoahaz called out to Obadiah, "Obadiah, right hand of Josiah the King, I bring you your *hoshen* and your sword and call upon you to come to the aid of your king. Come, look at my back, for I have confessed my sin toward my father and I have replaced the gold of the Rechabites to the school in Jerusalem. Now the Masoretes have use of the gold as do the scribes and prophets assigned to the school by the king."

Prince Jehoahaz considered that while he would please Obadiah by returning the gold, the throne would be his reward after the death of the king and the death of Obadiah. The prince knew that once restored to the service of Josiah, Obadiah could not refuse the request of his king to fight. Jehoahaz had his servant take off his robe and the servants of Obadiah saw the wounds of Jehoahaz. Obadiah went out and brought Jehoahaz into his house and a feast was prepared. But Obadiah could not see the deceit in the heart of Jehoahaz, for Jehoahaz thought, "Is not the throne worth fifteen lashes?"

"Does now the king assign and control the scribes at the School of the Prophets?" asked Obadiah.

Jehoahaz responded, "And why not? Is not Jerusalem the City of David and therefore the City of Josiah? Why should it not be the School of Josiah?"

"Because it is the School of He Who Is. How will the Word change by the prophets when it is the king they serve and not He Who Is? Why does the Word say 'When you sit to feast with a king, carefully consider what is before you, and put a knife to your throat if you have desires?' One wonders if the prophets serve the king or the princes or the Almighty."

"Is that not the same, Obadiah?"

"It depends upon the king and it depends upon the son. Just as the Word of Hilkiah the chief priest is different from the word of Azariah his son. Why is it that those now gone whom we called Prophet spent their days in fear of the kings, while our new prophets feast with the king?"

"You speak only to protect the troublemakers! When do Prophets ever speak a good Word? When does the Word please the King?"

"Maybe the Word cannot please the king because the king wishes to usurp the authority of He Who Is! If the Word is with the Prophets, how can it be with the king? If it is with the king, what need are the Prophets! Now if the king turns away, the school will turn away, and where will we find the Word? Will we find it in the word of the king?"

"While I humble myself to you, Obadiah the Zadikite, I could not tolerate your insolence!"

"The words now end, for you are to be a guest in my home, and receive the protection of my house and clan. But if I become blinded by your words and evil befalls us, may you end your days without light! Now, no further will we talk of these things."

Jehoahaz sat next to Berechiah, son of Obadiah. Next to Berechiah sat Tibni, the priest and advisor of Jehoahaz. Next to Tibni were the pillars of the house of Berechiah, Chebel and Nehi, both a head taller than all others, and newly considered men according to the traditions. And Berechiah, son of Obadiah, studied Tibni's face, for there was a scar from eye to ear, a double cut. And Tibni saw Berechiah note his scar.

Then Jehoahaz asked Obadiah as to his family and clan. Obadiah promised to bring to Jerusalem one thousand on horseback, two hundred on chariot, and one thousand on foot. Jehoahaz asked Obadiah how many other clans would come to Jerusalem upon his bidding, so that Jehoahaz considered the king's army to be fifteen thousand men. Jehoahaz spoke to Obadiah of his calling for an army to guard Jerusalem from the south, west of the Jordan; and he considered there would be seven thousand who would respond to his call. And Obadiah questioned Jehoahaz about the second army of Pharaoh Necho, as he had no report of this. Jehoahaz spoke to Tibni, and Tibni spoke of traders who had brought him word out of the Valley of Arabah.

Obadiah took Chebel and Nehi aside and spoke to them. Chebel and Nehi departed from the house and took horses and went to where there were Rechabites camped four days south of En-Gannim. Jeremiah the Rechabite sent Chebel and Nehi with servants, and they watched for the approach of the second army of Pharaoh Necho. Chebel and Nehi waited. With them was Jaazaniah, son of Jeremiah the Rechabite. As they waited, Jeremiah drew his tents near and through messenger to Obadiah, gained a favor and permission to offer to Chebel and Nehi daughters of his clan.

Chebel and Nehi were pleased with the daughters of the Rechabites as they watched the desert. Chebel and Nehi chose well, and the Rechabites celebrated. And Chebel and Nehi desired that their grandmother be with them in their joy and she joined them, but she was ill. She died with Chebel and Nehi at her side. Chebel and Nehi began their families, blessed with sons of the Zadikites. Jeremiah the Rechabite spoke to Chebel and Nehi about the king, and about the princes. Chebel and Nehi continued to watch, but there was no army of Pharaoh coming out of the desert.

So it was that Jehoahaz and his party departed from the house of Obadiah, Nagid of the Zadikite. Jehoahaz returned to Jerusalem with Tibni, the priest and advisor. He then sought his father Josiah and told him all that Obadiah had said.

In time Obadiah departed with Berechiah, his son, to Jerusalem, and all the Zadikites who had been called went with him. Josiah called Obadiah to his chamber, and the king spoke to Obadiah and Berechiah of his loneliness and his pleasure that Obadiah was in Jerusalem. The king also asked about the Rechabites. But the Rechabites were not sending a man to defend Jerusalem, and the king was angry with them, so the Rechabites outside the city withdrew.

The king appointed Berechiah, son of Obadiah, the bearer of his arms. The king asked Obadiah, "Do you trust me? Do you think what I am doing is righteous?"

Obadiah responded, "You have called me; I cannot judge what is righteous in this situation. I must trust your discernment in this. What do your prophets say?"

"I have been told it is the Will of He Who Is to defeat Necho so that I may claim kingship over all of Israel and rule as did Solomon and David his father. For the Asshur and the Bab'el will weaken each other. Should this not be the Will of our Elohim? Am I not a righteous king, and will not our righteousness be rewarded by the Almighty? It must be! Think of the opportunity!"

"The opportunity is great for both victory and defeat. How large is your estimate of the army of Pharaoh Necho?"

"I have been told the army now approaching the Valley of Jezreel numbers twenty thousand, and that his army to the south numbers fifteen thousand. Of both armies, five thousand are on chariot and five thousand are on horseback. The rest are on foot and carry sword and bow."

"And our forces?"

The king spoke, "We are almost twenty thousand to defend the North and seven thousand to protect the South. If our timing is good, we can defeat Pharaoh and march to defend Jerusalem with my son. This must be before Pharaoh's army is joined into one."

Obadiah, knowing the Jeshurun, said, "But how many are here at Jerusalem, ready to march?"

"There are fifteen thousand here, now, ready to march, including your clan."

"And chariot? And horsemen? And sword and bow?" asked Obadiah.

"There are four thousand chariot, four thousand horse, and seven thousand with sword and bow," said the king. "And there are to be five clan to meet us at Carmel, of Ephraim."

"We then shall, by your report, be more than Pharaoh and be fighting in our own land. Then let us march, and may He Who Is be with us!"

The armies prepared themselves at the gates of Jerusalem, and Josiah went out to depart from the Gate of Ephraim. At the gate stood Jeremiah the Prophet, son of Hilkiah the priest of Anathoth, saying, "... in the cities of Judah and in the streets of Jerusalem and say, 'Hear the Words of this Covenant and do them. I have solemnly warned your fathers in the day that I brought them up out of the land of Egypt, even to this day, saying, 'Obey My Word!' Yet they do not obey nor do they hear. Therefore I will bring upon them all the Words of this Covenant which I commanded, but they will not do...'"

"Am I never to rid myself of this troublemaker?" asked the king of Obadiah. "Why did he have to wait until I am at the gate to speak what he considers the Word? Why did he not come to my chamber when I called upon him."

Obadiah answered the king saying, "With respect to you, my king, you need to speak to your sons . . ."

And Jeremiah continued, saying, "A conspiracy is found among the men of Judah and among the inhabitants of Jerusalem! They have turned back to the sins of their forefathers, who refused to hear My Word..."

The king exclaimed: "Out of my sight, Prophet! You were called upon and did not say 'yea' or 'nay'! And still you do not say 'yea' or 'nay'! Before the Sabbath we will defeat Pharaoh! Have not the prophets decried alliances with Egypt? So now we will defeat Egypt!"

But Jeremiah ignored the king and said, "Behold, I am bringing disaster upon all the people; no one will be able to escape!"

"Yes! Yes! Disaster is coming!" spoke the king. "But is it this week? Why do you not say 'yea' or 'nay?' Come with me, Jeremiah! Come stand with my fifty prophets!" But Jeremiah ignored the words of the king.

And Berechiah, Nagid of the Zadikite, asked the king, "Where are these fifty prophets?"

"They will stand behind us in battle! They now understand that their lives depend upon the Word they delivered to me!" Then Josiah departed the gate, and his soldiers saluted him and called his name. Fifteen thousand departed with Josiah that day.

Jehoahaz also departed from Jerusalem, and proceeded to Anathoth, and there he camped.

Josiah came to the vale which approaches Megiddo in the Valley of Jezreel. There he camped as Pharaoh's army approached. There the five clan joined Josiah the king so that Josiah's army numbered 21,000 men.

And Pharaoh sent to Josiah the king a messenger requesting a meeting at his tent. Pharaoh left with the army of Josiah two of his sons, and Josiah went with his servants, Obadiah, and the counselor Malluch to the tent of Pharaoh.

Pharaoh Necho said to King Josiah, "Why have you come out to do battle with me? Have you not heard the Word of He Who Is? Have you not heard that this Holy One of yours that has been the bane of Egypt has come to me and directed my action? Have you not been told to remain in Jerusalem?"

Josiah said to Pharaoh, "I have fifty prophets who have come with me this day that have instructed me that I am to do battle and that the battle will be mine."

BERECHIAH

"Is there not one who has said differently to you? Does your heart not burn at his Word?" asked Pharaoh.

Josiah said, "There is one who speaks a different Word, but he always speaks differently. Though I have sought to be righteous in my dealings with all and have kept the Covenant our conquering One has provided for us and searched diligently for Him, I hear nothing from this man. He refused to say 'yea' or 'nay!' I, the king, begged for a clear Word! But nothing. Therefore, I am here to defend Judah! Evil comes no matter what I do! Without a Word, to not be here would be dishonorable!"

And it was then that Pharaoh said to Josiah the king, "Hear me! Withdraw from this battle, for I was told that the number I brought to this valley would not matter, but that the hand of your god would be with me. To what advantage is it for me to do battle with you? I wish to get on to Asshur. I consider it not in the interest of Egypt to spill the blood of its sons here, so far from our goal. I would not have stopped here but for the Word I received. I believe what I have heard.

"To ensure your understanding, I am to also say to you, 'Where are your sons? Have they not all gathered in Jerusalem to await word of your death? Have they not betrayed you and your chief priest and your governor? For is not Hilkiah your chief priest dead this day, and will not the bones of Maaseiah be found? Is not the governor of Jerusalem with you? Where is there a righteous man in Jerusalem? Has not your Prophet fled Jerusalem from the Gate of Ephraim? Has not Obadiah given his daughter Deborah in marriage to Lemuel? Is not Lemuel delivering a message to Chebel and Nehi, and are they not returning here?'

"Listen to me, King Josiah. I am no god to any but my people, and I know what I am. I am confounded by this which I have been told to say and do. Hear my Word to you and depart from here and let us be brothers in our belief, for surely He Who Is, is. I now understand many things! The greatest is that I can do nothing but what He Who Is commands of me! Dare I do otherwise and lose my firstborn as did the pharaoh of old? I would rather be in deepest Africa, but have I a choice?"

Obadiah saw that the king had no words to say and Obadiah said to Pharaoh, "If a thief broke into your house in the night, would you listen to him as he said, 'Your Elohim told me to break into your home and steal from you?' Would you not call your guards and say to your guards, 'Execute this worthless thief?' And would it not be done? Has not Josiah my king said the same to me? For have we not caught the thief in our house and are we not now about to execute him?"

"Obadiah, Nagid of the Zadikite, once friend of Berechiah the Rechabite, my friend, hear my words to you," said Pharaoh. "Did I not purchase all that this army has eaten in this land? Where is it that any has stolen from the people of Israel? Accuse me and I will blot out that man and his family! We have come not as a thief in the night or as an army of marauders, but the sun shines on all that we do and you see what we do. Where is it that you can find fault with me? Tomorrow let your son stand with the king and let your son stand with Malluch the Rechabite at his side. Wrap your son in your *dagal*, and let the *dagal* of the Rechabite protect your son's head and he will be saved. This I know. But still, turn away from this vision, and I will not need to protect your son!"

The Word of Pharaoh Necho burned in the heart of Obadiah the Zadikite. Berechiah his son was also amazed. Malluch remembered the Word from Pharaoh.

Josiah the king asked Pharaoh Necho, "Has your Word informed us as to our fate?"

Obadiah said to the king, "Do not ask him as to our fate, for if the Word is true, then we know our fate. If this Word is from a seer, we condemn ourselves as Saul condemned himself. We believe or do not believe; we do or do not do. There is no fate but that which He Who Is knows, which is that which we choose, which is or is not contrary to Elohim's Will. I place my life in the hands of He Who Is. If I am wrong, I will die with Elohim having to know that I thought I was doing His Will. I may be chastised for doing this, but I cannot be chastised for lack of faith or lack of righteousness as far as I know it to be, or for lack of honor."

"It is good you have not asked" said Pharaoh. "Will you not depart from here?"

Josiah stood and said to Pharaoh, "I can do only that which I think is the Will of my Elohim."

"Do you not know the soldiers in my army?" asked Pharaoh. "Do you not know that I have 15,000 foot soldiers and bowmen, 8,000 on horse and 7,000 on chariot? You have 5,000 on chariot, 6,000 on horse, and 10,000 on foot. Does not your son now return to Jerusalem? Not only is your god not with you, but you are being betrayed. Go, Josiah! Return to Jerusalem!"

Josiah was angry with Pharaoh, and said, "Why could not my Elohim come to me and speak these Words? Why does my Elohim confuse men so? Does He Who Is have sport with us? Have I not been righteous? Even if all this is true, can I leave this field? Where would I find honor? From whom would I find respect? Would they not say, 'There is Josiah the fearful'? And when the Asshur come to Judah, would not the king say, 'Go home, Josiah, for your god has sent me to take what is yours?' And would not the king of Bab'el come to Judah and say, 'Go home, Josiah, for your god has sent me to take away your daughters'? Can I only know the truth when my blood is spilt? Then so be it. The other choices I have cannot be. If my sons are betraying me, why would I want to go to Jerusalem? Would I not have to kill them? No, stand and fight, Pharaoh. Tomorrow my Elohim will see his servant die or live; it is not in my hand."

And Pharaoh Necho said to Josiah, "Go, and may we all understand why we live."

So Josiah withdrew from the tent of Pharaoh Necho and returned to his tent, and sent the sons of Pharaoh to the tent of Pharaoh. Josiah called Obadiah the Zadikite to him to determine the battle.

Then Obadiah asked the king to send a messenger to Jerusalem to uncover the truth of what was happening. A messenger of the king was sent. Obadiah asked the king to send a Rechabite as well, so the king also sent a Rechabite to Jerusalem. The messenger of the king was killed, but the Rechabite passed, as the spies of the prince did not understand that the king had sent the Rechabite, and the *dagal* of the messenger protected the Rechabite, for no one would fall on a Rechabite.

And Obadiah presented to the king a battle plan, saying, "Tomorrow send the chariots to the left third of the army of Pharaoh. Have them strike through the army as a funnel fills a jar. When the first chariot reaches the middle of the foot soldier, have them turn to the left and proceed up the wall of the Valley of Jezreel. Have the bowmen second in rank shower the right flank with arrow to hold them in position. When we see the chariots reach the valley wall and turn, blow the trumpet and let the horse through the bowmen and have them split the right two-thirds as the chariots come down and split the middle of Pharaoh's army. If the chariots are able to destroy the left third in the original attack and descend from the wall, the other two-thirds will be disheartened. If Pharaoh's chariots attack along the front, our chariots must ignore them and continue on their task. The bowmen must either use their arrows or use their swords, but they cannot break. Our horsemen must be able to attack through the foot soldier at the trumpet sound."

Josiah asked, "And where shall we be?"

"On the left ridge above the horsemen, my king, will be your stand and banner, with the *dagals* of the clans. I will lead the chariots at the first attack, but once on the valley wall, I will return to your side."

"It is to be done. Call for the captains and have them remain with me this night." But the priest Tibni, advisor of Jehoahaz, whom he did not call, was no longer to be found in the camp.

Then Obadiah departed from the presence of the king and went to his tent. Chebel and Nehi came to the tent of Obadiah and reported to Josiah all they had heard and seen. Obadiah went to the tent of the king and said to Josiah, "My king, hear the report of my messengers that have just come to me."

The king said, "Let them come to me and speak their word to me."

And Chebel and Nehi came to the king and Chebel said to the him, "King Josiah, hear our word and do not be angry with us for the information we bring to you."

"You will be spared, for I will need you tomorrow at the side of Obadiah."

So Chebel said to the king, "For two moons we waited in the Valley of Arabah and we did not see an army of Pharaoh, nor did the men of the desert see an army of Pharaoh, nor did the Rechabites beyond report an army of Pharaoh. But the army of Jehoahaz is in Jerusalem and no one knows where Hilkiah the chief priest is. It is said that the party of Jehoahaz has control of the Temple and the house of the king and his concubines. No one knows where the king's other sons are. They are thought to have fled. Have they come here?"

King Josiah said, "Am I as Pharaoh, to have my sons at my side? Is it his authority they fear, or is it love? Is it not apparent how much my sons love me? Depart from me. I believe your words and must consider my action."

And Obadiah called Chebel and Nehi and told them to leave the camp of the king, as according to the law they were to enjoy their new wives for one year.

But Chebel said to Obadiah, "How could we now abandon our father in his hour of need. Our wives are with child; if need be we shall be remembered as is our father Nathan." And Chebel and Nehi remained at the right hand of Obadiah, Nagid of the Zadikites, until the end.

Then Obadiah said to the king, "My king, will we depart from Pharaoh?"

Josiah the king said to Obadiah, "We can do nothing but what we do. What we have planned will be done."

So Obadiah departed from the king. He sent his son Berechiah to the tent of the king, and Berechiah stood at the door of the tent of the king with the *dagal* of the Zadikite.

Before the morning, Josiah rose and called to Obadiah, Nagid of the Zadikite, and his captains, and the army prepared for battle. Across the Valley of Jezreel stood the army of Pharaoh, with the foot soldiers in divisions across the front, the horsemen, and then the chariots. And Josiah ordered the deployment of his troops.

And Obadiah said to Josiah the king, "My king, Pharaoh spoke the truth. I think his numbers are beyond ours and his troop deployment is crafty, almost as if he knows our plan."

"How could he know? Did we not first speak of it only last night? Were not our captains with us all night?"

"Yes, my king." And there was quiet.

BERECHIAH

Then Josiah asked of Obadiah, "If you think we may die this day, why do you remain at my side? Why are you not with my sons?"

"My king, I serve you! You have never understood! It is the faith that makes the act, not the act that makes the faith! As an old man said to me, 'Our lives are like a fruit: Most taste the peel and say 'This is bitter!' and throw it away, but we enjoy the peel in order to wallow in the meat of the fruit where it is sweet.' With our lives we do things contrary to the wishes of the flesh and this is seen as bitterness to others, but it is necessary for our survival. Could there be fruit without the peel? Could there be fruit without the meat and seed? No. But this day I eat the peel and celebrate. I can do no other."

As the king pondered this, he asked, "Who will know what we have done here? Who will care?"

And Obadiah responded, "Certainly it will not be told by us!"

Then the king said, "I must say something worthy of a king." And the king was silent. Then the king quietly said, "Is it not a glorious day to be with our He Who Is?"

Obadiah responded, smiling gently, "I would rather be in bed with my wife."

Josiah also smiled and Obadiah the Zadikite departed from his king. When he reached the chariots of the Zadikites, *dagal* flying, the yobel of the king spoke to the chariots and they attacked. Pharaoh watched from the right of the field.

And Obadiah the Zadikite led the chariots into the left third of Pharaoh's army, and, as he rode through, his driver and he and his servant smote the Egyptians, and the chariots of Josiah followed Obadiah, Claw of Josiah, into the gap created by the charge.

But Pharaoh's foot soldiers moved to their left, behind the horsemen of Pharaoh, so that by midway through his expected charge, Obadiah was forced to turn left and move up the wall of the valley. While the bowmen shot arrows, they fell on the shield of the foot soldiers of Pharaoh, not on the horses nor on the chariots.

While Pharaoh's own right flank struggled for survival as the chariots of Josiah went through them, the horsemen of Pharaoh charged their right flank where Obadiah had turned, but not all his chariots had yet turned, so that Obadiah's signal to turn and prepare to charge down into the valley was not seen by the chariots.

The trumpet of Josiah saw the signal of Obadiah and blew just as the trumpet of Pharaoh ordered the horsemen to charge. The horsemen fell upon the backs of the chariots of Josiah, followed by a trumpet of Pharaoh, and so the chariots of Pharaoh went through the gap created by Obadiah which separated his center from right flank, and the chariots of Pharaoh split the army of Josiah in two.

When Josiah's trumpet ordered the horsemen to attack, they could not attack, as the center and right flank of Josiah collapsed on each other when the horsemen tried to force their way through. The right flank of Josiah felt the chariots of Pharaoh and their own horsemen and their spirit collapsed. But the left flank remained stable.

Obadiah saw this from his vantage point and took to the ridge and found the king. "My king! Order the chariots to the top of the wall of the ridge! All is not yet lost!"

"Order it! said the king.

The army of Josiah heard the yobel, but was in disarray. Then Josiah saw the battle as it really was and said to Obadiah, "Come, my friend, let us fight where death is most certain, with the *dagal* of the tribe of David and the *dagals* of the clans of Judah at our side. Come, let us meet our Holy One of Israel, for there are questions I must ask of the Almighty. I think our blood will soon be spilled here at Megiddo."

So Josiah and Obadiah descended into the fray with Malluch, Berechiah, Chebel and, Nehi, with the *dagal* of the House of Judah and the *dagal* of the Zadikite and the other clans by their sides. And they were surrounded by Pharaoh's army. The arrows of Pharaoh struck Josiah so that he was mortally wounded. His servants withdrew the dying Josiah in his chariot and he died as he left the field of battle.

Malluch took Berechiah, son of Obadiah, and covered him with his *dagal*l, but Berechiah took the sword of the king and used it on his enemy. Egyptians fell back from the youth as he protected the body of his father. Chebel and Nehi fell with sword in hand, and Judah groaned as her *dagal* fell.

Then Berechiah, being the only one of the king's party alive, ordered the yobel to blow retreat, and the army of Josiah fled.

Berechiah ordered the false prophets to be put to death, and they were. And Berechiah the Zadikite saw Tibni, servant of Jehoahaz, in Egyptian uniform, and, though the priest hid his face, his scars betrayed who he was. And Berechiah the Zadikite remembered the traitor.

And Berechiah was surrounded by Egyptian troops, and he and Malluch stood alone in the field. As was the custom, those near death were relieved of life. Berechiah saw the Egyptians would not advance and would not fall back. He dropped the sword of King Josiah and knelt by the body of his father and he wept.

When Pharaoh saw Berechiah he was pleased his soldiers had done as he had ordered, and Pharaoh allowed the body of Josiah the king to be carried away from the battlefield to Jerusalem to be placed with his fathers. And he ordered the body of Obadiah to be taken to the house of Obadiah so that his wife could do as she wished. The bodies of the dead were buried

BERECHIAH

in the Valley of Jezreel, and Pharaoh drove his chariots over the burial place so that no one could find the bodies of the 8,000 of Judah who fell, nor the 5,000 of Egypt.

And Pharaoh Necho sent a messenger to Jerusalem, saying, "Do not make a king for yourselves until you hear my words to you."

But in Jerusalem Pharaoh's word was disregarded, and the party of Jehoahaz assigned a new chief priest and new governor by Jehoahaz's word, and Jehoahaz was anointed king of Judah. While the righteous feared for their lives, evil men plotted and were pleased with their accomplishments. The Temple was desecrated, and while Josiah's blood was not yet dry on the ground of Israel, wine flowed through the veins of his son Jehoahaz.

And Jeremiah, son of Habaziniah the Rechabite, went to the house of Obadiah the Zadikite, and the tents of the Rechab protected the wife of Obadiah and Deborah, the twin of Berechiah the Zadikite. Jeremiah, Nagid of the Rechabite, took Deborah the Zadikite to Lemuel, son of Zephaniah the Zadikite of the city of Tirzah. At the appointed time, Lemuel wed Deborah, daughter of Obadiah, and Hannah wept for her husband Obadiah, but heard of the well being of her son, Berechiah, and her daughter, Deborah. Two *dagal* flew over the house of Hannah, that of the Zadikite and that of the Rechabite.

The wives of Chebel and Nehi both were with child. And Jeremiah the Rechabite sent these two women out of Judah, for *nokri* from the Moab entered Judah as she was wounded, and laid waste the fields of Judah and her smaller cities.

For a fortnight Berechiah and Malluch were held in a tent awaiting audience with Pharaoh. Berechiah heard much, as servants of Malluch came to him and reported daily.

And Malluch sent word to Jeremiah the Rechabite as to Berechiah. So Jeremiah the Rechabite sent to Pharaoh a messenger with a request along with 8,000 rams.

Pharaoh received the messenger and the messenger said to Pharaoh, "Where is Berechiah the Zadikite? Is he now with his father that I have not seen him? Here, take one ram for each man of Israel that fell, and send me word as to the new Nagid of the Zadikites, Berechiah, son of Obadiah."

And Pharaoh answered, "Who are you? And who has sent you?"

"I am Lemuel, betrothed to the sister of Berechiah, sent by Jeremiah the Rechabite. I am here to beg for a word from Berechiah."

"Do you think I do not know that Jeremiah knows exactly what happens in my tent? Tell the young fox that he only needs to listen to the reports of his spies," said Pharaoh.

"But Jeremiah does not know what is in the heart of Pharaoh!"

"I am surprised this god of Judah has not told him that! I consider that soon I will be mad or out of Israel! I tire of hearing from gods!" Pharaoh was provoked.

Then Lemuel presented a gift wrapped in the *dagal* of the Rechabite. Pharaoh unwrapped the *dagal* and found his own dagger.

Pharaoh was angry, and he said, "Is there only intrigue in this land? Traitors and spies and boys that rule clans who govern better than my captains! No wonder armies burn this land to the ground! Can they do otherwise? Send the boy Berechiah to me! Let us see who he is!"

Chapter Eight

✳ ✳ ✳ ✳ ✳

The Court of Pharaoh at Riblah

So Pharaoh brought Berechiah the Zadikite before him. Pharaoh's sons, his captains, and his guard were around him in the tent of Pharaoh. As Berechiah entered Pharaoh's presence, from behind a screen he saw eyes with a double cut to the ear. And Berechiah knew the design of the traitor Tibni, advisor of Jehoahaz. Berechiah stood before and awaited word from Pharaoh.

"Who is this sparrow that fights like a hawk?" asked Pharaoh. "Who is it who has friends that send me my own dagger? Is he a boy or a man? Is he Nagid of the Zadikite or not? Let me see his eyes and I will know his heart!"

And Berechiah said to Pharaoh, "Does a boy take his father's place in battle? Does a boy protect the body of his king? Does a man claim the protection of Pharaoh by accepting the protection of a *dagal* spread by a friend? Does a man want to live when his king and his father and his family lie dead around him?"

"My sparrow has a sharp beak! He pecks at Pharaoh to gain attention. What does this sparrow want?"

"I want righteous judgment against the enemy of Israel!" said Berechiah.

"Who is that enemy? Is it I?" asked Pharaoh.

"It is who I know it is!" declared Berechiah.

"Let us play with this sparrow and have him learn lessons of authority," said Pharaoh. "Bring the captain of my archers!"

And the captain of Pharaoh's archers was brought to Pharaoh.

Pharaoh said to the captain of his archers, "Stand before me thirty paces and shoot three arrows at me!"

So the captain of Pharaoh's archers stood thirty paces from Pharaoh and shot three arrows at him. Pharaoh's guard stopped the arrows, one through each hand and one in his shoulder. The guard's blood was spilled before Pharaoh; and he was removed from Pharaoh's presence, and another guard took his place.

"Do you understand what has happened before your eyes, Berechiah, soon to be Nagid of the Zadikite, and friend of the Rechabite?"

Berechiah considered the authority of Pharaoh, and he wondered to himself, "Is this 'good?' Is this not evil? Is this not one of the horns of Ba'al?"

Pharaoh said to Berechiah, "Take the bow of my captain, and shoot your arrow. If it does not reach me, you will know that your god sent me to this land! You will then say to me, 'Pharaoh, you are not my enemy.'"

"Am I not to have three arrows as did your servant? If I am a sparrow, what fear is there of me having a sting to poison or a claw to tear?"

"Take your three arrows, and let us see the training that Obadiah, the Claw of Judah, gave his son!"

So Berechiah took the bow and took three arrows and took thirty paces.

And the guards were afraid, for they did not understand the god of Judah. Pharaoh's sons went and stood close to the royal throne, but Pharaoh smiled before his servants for he was not afraid.

Berechiah took the arrow and placed the arrow and aimed toward Pharaoh. Then he turned to the screen that hid Tibni and shot the arrow, and the second, and the third. Three arrows entered the neck of Tibni the traitor, and he died, gasping for breath, as all three had pierced his throat. It was a painful death.

There was silence.

No one moved toward Berechiah; and no one said a word.

Tibni died alone, and his body was thrown out of the camp.

Then Berechiah said, "Pharaoh, you are not my enemy."

And Pharaoh said, "You have spoken truth. Your wit is as sharp as my arrows. The Claw still lives!"

And Berechiah said to Pharaoh, "Does Pharaoh need traitors to complete the Word of He Who Is? Does Pharaoh regard traitors to be worthy to be in his presence?"

Pharaoh said, "Your god came to me in a vision and said to me, 'Go to Judah' so I went to Judah and did as I was bid. Your god did not tell me how to do it! I must be sure! How did I know that what I saw was not a nightmare? Or a trick! How many kings do you know who have had visions from foreign gods? I did my bidding out of fear! I pray your god does not care why I came to Judah! Just as I do not care why my guard held out his hand and took an arrow meant for me! I came, I did. The guard did. Why? Does 'why' make a difference?"

"That I do not know, but I do inquire: How long until you will depart from Judah?"

Pharaoh said, "Why is it you are concerned about when Pharaoh will leave Israel? Did not your father Abraham come to Egypt to the house of my fathers? Was not Joseph a servant of Pharaoh? And has not Israel fled to Egypt to find safety?

"Why is it you hate Egypt? We have hurt your people, yes, but we have helped your people! You come to us often, and now I come to you! Who would you be if we had not helped your father Jacob? Has not your Prophet Isaiah said, 'Out of Egypt will come Emmanuel?' Do you think us fools? Do you think we are accursed, and yet we are vital to your Story and necessary to your future! How can you hate me?"

And Berechiah said, "I do not hate Egypt. Tomorrow I may need to clean my wounds in the Nile if my Elohim points me there; but if so, will Pharaoh still be in Israel?"

Pharaoh said, "You must have patience. I still have tasks to perform, not only for your god, but a good task asked of me by Berechiah the Rechabite, Obadiah the Zadikite, and Josiah, king of Judah. You have taken care of one of my problems with wisdom and trickery beyond your years. Now I set before you another task: Advise me what I am to do with the pretender Jehoahaz, sitting on the throne of Judah without the blessing of your god. I must do this task before I leave Judah."

"I cannot counsel Pharaoh as to how to depose the one who declares the Almighty One and Judah have declared him king of Judah. He may be evil, but so were his fathers, other than the great Josiah, and even he had his sins, as did our great King David. Would I counsel an enemy of yours how to remove you from your rightful task? I can say: If he be of Adonai, he will not be deposed. If he is not of Adonai, you will depose him, and remove him from Judah to the safety of Egypt, where Asshur or Bab'el cannot reach him, and yet his blood will not be on your head."

"Your lack of counsel is wise," said Pharaoh. "But does this mean that King Josiah was not of your god?"

"No."

Then Pharaoh was perplexed, for he could not understand how, if Josiah was good, he was now dead. So he said, "Yes, you speak with wisdom. As for now, come, step forward—without bow or knife—and present yourself to Pharaoh, for we will become friends. I will be your protector! And we will speak of this strange god."

So Berechiah the Zadikite went and was seated next to Pharaoh, and Pharaoh presented to Berechiah the *hoshen* of Obadiah his father, the sword of Obadiah, the armlets of Obadiah, and the *urim* of Obadiah, which, as with all things, were from Obadiah's father and his father's father. The servants of Pharaoh placed on Berechiah the things of his father, and Berechiah wept.

And Pharaoh said to Berechiah, "Would that my sons weep over me when my time comes! Is there love such as this in the hearts of my sons?" And he gazed into the eyes of his eldest son.

And Berechiah said to Pharaoh, "For this thing that you have done, I, Berechiah, Nagid of the Zadikites, will never lift a sword again against Egypt. Neither I nor my people. If Pharaoh needs safe passage, for himself or his servant, it will be Berechiah of the Zadikites that will provide the safe passage. If Pharaoh calls for service, Berechiah will respond. This I swear before my Elohim this day!"

Pharaoh rose and took his linen *dagal* of gold and green and placed it around Berechiah and Pharaoh said before his captains, servants, and warriors, "Hear and believe this I say this day before the god of Judah: I, Necho, Pharaoh of Egypt, protector and ruler of the living and the dead! I order the royal protection of Berechiah, son of Obadiah the Zadikite of the House of Judah, until his death. This protection binds this Pharaoh and the next and the next until Berechiah is no more. If a hand is raised against Berechiah or his family or even his empty house, Egypt will cause terror on that person, his family, his clan, his tribe, his city, and his people! They will be blotted from the earth."

And Pharaoh looked to his guard and asked, "Who would serve me by being my eyes over Berechiah the Zadikite?"

From the guard a man stepped forward and said to Pharaoh, "I am Etutu-Ebuh, captain of Pharaoh's southern army; I am of the Sukkiim; I will do as Pharaoh commands."

"It is done. You will be provided for by the hand of Pharaoh."

Then Pharaoh stood and took the sword of Obadiah and held it with his hand so that he bled. Pharaoh ordered messengers to take the oath of Pharaoh to each city of Judah, to each city that had interests in Judah, to Egypt, and to all at the court of Pharaoh in Egypt.

And Pharaoh took white linen and cleaned his hands with it so that there was blood on the white linen. Pharaoh took the linen and placed it on a spear and on the *dagal* of Pharaoh and gave it to Berechiah.

"This I do as compensation for the loss of your father and the loss of your king whom you loved, and those of your clan whom you loved. I came at the behest of your god. I did not wish to do this thing, but I did as I know I was told, as I believed I was told. I have fear for what I have done.

It had to be done. But to you, Berechiah, I swear my love and eternal debt. I ask you to understand the imperative for what I have done, but you may not understand what I now must do."

And Pharaoh ordered that a guard be brought to him of two thousand men. He ordered the captain of his archers to go to Jerusalem.

Pharaoh said to his captain, "Say to Jehoahaz, pretender to the throne of Judah: 'I am Necho, Pharaoh of all Egypt and beyond, brought to Judah by your god, the same one who defeated your father in battle at the behest of your god. Hear this, people of Jerusalem and Jehoahaz, pretender to the throne of Judah: I, Pharaoh, require Jehoahaz to stand before me, him and his family and his brothers and their families. Come to Riblah in the land of Hamath, or I will descend upon Jerusalem in the same manner as I scattered the army of King Josiah at Megiddo.'"

When the people of Jerusalem heard these words they were fearful. Jehoahaz took counsel with his party, and his party turned on him, placed him in chains, and took him to Pharaoh Necho at Riblah in the land of Hamath. They brought all the family of Jehoahaz to Pharaoh, as well as the sons of Josiah.

And Pharaoh said to Jehoahaz, "Did you not hear the word I sent to Jerusalem that I am to appoint the King of Judah?"

"Great Pharaoh of the Nile," Jehoahaz said to Pharaoh, "do kings not say things today that they forget tomorrow, and do not gods say things today that they forget tomorrow? I am first of the sons of Josiah. I have earned the throne of David. It is my right and I claimed my right! Did not Josiah on his deathbed confirm my throne?"

"You lie well!" said Pharaoh. "But do not believe your own lies! I know and you know that Josiah died before he left the field of battle! Do your dead kings speak? Who buried Josiah?"

"A minor point which does not matter. Josiah himself would have placed me on the throne had he been in Jerusalem. It is my right. So he was in Jerusalem!"

"What if it was not your right? Who is it that places princes into the chair where they are then called king? I am to say to you, 'Is it not your god that makes a king?'"

"What god put Pharaoh on his throne?"

"My gods do not punish their own kingdom nor send Pharaoh on assignment to imperil his own people. It is only your god that does this! And my god does not send foreign kings to punish me! How strange is your god. This warrior god killed our firstborn! Yet Berechiah the Zadikite speaks of your god as love, as the beginning and only meaning of life!

"This I do not understand, but I do understand that you are not of this god! Even I hear of your behavior in Jerusalem! You stole the throne of your father! You forget to whom you speak! See now the body of your servant Tibni. I consider that you are an affront to nature, let alone your god!"

"Is Pharaoh the judge of who I am and what I do?"

"Yes! For it is your god that has told me to do so."

"I think I fear Pharaoh more than I fear this Holy One of Judah!"

"Then fear Pharaoh and die in fear! Hear this that I command: Out of my sight, false prince and thief! The curse of Obadiah the Zadikite comes back upon you!"

And Pharaoh bound Jehoahaz in his chains and had a burning rod placed through his eyes so that Jehoahaz could no longer look on his sons nor find pleasure in the earth, and his soul burned within him. Then Pharaoh sent Jehoahaz to Egypt where he was to die living in a house of servants, and the sons of Jehoahaz did not know they were princes, and they were forgotten. Jehoahaz had ruled Judah three months.

And Berechiah observed all the things that occurred with Pharaoh.

So Pharaoh called to him Eliakim, son of Josiah, and Eliakim was afraid. Pharaoh asked of Eliakim if he were of this god of Judah, and Eliakim answered that he was of the same mind as was his father. And Pharaoh gave Eliakim the name Jehoiakim and placed the crown of Judah on his head. Jehoiakim returned to Jerusalem with his family, and with the burden of tribute that Pharaoh had assigned to Jehoiakim to be delivered to Egypt each year. Judah was burdened greatly by the tribute.

Then Pharaoh spoke to Berechiah the Zadikite about the god of Judah. Malluch spoke as it was spoken of old, and Pharaoh was troubled.

Berechiah the Zadikite said to Pharaoh, "It is time for Pharaoh to return to Egypt. His task has been completed."

But Pharaoh said to Berechiah, "It is the curse of kings to do those things that they should not. I have been called upon by my one-time enemy, Asshur, who is now my friend and is soon to be attacked by the Bab'el. I need to return to Egypt, but I cannot do so. I must go to the place of my enemy and there either establish Egypt as a kingdom as she once was, or return to a kingdom only of the river Nile. I have dreams of being as were my fathers, and I must do as I have said I must do. If I protect the Asshur, I will fear no king to my east nor to my south nor to my west. My people will be secure and will remember my victories. Egypt will be as it was!"

And Berechiah said to Pharaoh, "You will be remembered for what you have done in Judah!"

"But that may not be the way I want to be remembered!"

So Berechiah asked of Pharaoh, "Why is it that I may not return to the house of my mother? Is there a service I have yet to offer?"

"No, my young friend," said Pharaoh. "But there is a service that I am to provide to you!"

BERECHIAH

Pharaoh asked Berechiah, "Do you not take pleasure in your manhood? Do you not find a passion in your body?"

"Yes, but there is much I do not understand!"

Pharaoh smiled and found pleasure in this young man. He brought out a curtain and placed it at the door of his tent and the sun shone through the curtain. Pharaoh called to his servants to play the instruments of his land and behind the curtain a figure danced for Pharaoh. And Berechiah took pleasure in the dance and in the figure of the dancer.

And Berechiah said to Pharaoh, "What is this that you do?"

"I present to you your wife, chosen for you by your father Obadiah and Jeremiah the Rechabite," said Pharaoh to Berechiah. "She is the daughter of a Jehudi of the Sukkiim brought to my court in compliance of treaty. Her skin and hair are as red as a dark sunset and shine as a river at night. Her eyes glow with the brightness of the moon! Your god must be the creator of this jewel, for only a god could create such beauty!"

"Is she as she should be according to our traditions?"

"She is as according to your Law," said Pharaoh.

"Then let me see her."

But Pharaoh said, "My friend, give me your word that you will take this one to be your wife before you see her! You have trusted me and I have trusted you! Now let it mean something between us!"

"So be it. She shall be my wife, if it is found acceptable with her parents and, as my father is dead, if she finds favor with my *zaqen*."

"Her father finds it acceptable, for it is this Sukkiim who is my representative to you and you have found favor with him! As for your *zaqen*, I have sent for them, as I know your customs," said Pharaoh.

"And her mother? Where is her mother?"

Pharaoh said, "Her mother died in childbirth with their third child. She was one of pale skin from across the sea to the land of hard water."

"Then I will take her as my wife, if she smiles at me and my *zaqen* find favor in her."

And the maiden danced to find favor with Berechiah. She danced hiding her face from Berechiah, and bowed and turned and brought herself face to face with Berechiah, and she smiled. Berechiah was warmed; he knew he had met his gift from the Holy One of Israel.

Berechiah looked upon his wife-to-be and turned to Pharaoh and said, "Her name is to be Rizpah, for her color is as 'burning coal.'" And Berechiah took the hand of Rizpah and stood and Rizpah stood with him.

And the court of Pharaoh remembered their childhood and the joy of youth.

So Berechiah the Zadikite learned the language of the Sukkiim and Rizpah learned the customs of the Zadikite.

Robert Hermanson

Then the *zaqen* of the Zadikite came to Pharaoh, and Pharaoh brought them to Riblah and Berechiah the Zadikite. Pharaoh stationed himself behind a screen so that he could hear the questions of the *zaqen* and the responses of Rizpah.

And the questions began: "How is it that you, a Sukkiim, come here to this land to be betrothed to Berechiah."

Rizpah answered, "I was sought by Obadiah the Zadikite and Berechiah the Rechabite and I was found in the house of my father, servant of Pharaoh of Egypt. While still a child I was chosen."

"Who are you?"

"I am Rizpah, as named by Berechiah. I am daughter of Etutu-Ebuh, captain of Pharaoh, warrior of the Sukkiim, whose name is known in all of Africa. Our clan goes back to the days before the great judges of Israel and we possess the Stories of you, our people."

"Are you then not of Canaan, cursed by Noah?" asked a *zaqen*.

"What is this insult? Was Moses' wife cursed? Was she not Ethiopian? In your Story does not the Song of King Solomon speak of his maiden stating she is black and beautiful? If we are cursed, I am cursed as are all! Are you not sons of Adam and Eve? We are now all sons and daughters of Cain, for have not all our people traveled to this land and that?

"Do not the daughters of princes travel from this land to that to wed kings? If a drop of blood comes from Cain, am I not of Cain? If a drop of blood comes from Canaan, are we not all of Canaan? How many daughters of our tribe have come to Israel? How many daughters of kings have come to us? We tell of thousands in five hundred years. And how many come to us from Israel who are as dark as we? How many come to you from Egypt and Asshur and to the north to the men who travel the seas and to the south to the men who travel to different lands? Did not those of Dan also sail the seas?

"Why the insult?" Rizpah said again. "Do you fear my lineage? Do you fear the sons of Moses? Is it lineage or faith that is the question? If it is clan or tribe, show me the twelve tribes. Where are they? Is Judah of Judah? Is Levi of Levi, or is it what one claims? Where is Zebulun or Manasseh or Simeon? Where is Reuben? Does not the blood of Reuben flow in the Moabites? If there are curses left from the days of our fathers, they are on all of us!

"I have the blood of the Rechab in me, and is not the clan of Rechabites now from all the twelve? And I have the blood of Deborah in me, as well as that of Pharaohs long forgotten, as well as that of the sons of Sheba.

"Yes, I may be of one cursed, just as you are of one cursed and lost," Rizpah spoke clearly. "We all have within us a lineage to Adam. You cannot show me who is of Simeon, nor can I say 'I am' or 'I am not' of Canaan. Is not the question a question of individual righteousness?

"Who is righteous? Do you judge a man guilty by who his father was, or by who he is? While I might bear my father's shame and suffer from his evil behavior, it is my own righteousness that our Holy One weighs. Do you love or despise a man by who his father was, or by who he is?

"Samuel was a man of faith; but were his sons? We understand King Josiah was a man of faith and righteousness. Was his father also, or his father's father? If you use a man's lineage to determine his value, would our Holy One of Israel ever visit one of us? If we are cursed would our father's friend, Isaiah the prophet, come and live with us three years? No! Because you have forgotten us, you want to refute us. We are you! We have not forgotten our faith! We have not forgotten our Story! We are Jehudi just as was Josiah, and of Israel as were David, Moses, and our father Abraham. I am your faith!"

"What do you know of our faith?" asked a *zaqen*.

"'Hear, O Israel, Adonai is one.' Hear the Story and Word I have been taught and believe and live, and compare it to your Word!" spoke Rizpah.

So the *zaqen* heard the Word and the Story of Rizpah's clan and tribe. And the sun went down and they slept and the sun came up and they ate and still they heard the Word. And the sun went down and came up a second day.

"What Words do you find most helpful?" asked a *zaqen* who now loved Rizpah.

"'A wandering Aramean was my father,'" answered Rizpah. "Is that not who we are? Is that not the beginning of our story? Those words are the gate to our identity and to faith. Who am I? 'A wandering Aramean was my father.' And why is that important? Because our He Who Is acted upon this people and still acts upon this people, be it in love or chastisement."

"It is good that you know these things and this Word."

"But that is not faith," Rizpah affirmed. "I may know the Word, and I may sometimes even do the Word, but I still may not have faith. Even knowing and doing may not mean understanding. Teaching does not provide faith; memory does not transmit understanding. Both are simply preparation.

"If I only chew on beeswax, what do I know of honey? Beeswax bears small resemblance to honey, golden and rich, dripping down my chin. The wax is tough and hard to chew and there is only small flavor of the sweetness of the honey. Faith and righteousness are the honeycomb which let us know the honey of our One.

"What does an uncut diamond tell of itself to the unknowing? When cut it sparkles and shines the colors of the rainbow! We can only describe the way; the path has to be walked alone. Then it is the faith that makes the behavior, not the behavior that makes the faith."

The *zaqen* considered these words, and one said to Rizpah, "What is good on this earth?"

Rizpah said: "The Will of Elohim is the only good. Therefore I must conform to that will and consider good only that which is the Will of Elohim. The Will is found in the Word, and the Word is the Will. I may lose my mother and it may or may not be the Will of He Who Is. Good is different from our pleasure; good is our One's pleasure. There is much good that is pleasurable, but all things pleasurable are not necessarily good.

"But are these not questions for the rabbis and those who have time to consider?" asked Rizpah. "Do they not deal with issues that make it impossible to act?

"Do rabbis ever die in battle? Are they not too important to die in service? I am here to serve and someday love my husband-to-be. Find in me righteousness. Find in me faithfulness. Find in me wisdom beyond my years. Hear and respect that I am a Possessor of the Word in our tradition. Let me make sons and daughters for Israel and you will know my husband and all that is his to be righteous before our Elohim."

Another *zaqen* said to Rizpah, "First, never let another hear the words you spoke of being a Possessor! We will fear for your life! Remember that! Now, my question: How do you consider Jerusalem? We know you are of a foreign land and we now know of your faith and words and accept your chastisement, but what about Jerusalem? What should she be to us?"

Rizpah responded, "Why is a place sacred? Is a place sacred because our men and women died there, or because our He Who Is was felt and seen and heard at that place? Is not a place sacred where worship occurs? Now all these are true, and more. If I erect a Mizbeach, a High Place, uncut stone by uncut stone, and worship our Elohim in faith and with righteousness, and if I know I am in the Presence of our He Who Is, is this place not sacred?

"Now outside of our Word which we remember, I have heard of Nathan, prophet at the time of David, who instructed David to build a house for our Elohim. But what Elohim had made sacred, men destroyed by their acts of cruelty, unfaithfulness, and unrighteousness. The Temple has been desecrated. Will the sacrifices to Ba'al tempt the nostrils of the Almighty? No. Our Elohim is no fool. Is it not for our own pleasure that we do these things? Does Elohim live in Jerusalem, or David, or Hezekiah?

"For me, Elohim is where Elohim Is. And that is everywhere." Rizpah was thoughtful. "I do not want my sons dying in a city and temple of cut stone! Is not Jerusalem condemned by the Word of our He Who Is? Are we to defend that city from the inevitable? We will go back and we will be sent

BERECHIAH

out and we will go back and we will be sent out! Why? Because we are a stiff-necked people, and bearded old men dream of glory that never was.

"What does He Who Is want of me? Defending Jerusalem is not righteousness. Building a Temple is not faithfulness. Isaiah gave us this Word while he was with our tribe when we were south of Ethiopia amongst the Sukkiim. Do you not know the Word of Isaiah?

"It is who I am that is important. How I live is important. It is the righteous man that is great; not a city, not a Temple." Rizpah paused.

"In many ways I consider language comparable to a Temple. Our words are our memory. Is not our memory sacred? Do we not create who we are by the words we use? If there comes a time when our Story is lost, will not our language no longer be sacred? If my grandfather is able to hear my words, am I not to be careful, for will he not know who I am by my word? Word is more sacred than Jerusalem ever will be. For the Word I will die; for our word together I would die. As for Jerusalem, she is a temptress over which the horns of Ba'al snag the unwary. And Ba'al will always be worshiped there. On this, my betrothed thinks differently than I; this I know. And this will be the last I speak of it. You have asked and I have spoken."

Then another *zaqen* asked, "What do we do with the written language that some now read and call sacred and call the Word of He Who Is?"

Rizpah answered, "My clan has a memory of the Word, which I have spoken. It is as I was told, stretching back before the judges, before Moses, and even to Abraham. Our Story is even before Abraham. But now I hear of a Word that is different than my Word. I hear of Prophets, and their Word comes to us and we see and know it to be true. I am confused by the different traditions and I am fearful of those who write what is their own will and not the Will of He Who Is.

"Where will it be remembered where Josiah the King died? Will we ever forget the evil of the other kings? If priests have their way, what tradition will be remembered? I fear this task is not of He Who Is, but of men.

"When I speak the Word of He Who Is, let my sons feel my breath on them as I have felt the Breath of He Who Is on me. We will remember by our words. The written Word will not enter our house. If it were to enter, would it not soon be that our children would be so bold as to actually say the name of our He Who Is? Oh! Elohim! Protect us from ourselves!"

And the *zaqen* of the Zadikite found Rizpah to be worthy of their son Berechiah. The Zaqen gave their blessing on the marriage, and they celebrated. Then Berechiah took Rizpah to be his wife, as was the custom.

When it was asked whether Berechiah was a man, Pharaoh answered, saying, "Is there one in Judah who stood with his king at the last and did not flee from his father's side? Surely this is a man in any nation."

Berechiah learned the customs of the Sukkiim and Rizpah learned of the prophets. Together they learned many things that were good and pleasurable. Rizpah came with child, and a son was born and was named Nathan by Berechiah and Rizpah.

And Pharaoh stayed in Israel. He called Berechiah the Zadikite the Claw of Judah, and sent him to cause righteousness where there was chaos. The Zadikites took pleasure in their Nagid, as friend of Pharaoh, husband of Rizpah the Sukkiim, and he became as was his father, Obadiah, righteous and faithful to He Who Is.

Rizpah bore Rachel the following year and Jehoshua the third year after marriage.

It was that year that Pharaoh moved his army out of Israel, and released Berechiah to his own house.

Pharaoh Necho moved his troop to Carchemish and there met Nebuchadnezzar and was defeated. And Pharaoh Necho fled from Carchemish and received safe passage through Israel by Berechiah the Zadikite, and Pharaoh returned to Egypt.

Pharaoh remembered Berechiah the Zadikite until the day he died and considered him to be a son. And Pharaoh's son ruled in his stead, and his son also became Pharaoh, named Hophra. All the Pharaoh remembered their obligation to Berechiah the Zadikite, even those who had not known him, as Pharaoh Necho had pledged.

And Rizpah bore a fourth child named Haggith, and a fifth named Mikaiahu, and a sixth child named Hannah. Berechiah was pleased with his three sons and three daughters, and he was pleased with his wife. Surely He Who Is had blessed him! And Rizpah slept with her husband and kept him warm, and he her, until the last.

Chapter Nine

✺ ✺ ✺ ✺ ✺

Jeremiah the Prophet

And Jehoiakim ruled in Jerusalem from the time as appointed by Pharaoh. Jehoiakim was the son of Josiah the king, and Zegbidah, the daughter of Pedaiah of Rumah. He was twenty-five years of age when he began to reign. He reigned eleven years in Jerusalem, the city of his fathers. He paid tribute to Pharaoh each year of his reign, even after Pharaoh was defeated by the king of Bab'el at Carchemish. He taxed his people so that he could pay the 100 talents of silver and the one talent of gold that he paid to Pharaoh.

And Jehoiakim did abominations in the sight of the Holy One of Israel, even in the Temple, as his brother had done before him. The priests and chief priest caused the worship of Ba'al and of the gods of the *nokri* in the Temple. The people of Jerusalem would not listen to her Prophets, and scoffed at the Word. The people did as they wished in the Temple and in the streets and in their own houses.

At this time, Berechiah, Nagid of the Zadikite, continued to live with Rizpah, his wife, in the fields and hills of En-Gannim. There Berechiah served as Nagid of the Zadikites, dispensing righteous judgment within the clan and as *zaqen* within his community. Berechiah longed for Jerusalem, but had heard he was not in favor with the king. And Berechiah defended Judah from marauders and the excursions of the Moabites and other *Nokri*, but he would not raise a hand for or against the city that chose not to serve the One of Israel.

Berechiah said, "What will befall Jerusalem as said by the Prophets will also befall the cities of Judah that are not faithful." Those who were wise feared the One of Israel and prepared for the Day of Judgment.

But the people were unable to hold to their faith and sold their birthright for the gods of the land and the pleasures of selfishness. Righteousness could not be found except for the faithful clans of Israel. Yet amongst the faithful clans and amongst the righteous priests there remained those faithful who remembered the Will of He Who Is, and in turn they were ridiculed and despised. Still, Berechiah defended the righteous with the sword and with swift judgment.

Berechiah upheld the law of Moses and celebrated the festivals and days of remembrance, but the unfaithful forgot these things. Poor men found no righteousness in the land, and widows and orphans found no haven. The widows of the men who died with Obadiah at Megiddo were cared for by Berechiah, as were the mothers who remained without support. Berechiah took those that were without inheritance and without a way to meet their needs and provided for them through his clan and the clans of the faithful. So the Zadikites were known and feared, as were the Rechabites, as righteous before the Holy One of Israel.

The Moabites learned not to enter southern Judah, for as by agreement among the clans, Berechiah was able to raise an army of 15,000 men of the Almighty. But this army was not at the service of the king, so that the king ruled in Jerusalem but the people did not know his word. And while the king knew the will of He Who Is, it was not done. The King found himself in disfavor with the parties of the princes and with the corrupt and dishonest, for one day he allowed abominations and the next he fell on his knees before He Who Is. One day he would encourage false worship, for it was profitable, and the next he would call for the Word from Jeremiah, son of Hilkiah of Anathoth. Who was this confused king?

And it was that the party of the princes and the chief priest and the priests of the Temple encouraged Jehoiakim in his desires, and Jehoiakim considered himself king of all Israel and of all tribes and clans. Jehoiakim desired to create an army as had his father, Josiah. Then he sent out word to the cities of Judah and to the clans of Judah, but the word of Jehoiakim was not considered by the great men of faith.

And Nebuchadnezzar heard of the desires of Jehoiakim and led an army out of Bab'el to Jerusalem. Jehoiakim was called out to serve Nebuchadnezzar, and he submitted himself to Nebuchadnezzar, so that he paid tribute to both Pharaoh and Nebuchadnezzar. The desires of the people were untamed in Jerusalem, and they did not know even to be shamed by the submission of Jehoiakim. There was only one voice in Jerusalem that spoke out against the sins of the people and of the king and of the priests, and he feared for his life. The Word that came to Jeremiah was heard by Berechiah the Zadikite and the *zaqen* of the Zadikite, so that there was fear for the king and fear that Jerusalem would be destroyed.

Berechiah

So it was that Berechiah, Nagid of the Zadikite, went to Jerusalem with his *zaqen*, his servants, Malluch, his advisor and friend, and Etutu-Ebuh, the Sukkiim and father of his wife and servant of Pharaoh. Then Berechiah requested that Jeremiah, Nagid of the Rechabite, come to Jerusalem and meet him there. Berechiah received word that Jeremiah the Rechabite would be at Jerusalem. Berechiah camped before the Gate of Ephriam with the Rechabites that were camped at Jerusalem.

And Berechiah went to the Temple and offered sacrifice according to the Law, and prayed as had his father before him in the place of his father. It was noted that the day Berechiah went to the Temple there was no sign of the gods of the *nokri* nor Ba'al, for the priests feared Berechiah. And Berechiah took his sons and daughters before He Who Is and dedicated them as *nazir*, in service to He Who Is. Then Berechiah went out from the Temple with his party, and they returned to the tents of the Zadikites.

Berechiah sent word to the tents of the Rechabites that he would approach their tents, and he was welcomed by Jeremiah, Nagid of the Rechabites, who was ill. The *zaqen* of the Rechabites were gathered at the Gate of Ephriam with Jeremiah. Then Berechiah was displeased that he had sent for Jeremiah and said, "If I had known that Jeremiah was not healthy, I would have come to him."

But Jeremiah the Rechabite said to Berechiah, "If I stay at the Holy Mountain or travel in my caravans abroad and our One of Israel calls and the Angel Abaddon is sent to me, will it matter where I am? I come to meet my friend and the friend of my clan, and if He Who Is calls me out, so be it."

So Jeremiah the Rechabite slept with his fathers. The *zaqen* of the Rechabites met with Berechiah and in his presence they called upon Jaazaniah, son of Jeremiah, son of Habazziniah, to be their Nagid, as they saw that his righteousness and faith was that of his fathers.

Then Jaazaniah, Nagid of the Rechabite, sent the body of his father, Jeremiah, to the Holy Mountain and he lay with his fathers' bones and with all his family. And Berechiah the Zadikite and Jaazaniah the Rechabite met together and discussed many things, and determined, as was their custom, that it was to be in the thirty-sixth year of Jaazaniah that Berechiah would meet again with Jaaziniah and his clan at the gates of En-Gannim. And Jaazaniah requested that Berechiah meet with Jeremiah, son of Hilkiah of Anathoth, as Jaazaniah considered that he heard a new Word, as was delivered by Isaiah and others, from the mouth of Jeremiah.

So Berechiah the Zadikite and Jaazaniah the Rechabite sent word to Jeremiah, son of Hilkiah the priest, to come to the tents of the Zadikites. Jeremiah the Prophet came to those gathered at the tent of Berechiah, the Claw of Judah, and was received, as was Baruch, his secretary and friend.

And Berechiah asked of Jeremiah, "What is it that makes you a Prophet? Why is it that our He Who Is has called upon you?"

Jeremiah said to the gathered, "Let it be known that I did not choose this path; it is an assignment that I have tried to avoid, and tried to sidestep, and tried to remain dumb, all to no avail. The Word came to me. It simply came to me. I did nothing. And I heard He Who Is say to me, 'Before I shaped you in the womb, I knew you, and before you were born, I consecrated you to speak to all the peoples.' I said then, as I would say today, 'O, my Elohim, I cannot, as I do not know how to speak, because I am a child.' And our Holy One said, 'Do not say, 'I am a child,' because everywhere I send you, you shall go, and everything I tell you to say, you will say.'"

"And you are not crazy? Are you troubled?" asked Jaazaniah, Nagid of the Rechabite. "I have rubbed the *urim* given to me, and rubbed and rubbed, and prayed and prayed, and the Holy One of Israel has never spoken to me. I have done His Will as I have seen it to be, I have acted and considered judgments and followed the path of my fathers, but I have not heard He Who Is. Is it a voice, a thought, an idea? Is it a pain? Does someone else say something to you and you think. 'Oh! That is what the Almighty is saying to me?'"

"It is a pain, it is a burden, and it makes me afraid! I fear for my life! But who can fear a king when one fears the Holy One?! I hear the Word as if you would be speaking to me, but I am alone! I can hear it when in the Temple, or when on the street, when being beaten, when praying, or when sleeping. I hear it, and I must stop and listen, and I do not understand why others do not hear, nor do I understand why they do not believe!"

"Is it not an honor to be the servant of the Almighty One?" asked Malluch.

"Is it not more an honor to be the one called to do what is asked by our Holy One?" returned Jeremiah the Prophet.

"And who is called to do what is asked?" questioned Malluch.

"You! Each one of us here! The king! The priests! All of Jerusalem! All of Judah! All of Israel, here or in the lands of the *nokri!* And now hear clearly: I was appointed as the one to deliver a Word 'to all peoples.' What does that mean? That means there are none that are not to listen!"

"And what are we to do?" asked Malluch.

"Listen to the complaint of He Who Is! Thus says our Holy One:

    'What fault did your fathers find in Me
        That they went far from Me and continually went after

Berechiah

        Emptiness, falseness, and futility and became nothing?
Nor did they say: 'Where is our One that brought us up
        Out of the land of Egypt,
            That led us through the wilderness

Through a land of sand and pits,
    Through a land of droughts and the shadow of death,
    Through a land which no one crosses and no one lives?'
And I brought you to this land of plenty
    To eat its fruit and all good things.

    But when you entered, you then defiled My land
    And My inheritance for you was made detestable.
    The priests did not ask, 'Where is the Almighty One?'
And those charged to speak and explain the Law forgot Me.
    And the kings also sinned against Me.
    And the prophets prophesied by Ba'al and acted deceitfully.'"

"Surely this is true!" said Malluch. "But we who are here, are we not servants of He Who Is? Do not our ways and our lives not demonstrate this? And do not our children know this?"

"But this Word is sent to those who need it! And while you may not be guilty, you need to hear it, because it is the Word! And hear more:

'For My people have committed two evils:

They have forsaken Me,
    The everlasting fountain of life-giving waters,
And have hewn cisterns for themselves
    Which cannot hold water.

Is My people a servant? Is Judah a slave?
    Why is she now a captive and prey?
Lions have roared and growled at her.
They have laid waste the land.
    Her cities are burned and deserted.
Also, the men of Memphis and Tahpanhes
    Have shaved your heads!

Have you not brought this on yourselves, O Judah,
    By forsaking the Holy One of Israel?

ROBERT HERMANSON

    But now, what are you and your silver doing on the road to Egypt?
        Will you drink of the river Nile?
    And what are you and your gold doing on the road to Asshur,
        Will you drink of the river Euphrates?

    Your own evil shall correct you,
        And your abandonment of the Faith will reprove you.

    Know therefore and see that it is evil and a bitter thing
        That you have forsaken me, the Holy One of Israel.
    The fear of Me is not in you,' says the Almighty.

    'As the thief is ashamed only when he is caught,
        so too the sons of Jacob,
    They, their Kings and Princes, their priests and their prophets.'"

"And what is it that we can do?" asked Berechiah the Zadikite.

"Nothing. Hear the Word, do the Word, fear the Holy One of Israel, and expect righteousness of all Jehudi and all our people."

"And what is the penalty?" asked Malluch.

"Hear the Word of the Holy One:

    'Wherefore will you plead with Me?
    You all have sinned against Me!' declares the One of Israel.
    'In vain I have struck your children,
        But they do not even recognize chastisement.
    Your swords have devoured your Prophets, like a raving lion.'

"O living ones, heed the Word of He Who Is!" Jeremiah paused as Baruch wrote. Then he continued:

    "Did you not hear Me in the days of Josiah the king?
        When I declared the Word in Jerusalem?

Did I not say:

    'Have you seen what My faithless Israel did?
        She went up on every high hill
            And under every green tree, and

Berechiah

> She was a whore there.'
> And I thought, 'After she has done all these things,
> She will return to Me.'
> But she did not return,
> And her treacherous sister Judah saw it.
>
> And I saw that for all the adulteries Israel committed,
> I gave her a writ of divorce;
> Yet her treacherous sister Judah did not fear
> But went and was also a whore.'

"I fear the time of the Holy One of Israel is at hand! The Word I am to deliver will be of no comfort! My life is already in jeopardy, and tomorrow I fear the king will end it," said Jeremiah.

"Is the king so blind that he cannot see what happens even in the Temple?" asked Malluch. "Does he think we are so stupid or so ignorant to not know that he cleansed the Temple this day, and sent the priests of his court away? Who was there this day? Our friends! But where was Immer, or Pashur, his son? We only saw the Nethinim, and they hid their eyes from us."

And Jeremiah replied, "It was only the king that protected you! If it had been the princes, you would have been taken this day and heard of no more! They fear you as it is only you who has tempered the unrighteousness of this kingdom!"

"And where do you hide?" asked Berechiah. "Is the school still open?"

"I live in the house, but there is no one else there but my friend Baruch, my scribe."

"Where are they?" asked Berechiah.

"After the fifty prophets were killed at Megiddo, the king who made himself king by the death of his father scattered the remnant. He wanted to be king by popular acclaim, and he could not do that with anyone reminding the people of how his plotting gained the throne. Now the false prophets gather at the Temple for instructions from Pashur, who gains his instruction from the chief in the Temple, his father Immer. And now Pashur even brings his son Gedaliah into the plot."

"Is there no one faithful in the Temple at this time? Is there no one to trust?" asked Berechiah.

"Azariah, son of Hilkiah, the chief priest, has disgraced himself with his weakness and tolerance and encouragement of abominations, and now he is about to die. And Seraiah, his son, will be chief priest soon. They do not know truth from lies, or harlots from faithful wives. Now, if they were to become faithful and righteous, they would surely die. They live as kings, and may have more power than Jehoiakim over the people," said Jeremiah.

"Then we are alone?" asked Berechiah.

"How are we alone, when He Who Is is with us?" responded Jeremiah.

"And why is it that Baruch writes down what you say? Why does he not remember, as does Malluch and those who are Protectors of the Word?" asked Berechiah.

"I am one, and if I am put to death, who will remember? Who hears me? And if Baruch is put to death, who will remember? I have Baruch write down the Word as I receive it; sometimes when it comes it is confusing; sometimes it comes at times when something is happening, but with Baruch, it comes and it is written. And we have several places where copies have been placed."

"Chosen Prophet, we beg that you provide a copy to us, that those who are in our charge to protect the Word will serve this Word as faithfully as we remember all things," said Jaazaniah. "But know that it pains us gathered here to consider a Written Word! Allow us a copy to consider what it is that is being done."

"This you shall have." So Jeremiah ordered Baruch to provide the Word as was delivered to him to be given to Jaazaniah, and Jaazaniah provided the Word to Berechiah.

Then Jeremiah said, "This is the scroll Baruch pronounced in the Temple this day, and sent to Jehoiakim."

"And what did you say to the king this day?" asked Berechiah.

"I have said nothing different since the early days of the reign of Jehoiakim, when the priests and the princes tried to kill me, and you will find in my writings, 'When the princes of Judah heard these things, they came up from the king's house to the House of the One of Israel and took their seat in the entry of the New Gate of the House of the Holy One of Israel. Then the priests and the prophets said to the princes and to all the people, 'This man deserves the sentence of death, because he has prophesied against this city, as you have heard with your own ears.'"

"Why did you not speak in the Temple? And, again, what is it you said?" asked Malluch.

"I have been barred from entering the Temple. See the scourging Pashur has given me!" Jeremiah disrobed, and all were aghast at the wounds on the body of Jeremiah.

"This was done to me because of the Word I deliver, and that Word is: 'Return to our Holy One of Israel!' We of Israel cannot escape the Covenant we have with He Who Is, and it is we who will be the guide to all nations. That Covenant is not of stone, but of flesh written in our hearts. The return to the One is complete submission in love as He has demonstrated love to us.

BERECHIAH

"Our love for He Who Is will be seen in what we do and say to each other, even those considered unworthy by the wealthy, for none are unworthy to He Who Is. It is the righteous of Israel who inherit from He Who Is, not kings, not priests, not princes. If we sin as a nation, there will be judgment, and we have greatly sinned! Lastly, there is no need for anyone but the Holy One of Israel, the one and only Creator."

And Berechiah said, "This is good! This is the Word! But what did you say to the king?"

And Jeremiah answered, "I have said to Jehoiakim what I was told to say, as I was told to say to his brother Shallum (Jehoahaz): 'For thus says the Lord concerning Shallum, son of Josiah, king of Judah, who reigned instead of Josiah his father, and who went away from this place: 'He shall return no more, but in the place where they have carried him captive, there shall he die, and he shall never see this land again.'

> Woe to him who builds his house without righteousness,
> And his upper rooms with unrighteousness,
> Who uses his neighbor's services for nothing,
> Refusing to pay them for their labor.
> He says, 'I will build myself a great house,
> With spacious upper rooms,
> And cut out larger windows in it
> And panel it with cedar and paint it red.'
> Are you a king because you make a great palace?
>
> Did not your father eat and drink?
> And do what is good and righteous?
> Then it was well with him.
>
> But your eyes and your heart are intent only
> Upon your usury and dishonesty and profit,
> For the shedding of innocent blood, for oppression and extortion.

"Therefore, thus says the Lord concerning Jehoiakim, son of Josiah, king of Judah:

> 'They will not lament for him,
> Saying, 'Alas, my brother! Alas, my sister!'
> They will not lament for him,
> Saying, 'Alas, the Lord!' or 'Alas, his glory!'
> He will be buried with a donkey's burial,
> Dragged off and thrown out beyond the gates of Jerusalem.

ROBERT HERMANSON

'Go up to Lebanon and speak out,
    lift up your voice in Bashan,
        cry out from Abarim,
Judah! All your lovers are crushed!
    I warned you when you considered yourself to be prosperous,
        But you said, 'I will not listen!'

This has been your way since a child;
    You have not obeyed my voice.

The wind will sweep away all your shepherds,
    And your lovers will go into captivity,
Then you surely will be ashamed and disgraced
    Because of your evil.

O people of Lebanon, living amongst the Cedars,
    How you will groan when death approaches you,
        With pain beyond that of a woman in childbirth!'"

"That certainly will not gain you favor with the king," said Berechiah. "It appears that you will be in danger. We will need to have the king hear a word of caution."

And Berechiah, Nagid of the Zadikite, heard that some of the princes had told Baruch to take Jeremiah and hide him, as they were fearful. And Jeremiah had refused to hide, according to Baruch, but Berechiah held Jeremiah in his tent, and Jaazaniah sent spies to hear what was happening in the court of Jehoiakim.

At this time word came to Jaazaniah that the king had taken the scroll of Jeremiah and burned it column by column, and had ordered the seizure of Jeremiah and Baruch. When Jeremiah had heard these things, he said to Baruch, "Take another scroll and write on it all the Word that was on the first scroll which Jehoiakim the king of Judah has now burned. And concerning Jehoiakim, king of Judah, you shall say:

"Thus says the Lord:
    'You have burned this scroll, saying,
        'Why have you written on it
            That the king of Bab'el will certainly come
            And destroy this land
            And will cut off both man and beast from it?'

Berechiah

"Therefore, thus says the Lord concerning Jehoiakim, King of Judah:

'He shall have no one to sit on the throne of David,
    And his dead body shall be cast out to the heat of the day
        And the frost of the night.

I shall punish him and his descendants
    And his servants for their guilt,
And I shall bring on them and the inhabitants of Jerusalem
    And the men of Judah all the evil
That I have pronounced against them
    As they have not listened.'"

And Berechiah was fearful of this Word which he heard from Jeremiah the Prophet. So Berechiah went to the king of Judah, to speak to the king, but the king's heart was hardened and fearful of Berechiah, for Berechiah was known to be righteous, and the king would not receive Berechiah the Zadikite. And Berechiah left Jerusalem and went to En-Gannim, but the king knew Jeremiah the Prophet was under the protection of the Rechabites and Zadikites, and he remained fearful of all, including his sons.

And Jehoiakim the king was told by his servants that Nebuchadnezzar was not to be feared. He decided he was able to defy Nebuchadnezzar, and he refused submission and did not send tribute. So Nebuchadnezzar sent an army to prepare the way for him to enter Judah. The army of Nebuchadnezzar burned and destroyed as it marched through Judah.

And Jeremiah the Prophet received the Word from the Holy One of Israel that said, "Go to the Rechabites and speak with them, and bring them to the House of the Holy One of Israel, into one of the chambers. Then offer them wine to drink."

Jeremiah the Prophet did as he was told, and took Jaazaniah, Nagid of the Rechabite, son of Jeremiah, son of Habazziniah. He took him and his brothers and all his sons and the whole house of the Rechabites at Jerusalem and brought them to the Temple into the chamber of the sons of Hanan, a man of He Who Is.

Jeremiah then set before the Rechabites pitchers full of wine and cups and said to Jaazaniah, "Drink wine."

But they answered, "We will drink no wine, for Jonadab, the son of Rechab, our father, commanded us, 'You shall not drink wine, neither you nor your sons or daughters, ever; you shall not build a house; you shall not sow seed; you shall not plant or have a vineyard; but you shall live in tents all your days, that you may live many years in all the lands where you sojourn.'

ROBERT HERMANSON

"We have obeyed the voice of Jonadab, the son of Rechab, our father, in all that he commanded us, to drink no wine all our days—ourselves, our wives, our sons, or our daughters—and not to build houses to live in. We have no vineyards nor fields nor seed, but we have lived in tents and have obeyed and done all that Jonadab our father commanded us and more. But when Nebuchadnezzar came upon this land, we said, 'Come and let us go to Jerusalem to see this army of the Chaldeans and the Syrians.' So we are here in Jerusalem."

And Jeremiah said: "The Lord has said, 'Go and say to the men of Judah and to the inhabitants of Jerusalem:

'Thus says the Holy One of Israel:
'Will you not receive instruction and understanding
      By listening to My Words?

The words of Jonadab, the son of Rechab,
    In which he ordered his sons not to drink wine, are observed.
      So they do not drink wine to this day,
        For they have obeyed their father's command.
But I have spoken to you
    Again and again and again and again,
      Yet you have not heard me!

Also, I have sent to you
    All My servants the Prophets, sending them
      Again and again, again and again,
    Saying, 'Turn now every man from his evil path,
      And change your deeds,
      And do not go after other gods
        To worship them,
    Then you shall dwell in the land which I have given to you
      And to your forefathers,
    But you have not inclined your ear
      To Me nor heard Me.'

Indeed, the sons of Jonadab, the son of Rechab
    Have heard and observed the order of their father
      Which he commanded them,
    But My people have not listened to Me!'

Therefore, thus says He Who Is,
    the Holy One of Israel, the Lord of all:

BERECHIAH

'Behold I shall surely bring
      On Judah and on all the inhabitants of Jerusalem
  All the disaster that I have pronounced against them
  Because I spoke to them, but they did not hear.
And I have called them to return to Me, but they did not respond.'"

And then Jeremiah the Prophet said to the house of the Rechabites, "Thus says the Holy One of Israel, Lord of All:

'Because you have obeyed the command of Jonadab your father
  And kept all his commands
    And done according to all that he ordered you
Therefore, thus says the Holy One of Israel, Lord of All,

'Jonadab, the son of Rechab, shall never lack a man
  To stand before me,
    Always.'"

And the Rechabites feared no one, for He Who Is had called them out and they were found faithful and righteous!

Chapter Ten

✹ ✹ ✹ ✹ ✹

The Fall

So Berechiah, son of Obadiah the Zadikite, dwelt with his family and clan at their fields and house in the south of Judah, outside the city of En-Gannim. And in the eleventh year of Jehoiakim, king of Judah, Berechiah, Nagid of the Zadikites, was called to judge the people of En-Gannim, and he and his wife and his children camped before En-Gannim. With Berechiah was Rizpah, his wife, his firstborn, Nathan, his second-born, Rachel, his third-born, Jehoshua, his fourth-born, Haggith, his fifth-born, Mikaiahu, and his sixth-born, Hannah. With Berechiah was Malluch the Rechabite, counselor and friend to Berechiah, and instructor of his children. The *zaqen* met to judge at the Gate of the Forgetful at En-Gannim.

To the *zaqen* was brought a man who had taken his daughter in the field and disgraced her and had been observed. The father was of Israel, by circumcision and the Law, as he had claimed judgment of a neighbor from the *zaqen* in years past. And Berechiah asked the daughter what had occurred, and the witnesses confirmed the testimony of the daughter. Berechiah asked the daughter, "Has your father disgraced you before?" In tears, the daughter spoke of other times in the house and in the fields.

Then Berechiah asked the mother when she had known of what was occurring, and the mother would not answer. So Berechiah spoke to the *zaqen* concerning this wrong and then spoke to the people, "Take this man to the cliffs of En-Gedi and throw him off. Let him die alone, cast out of Israel, and let his bones be picked by buzzards and be scorched by the sun, and the dust of his bones be blown into the Sea which is Dead. May his name never be spoken again."

And there were no tears but from the daughter.

Berechiah continued, "And let this woman also bear guilt, for she knew but did not speak. She allowed her daughter to continue to be shamed, and now Israel bears her shame. Remove the clothes from her back and she will receive four lashes. For sin not uncovered is sin continued. Sin of the individual is sin of the people, and before our Holy One of Israel we then are all guilty. And the field of her shame is given to this daughter of Judah, to hold or sell as she determines. Let her be taken to the Jordan and cleansed seven times, for as Na'aman was cleansed of leprosy, cannot this our daughter be cleansed of the evil which has befallen her?"

Then the men of En-Gannim did as the *zaqen* judged, and Berechiah took the daughter out of the house of her father and her mother and her brothers, and she sold the field and purchased a new field with a house, and she was righteous and faithful in the sight of the Holy One of Israel.

There was also a boy of ten years brought to Berechiah who had been caught stealing from a neighbor. The neighbor came to the *zaqen* and asked for compensation, as this was the sixth time the boy had stolen from him and others.

Berechiah called for the father of the boy, and the father presented himself before the *zaqen*.

Berechiah asked the father, "How is it that your son, a boy, continues to steal from your neighbor?"

"Who is it that can control a son?" asked the father. "Does the king of Judah control his sons? If a son goes here or goes there, am I to stop him?"

Berechiah asked him of his trade, and he said he was a sheep herder. Then Berechiah asked how it was that he had two hundred sheep and none would wander off.

"But, Nagid," he responded. "they do! And the lambs are the worst!"

Berechiah asked, "How do you stop a lamb from wandering off?"

"It depends upon the lamb," answered the father. "Some will respond to my voice, some will learn to respond to a twig, some will respond to a pebble, and some will respond to a stroke of the hand. It depends on the lamb!"

Berechiah then asked, "What happens if a lamb continues to wander off?"

The father said, with pain, "I then wound the lamb by breaking a leg, and the lamb stays with me, and I feed it by hand and I carry it, and the lamb becomes attached to me."

Berechiah asked, "How is it that you know so well how to protect and train your sheep, but this your son, the one by whom He Who Is will transmit the Covenant from this generation to the next, you do not understand nor protect nor discipline so that he understands what is important and what is not? Does not a child ask for discipline? Does this not begin at birth? And if you do not discipline, will you not create a son who thinks he can do anything?

"Also, if you do not discipline your son, do you not force us to discipline him so that he thinks evil of us? If he thinks evil of us, what will become of his sons and his daughters, or his grandchildren or great grandchildren? Will he not think ill of our Holy One? Will not his sins be visited upon his great grandchildren? What will he understand? Your lack of disciplining is selfishness. You find your sheep of more value than your son."

It was then that Berechiah spoke to the *zaqen* and they consented that Berechiah speak for all of them and he said to the father, "Take this boy, and do with him as you would do a lamb. Let there not be a moment he is not with you and that you do not provide for him or he does not provide for you, during the day and at night. A rope will attach you and you will not take off the rope until this boy is a man.

"You will also compensate your neighbor double, for is it not said, 'If a man steals an ox or a sheep and kills it or sells it, he shall pay five oxen for the one stolen and four sheep for the one stolen. He will make full restitution. And if he himself has nothing, then he will be sold for the theft. If the stolen beast is found alive in his possession, whether it is an ox or an ass or a sheep, he shall pay back double.'

"As your son has been caught six times, for each time you will provide double the value of the theft to any that were stolen from. For a child acts from the hand of the father, be that the father is present or not. If the father cannot be found or is dead, the uncle is held, and if not the uncle, the cousin, but there is a man to be held accountable. And if there is no man, the community will assign a man. Here, it is the father that is to be held to account."

The father objected, saying, "Zaqen, I am but a poor man! Is there not relief? Do not take my livelihood from me!"

"Did your son not try to take the livelihood of your neighbor? How many times was he successful in his theft? Where was your concern the six times we know of? And yes, there is a choice: five strokes of the whip for each theft. You may take thirty strokes! You will receive them from five neighbors, and then you will be given five strokes by your son!"

"But at thirty strokes, will I not surely die? Let the king hear my complaint!"

"And if your son was struck down while in your neighbor's house, who would mourn for him and from whom would you seek compensation? Does a child know the value of life? Do the ignorant know righteousness? Or is righteousness what I want when I want it! No! You have placed the life of your son in jeopardy, and you are placed in jeopardy as you place this people in jeopardy!

"May we all remember the cost of not disciplining our children. Not only does the child not understand and fall into ignorance, but the people are all held accountable! This is not a thing for a king to decide! It is for the *zaqen* of the community to decide. Is the law of a king righteous? No. Righteousness is found with the *zaqen*. If there are no righteous *zaqen*, there is no Covenant. Then we are all lost and will have the land taken from us and we will not be a People. You have heard the decision: Take your choice, and may He Who Is have mercy on your son!"

And the father compensated his neighbors, and his son was changed, for even in suffering begins wisdom.

And a *zaqen* asked Berechiah, "Son of Obadiah, it is apparent you possess the wisdom of your father whom we knew and loved and feared. We have heard of your righteousness in the land and with your clan and now see and hear your wisdom. Answer a question for me that I have not been able to understand: If I sin before my family and clan and city and Judah, and the *zaqen* cause judgment and I compensate as is required and truly seek forgiveness of He Who Is, according to the Law, am I not forgiven by the One of Israel, and should I not be forgiven by my neighbors?"

"Yes," answered Berechiah. "You are to be found as before the sin."

"But what if I am not uncovered? Will not He Who Is cause the sin to be punished, even if I offer sacrifice and privately seek forgiveness?"

"Yes, He Who Is will hear your beseeching but public righteousness is to be sought."

"Then it is, is it not, that the righteousness and judgment of Israel impacts on the judgment of He Who Is? As this man, as we found him guilty of disgracing his daughter, will he be found innocent upon his death? For has he not paid the price of his sin?"

Berechiah considered this question and responded, "While our judgment may or may not cause the wrath of He Who Is to subside, the judgment of men is only a reminder of the righteousness of the Holy One of Israel. The punishment or judgment of men is a call to the guilty to return to righteousness. When the penalty is final, it is for He Who Is to determine what will happen beyond. This we do not know! Righteous judgment causes fair compensation and punishment only for the living. The price of sin that is known is set; but that which is not known is not set.

"For myself, I would fear the Holy One of Israel's judgment far more than the judgment of men, guilty or innocent! I would, where five strokes are called for, take ten, to satisfy my He Who Is, rather than wait until my death and face the wrath of our Holy One! Only the foolish say, 'Let me escape the judgment of men,' and so compound the sin with lies and hardened heart. Do you deceive the Holy One of Israel? Can you avoid accounting? Is He Who Is a fool whose words of forgiveness encourage sin to multiply? No, the Word creates, the Word knows! But if you wait for the righteous judgment of He Who Is, is there righteous compensation here? If I were truly angry with someone, I might even think: Pray no man finds him out, that Adonai might cause righteousness."

"I still do not understand," said the *zaqen*. "Will you make it easy for us to remember?"

"Yes." Berechiah thought. "Hear this: The judgment of men does compensate for sin, as does sacrifice and supplication in righteousness and faithfulness. But the judgment and compensation demanded by men may not satisfy He Who Is. Then, where there is sin and there is no uncovering, that man should fear the Holy One of Israel, not only for himself, but for his children and his children's children. Is it not said, 'I am a jealous One, visiting the sins of the fathers to the children to the third and fourth generation of those who hate me!' The sins of the one will be remembered. For there is finding out beyond the touch of the Angel Abaddon. Not only will the sin of the one be remembered beyond presence with us, but the sin will be held against Israel."

And the *zaqen* said, "This is certainly a jealous Holy One! At times I feel that our Elohim is more a burden than a blessing!"

"Only for the unrighteous one! And, I wonder what He Who Is considers of us! Has the love of He Who Is for us not been painful for Him? And why is that? How much better it would be if we were able to control ourselves and do righteousness and be faithful! But we cannot! And who pays for our sin? I fear all our children will pay, both the children of the righteous and the children of the unrighteous. We are chosen! We need to learn to accept that and live accordingly! Let us do our tasks in love with our One as we received from our parents and do with our children."

The *zaqen* remained silent, considering these thoughts.

And many came to the Gate of En-Gannim to see Berechiah the Zadikite, the Claw of Judah, for his defense of Judah and his story were known by all in the land. Many came to observe the beauty and hear the words of Rizpah, wife of Berechiah. This pleased Berechiah.

Many considered En-Gannim a safe haven from Nebuchadnezzar and his army, for Nebuchadnezzar had heard of Berechiah and his honored position and Nebuchadnezzar chose not to confront one whose god had chastised Josiah the good king and his servant Obadiah, and yet raised up the son, friend of Pharaoh. And while Pharaoh was defeated and remained beyond the Nile, Nebuchadnezzar understood the oath that Pharaoh had taken to defend Berechiah the Zadikite.

Berechiah

While Berechiah was judging, word was sent to him by Nebuchadnezzar, who was about to enter Judah, for Berechiah to come to him, for Jehoiakim the king of Judah had rebelled and defied the orders of Nebuchadnezzar.

But while Nebuchadnezzar moved his army, there were those that took advantage of the chaos and struck into Judah. It was the Moabites and Ammonites and marauders from Syria, and they ravaged Samaria.

While awaiting the appointed time to meet with Nebuchadnezzar, Berechiah responded to the people and the *zaqen* of En-Gannim. Some of the clan of Zadikite came to Berechiah to gain judgment and compensation, and Berechiah dealt fairly with all. In the Clan Zadikite, the poor, the widows, the orphans, and the elderly were cared for by all, and no one hungered nor slept without shelter. The wealthy of the clan righteously provided for those who served them, and they remembered the year of Jubilee and sent the freed on their way with a fair share so that among those who dealt with the Zadikites, there was no complaint. And there was no one with complaint against the Rechabites as well, for the Rechabites were men of honor.

And Berechiah, Nagid of the Zadikite, took 100 chariots and 300 horsemen to the tents of Nebuchadnezzar. There he found Nebuchadnezzar dressed in armor and protected by his captains. Nebuchadnezzar saw Berechiah and understood, as he could see his soul. And Nebuchadnezzar said to Berechiah, "Sit and listen to the tale of Obadiah and Berechiah the Zadikite, and tell me if it is true."

Berechiah listened to the story of all that had happened, and considered it to be true. Then he said to Nebuchadnezzar, "You have heard all that was and is."

And Nebuchadnezzar asked Berechiah, "Have you heard the words of your prophets Isaiah and Jeremiah of Jerusalem? Hear what I have heard."

Berechiah heard the words of Isaiah and Jeremiah, and Nebuchadnezzar asked Berechiah, "I hear that you are a righteous man, a faithful man to your god. If this is true, and you know what will befall Jerusalem when I now go to Jerusalem, will I find you or the Rechabites at the gates?"

Then Berechiah said to Nebuchadnezzar, "You will not find me at Jerusalem. My heart grieves that you will not find me at Jerusalem, but I have learned the Word of He Who Is is to be trusted. I find this Word is fair judgment for the sins of the kings and the sins of this people. I cannot defend Jerusalem. I do ask two favors of the great King Nebuchadnezzar."

"Do not falsely praise me if you wish to be my friend. I do what I think; I do what I can do; and I fear that what I do may not be in my control! This does not make me great. It makes me a man as you. I pray I be honored by my people as you are honored."

"Then, friend Nebuchadnezzar, you know the *dagal* of the Rechabite and the Zadikite. Let the Zadikites and Rechabites pass within your borders. If you find a Rechabite on your way, have mercy on him and his! You know the Rechabites fear He Who Is and treat all with righteousness, and serve all without evil. Know their *dagal* and honor those that carry it. And secondly, with your leave, I will defend Judah from the Moabites, the Ammonites, and the Syrians."

"First, I have heard of the Rechabites as traders and cattlemen who have assisted the Asshur, and the Egyptians, and the wanderers," answered Nebuchadnezzar. "My servants know the Rechabites as honorable men. I have heard that their tent is open to all who enter without evil in their hearts. I have heard that they returned to Pharaoh his own dagger. Someday I will meet the Rechabites and test their faith. I wish I had one as a servant, for I hear their word is as their eyes see, and they see more than any man. Regarding your second request: Defend Judah from these marauders, for they are not of Nebuchadnezzar. If they destroy Judah, how will I gain tribute and keep order?"

"Thanks is given and I will deal with the Moabites, Ammonites, and Syrians as they deserve. And, honored friend, here is Malluch, the Rechabite, my servant and instructor. It is he who has guided my hand! It is his fathers who have brought honor to the name of Zadikite. Ask of him and he will speak."

"Come forward, Malluch the Rechabite, and speak to me."

So Malluch went forward, and found favor with Nebuchadnezzar. Nebuchadnezzar asked Malluch, "Is there not one as you available to be my servant? Is there one that you can send to me?"

Malluch said, "I am not Nagid of the Rechabite; that has not been my chosen path. But presently, at the gates of Hebron where the Rechabites have been encamped, you will find Jaazaniah. Jaaziniah will be moving his own tent to Jerusalem to again protect the Prophet Jeremiah. There may be one of us called Daniel encamped with Jaaziniah worthy to serve you. And there are with him three brothers, of the Rechabites of the tribe of Judah. We consider that our Holy One has called out our Daniel to speak the Word."

"Hear this!" Nebuchadnezzar spoke to his captains. "Let us break camp and go to Jerusalem and do as I am to do with this rebellious servant, King Jehoiakim."

So Nebuchadnezzar went to Jerusalem with his army, and Jehoiakim died and it was done to him as Jeremiah had prophesied. There were many taken from Jerusalem, but taken to serve Nebuchadnezzar were Daniel, Hananiah, Mishael, and Azariah.

But in Jerusalem, Jehoiakin was established on the throne. His father was Jehoiakim and his mother was Nehushta, daughter of Elnathan of

Jerusalem. Jehoiakin was eighteen years old when he began to rule, and he ruled for three months. Jehoiakin did what was evil in the sight of the Holy One of Israel, and he believed in the words of the party of princes, and betrayed the treaty with Nebuchadnezzar.

Then Nebuchadnezzar went back to Jerusalem and took the gold and silver of the king and of the Temple, and he took the jewels and fine things of Jerusalem. He also took the princes and the leaders of the people. Ten thousand were taken out of Jerusalem. Among the ten thousand was Jeconiah, son of Jehoiakim, once king of Judah.

And Nebuchadnezzar made Mattaniah king of Judah and called him Zedekiah. Zedekiah was also a son of Josiah and his mother was Hamutah, daughter of Jeremiah of Libnah. He could do no different than those before him, and he sinned before He Who Is, in his own house and in the Temple.

In the beginning of Zedekiah's reign, Jeremiah the Prophet spoke the Word, saying to Zedekiah and to the kings of Edom, Moab, Ammon, Tyre, and Sidon:

"Make a yoke out of straps and crossbars and put it on your neck. Thus says the Holy One of Israel: 'I have made the Earth, the men and all the animals that are on the face of the earth. By My mighty hand and by My outstretched arm this was done. I will give it to the one who is pleasing in my sight. And now I have given it into the hands of Nebuchadnezzar, king of Bab'el, my servant, and I have given him even the animals to serve him.

"'And all peoples shall serve him and his son and his grandson until the time of his own land comes, then many nations and great kings will make these their servant. And it will be that the nation that does not serve Nebuchadnezzar, the King of Bab'el, and that will not put their neck under the yokes of the King of Bab'el, that nation will be punished,' says the Almighty. 'This will be done by sword and with famine and with pestilence until I have destroyed it by his hand.

"'So, as for you, do not listen to your self-serving prophets, your diviners or your dreams, your soothsayers or your sorcerers, who say to you, 'You shall not serve the King of Bab'el.' For they prophesy a lie to you which will cause you to be removed far from Judah and you will die there. But any who bring their neck under the yoke of the king of Bab'el and serve him, I will let them remain in that land and they will till it and dwell there.'"

But Zedekiah heard the Word and was hardened against it and harassed Jeremiah, and yet was fearful of Jeremiah, son of Hilkiah. And Jeremiah was beaten and was shut up in the court of the guard. And Zedekiah threw off the yoke which He Who Is of Israel had placed upon him. So it was that Nebuchadnezzar sent his captains Nebuzaradan and Nergalsharezer, and Jerusalem was surrounded.

Gedaliah, son of Ahikam, son of Shaphan, remained in Jerusalem and protected Jeremiah as he could. And Gedaliah protected all the Prophets who were like Jeremiah as well as Baruch, the scribe of Jeremiah, of the School of the Prophets.

And Jeremiah continued to declare the Word of He Who Is. So the princes and Shephatiah, son of Mattan, Gedaliah, son of Pashur, Jucal, son of Shelemiah, and Pashur, son of Malchiah, went to the king and said, "Let this man be put to death, for he weakens the hands of the soldiers and destroys the will of the people."

Zedekiah said, "So he is in your hands, for the king will do nothing against you."

They took Jeremiah and threw him into the cistern of Malchiah, the king's son, and Jeremiah sank in the mire. But Ebedmelech went to the king and begged for the life of Jeremiah, and the king relented and told Ebedmelech to release Jeremiah. The king sought Jeremiah and Jeremiah went to him and spoke the Word to the king.

And Jeremiah said, "Thus says the Holy One of Israel:

"'If you surrender to the captains of the king of
Bab'el, you will be spared and this city shall not be burned
and you and your house shall live. But if you do not, then
the city shall be given into their hands and they shall burn
it with fire, and you shall not escape from their hand.'"

The king spoke to Jeremiah saying, "I am afraid I will be given to those who have deserted me and they will abuse me."

Jeremiah assured him saying, "You shall not be given to them. Obey now and it will be well with you."

But the king chose a different path, and he said to Jeremiah, "Let no one know of these Words and you will not die."

The princes discovered Jeremiah and asked him what had happened, but he did not respond. And they took no action, for the conversation had not been overheard.

And Zedekiah defended Jerusalem from the captains of Nebuchadnezzar until the city starved, and a breach was made, and then the captains of Nebuchadnezzar entered Jerusalem and had no compassion. They slew the old and young, male and female, and took all the treasures of Jerusalem and sent them to Bab'el. Jerusalem was burned and destroyed, and buildings were razed. In the Genizah, all the sacred manuscripts were burned.

And Zedekiah ceased to be king in Jerusalem in the eleventh year of his reign.

At Riblah, at the camp of Nebuchadnezzar, king of Bab'el, the sons of Zedekiah were slain before his eyes and then his eyes were put out and he was taken to Bab'el. Then Nebuchadnezzar went up to Jerusalem and burned the Temple, and he burned down all the great houses. The walls were made to crumble, and the rest of the people were carried into exile to Bab'el. Only the poor and destitute were left in Jerusalem.

In Jerusalem, Seraiah, the chief priest, and Zephaniah were found out, as were the men of Zephaniah's council and the leaders of the men of war. Nebuchadnezzar withdrew these men from Jerusalem to Riblah, and there he ordered their execution. The unrighteous were either smote or removed from Judah to Bab'el. Even among the ones sent into exile were families of faith, righteous before the Holy One of Israel.

And Nebuchadnezzar, king of Bab'el, appointed Gedaliah, son of Ahikam, son of Shaphan, as governor, for he knew of Gedaliah's defense of Jeremiah.

And Nebuchadnezzar found Jeremiah and said to him, "Your god pronounced this terrible evil against this place, and he has brought it about, and has done as was said in all your words: 'Because you sinned against your god and did not obey his voice, this has come upon you.' Now, behold, I release you, Jeremiah, today, from the chains on your hands. If it appears good to you to come to Bab'el, come and I shall look after you, but if it appears wrong to you, do not come. See, all the land is before you. Go wherever you think it good and right to go. If you remain, go to Gedaliah, son of Ahikam, son of Shaphan, whom I have appointed governor of the cities of Judah, and dwell with him, or go wherever you consider it right to go."

So it was that the captain of the guard gave Jeremiah food and a present and let him go, and Jeremiah went to Gedaliah's encampment and lived among the people.

But when Nebuchadnezzar withdrew from Jerusalem, the party of the princes remained hidden. And Johanan, son of Kareah, warned Gedaliah that Ishmael, son of Nethaniah, son of Elishama, plotted his death, but Gedaliah did not heed the warning. So Ishmael, of the royal family, went with ten men to Gedaliah at Mizpah and smote Governor Gedaliah and the party of those left to assist him, and the Chaldeans who were to be his servants.

That same day eighty men of Shechem came to Gedaliah, and Ishmael slew all but ten. And Ishmael took the remaining people of Mizpah and fled to the Ammonites, but Jeremiah was not found. Along the way they saw Johanan, son of Kareah, with men of war. The people of Mizpah were saved, but Ishmael escaped. And there was great fear among the people, and the remaining captains of Judah and their men of war fled to Egypt, for they were afraid of the wrath of Nebuchadnezzar and the quick sword of the Claw, Berechiah the Zadikite.

A remnant found Jeremiah and they went to him and said, "What do we who remain and are righteous do? Call upon the Holy One of Israel and inform us of what is expected of us."

And Jeremiah heard the One of Israel and Jeremiah said:

> "'If you remain in this land, then I will build you up and not pull you down, I will plant you, and not pluck you out, for I now repent of the evil which I have done to My people. Do not fear the king of Bab'el. Do not fear him, for I am with you to save you and will deliver you from his hand. I will grant you mercy, that he may have mercy on you and let you remain in your own land. But if you say, 'We will not remain in this land,' and disobey the voice of the Holy One of Israel and say, 'No, we will go down to Egypt, where we shall not see war nor hear the sound of the trumpet nor be hungry for bread and we will dwell there,' then hear the Word of the Holy One of Israel:
>
> "'O remnant of Judah.' Thus says the Holy One of Israel: 'If you set your face to enter Egypt and go there to live, then the sword which you fear shall overtake you in the land of Egypt and there you will die. All who go to Egypt to live there will die by the sword or by famine or by pestilence, and they will have no remnant remain from the evil which I will bring upon them.'
>
> "For thus says the Holy One of Israel: 'As My anger and My wrath were poured out on the people of Jerusalem, so My wrath will be poured out on you who go to Egypt. You will be cursed and a laughing stock. You and your children will see Israel no more.'"

But those who heard Jeremiah did not believe him and called him a liar and they took their people with them and went to Egypt. Even there the men and women of Israel sinned against the Holy One of Israel. And what Jeremiah prophesied came upon those who had fled to Egypt.

It was then that the Rechabites found Ishmael in the land of the Ammonites, and the Rechabites slew Ishmael and slew the ten who were with him. When Nebuchadnezzar heard this thing he was satisfied and he knew the righteousness of He Who Is and found pleasure and assurance in his servants. The Ammonites were afraid, as they feared they had provoked the Rechabites by offering sanctuary to Ishmael, son of Nethaniah of the Royal Family.

And Berechiah the Zadikite sent word to the king of the Ammonites: "While we are wounded, the Lion still roars. Take what is yours and live; take what is not yours and you will surely die."

The Ammonites believed Berechiah the Zadikite, friend of Pharaoh, Nebuchadnezzar, and the king of Bab'el. But the Moab did not understand the strength of the Zadikites nor the reach of the arm of the Rechabites.

Marauders from Moab fell upon Judah and sought out the remnant and slew them along the road and as they plowed their fields and tended the vine and watched their flock.

And Berechiah brought order to southern Judah out of chaos. He did righteousness and was faithful to He Who Is, both he and his clan. He taught his children and their children, remembering the Word of Isaiah: "When all of your children are taught of the Holy One of Israel, great will be the peace of your children."

Now Berechiah had brought Deborah, daughter of Gedaliah, to his son Nathan, and Deborah bore a son, Hananiah. A second child, Cushi, was born, but was killed. Then Deborah bore a third male child, Elisha.

And Jaazaniah, Nagid of the Rechabite, asked Berechiah for the second of his children, Rachel, to be wife of his cousin's son, Hilkiah, who dwelled and traded in caravan in the land of the Sukkiim. So Hilkiah took Rachel, daughter of Berechiah, and wed her, and was a good husband to her and she a good wife to him. Rachel bore Amaziah, Hannah, Jedidah, and Tamar in the land of the Sukkiim. In the difficult days that followed the troubles, Berechiah did not see his daughter Rachel nor his grandchildren, nor had he word of them until his death. For Hilkiah and Rachel took caravan to the sea below the Nile. Hilkiah was comforted by the Word remembered by Rachel, and the Word was remembered by their children and their children's children. And there came a time when the sons and daughters of Hilkiah the Rechabite returned to Israel, but Israel did not remember who they were.

And Berechiah's third child, Jehoshua, found a woman in the fields of En-Gannim, the granddaughter of the farmer of the servant of Berechiah the Rechabite. So Berechiah the Zadikite spoke to the father of the daughter of Israel, and the father was pleased with the request of Berechiah, and gave Naomi, his daughter, to Jehoshua to be his wife. Naomi bore a child that did not live beyond the first day, and it was buried with the body of Obadiah. Then Naomi bore Rachel and Hannah and then bore a son, Jesse.

Berechiah searched for a husband for his fourth child, Haggith. He found Elkanah, and she bore two children, Hilkiah and Berechiah. Elkanah remained near the house of Berechiah so that Berechiah found pleasure with Hilkiah, his daughter, and his grandchildren.

And Berechiah, Nagid of the Zadikite, found pleasure with his son Mikaiahu, who demanded that Berechiah find for him 'a wife as beautiful as Rizpah,' his wife, with the hair of Rizpah and the color of Rizpah. So Berechiah sent word to Jaazaniah the Rechabite, now encamped in the Valley of Arabah, and asked Jaazaniah to find his son a daughter of the Jehudi, along the caravan trails, whose name was Rizpah! Mikaiahu would not have any other, and at age seventeen, a wife was brought up from the land beyond the Sukkiim. And Mikaiahu found pleasure in his Rizpah, and his Rizpah bore him eight children: Hosea was firstborn; Jeshua was second; Shemaiah was third; Nathan was fourth; twins, Rhoda and Ruth were next; then Cushi; and Rephaiah was last.

Lastly, Hannah, the favorite of Berechiah, sought a husband. And Zerah the Rechabite went to Berechiah and spoke to him. Berechiah brought Zerah into his house and into his fields, and Hannah found pleasure with him. Jaazaniah the Rechabite and Berechiah the Zadikite spoke to Zerah and Hannah, and Zerah understood that Hannah was a Possessor of the Word. Zerah took the assignment to go to Bab'el and find Daniel and keep the Word in Bab'el. But before they went, Hannah bore a child that died in childbirth. Her second child was a son, Obadiah, and the third was named Amariah. And Berechiah the Zadikite did not hear from his daughter, Hannah, nor did he hear of her husband Zerah.

And Berechiah, Nagid of the Zadikite, the Claw, found pleasure in his wife, Rizpah, and in his children, and in his children's children. Berechiah remained a friend of the Rechabites and remained faithful to the celebrations and holy days of Israel. He went up to Jerusalem each year and entered in the mist and departed in the mist. And Etutu-Ebuh remained with Berechiah and kept the *dagal* of the Pharaoh of Egypt in the courtyard of the house of Berechiah. Malluch also remained with Berechiah, and his hair and beard were now white as the clouds of a crisp and clear day. Malluch sought to teach the grandchildren of Berechiah as he taught his own children. He found among the grandchildren those who would be Possessors of the Word. And Malluch remembered the Word from Isaiah and Jeremiah and taught it to the children and to the faithful.

Chapter Eleven

✳ ✳ ✳ ✳ ✳

Survival

In the year that Jerusalem was captured by the captains of Nebuchadnezzar, the princes were removed, the people were taken into captivity, Gedaliah was murdered, and Jeremiah was removed from Jerusalem, there was great weeping among the people, there was famine, there were marauders, and there was chaos in the land. And Berechiah the Zadikite provided as he could for his clan and the clans that remained in Israel. He protected the weak and provided for the infirm. The Rechabites assisted the Zadikites and brought in cattle and bread, bred cattle, and provided grain from foreign lands to seed Israel. The people would build up and marauders would tear down.

In the second year after the fall of Jerusalem, Berechiah the Zadikite sent messengers through the land and asked that the Nagid of the clans and the righteous of the families remaining come to Hebron. The righteous came together and the clans were represented, and while some would say, "We are of Asher," or "We are of Judah," or "We are Levi," there were no tribes and no leaders of the tribes.

Berechiah said to the gathering, "What is it that now troubles us? What is it that we are to do?"

There were those who said, "We need food and clothing and a roof over our heads."

Then Berechiah said to them, "Is this not the day that He Who Is tests us? Is this not the day that we who have little still open our door to the sojourners, the poor, and the widow? Is our measure taken when we are satisfied, or is our measure taken in troubled times? Because you hide yourself from the widow or shield yourself from the inquiry of the sojourner or the poor, do you think you escape the Will of He Who Is? If your neighbor is without food, search him out! If your widows and wounded warriors are unable to care for themselves, search them out! If your eyes are shut and you do not see, does your responsibility disappear? Does not He Who Is know your tricks? There is grain to grow grain in Israel. There are cattle to make cattle in Judah. Let us do as the Holy One of Israel wants of us."

"But we are not as rich as you!" a man said.

"Where do you see my wealth?" Berechiah asked. "Do you see rings of gold and stones? Do you see clothes of kings on my body? When have you seen these on me? Yes, I am responsible for much, but I have many to be responsible for. These things which you think I have are not mine, but belong to the clan! Do I hold wealth for myself? Tell me, in all the land, is there one ever turned away from my door? Even the sojourner, whose fathers entered this land to take it, I have brought in and fed. For were we not sojourners in Egypt and in need, and did not the Hand of the Holy One of Israel open for us?

"What is rich? For us, there is no rich, and if there is, it is sin. For what I have all comes from He Who Is, and even that which I turn back to He Who Is was His to begin with. When what I have I have only in custody for He Who Is, I am not rich. And when I hold in custody, what are the things I hold for? Yes, I have a chariot; I have many chariots. Would you have me sell them? Yes, I have horses, and there are those who have even had to eat our horses. Yes, I have a shield and I have a *hoshen* of gold, and that shield and *hoshen* protect you this day. For have not my fathers used that shield and used that *hoshen* and died holding that shield and that cover for the heart?

"And are not you rich?" Berechiah sought to teach. "Are there not Jehudi this day unable to walk here because they do not have food? To them, you are rich! What is rich? If you feed yourself and have a rag on your back and are protected from the cold and rain, He Who Is has given you all you need! If you can feed your children, you have what you need. Those who store up goods for themselves are in need of fearing He Who Is. Those who want to give gold and silver, land and cattle, wives and concubines to their children, condemn their children. For it is knowledge that must be given, it is faith that must be provided, it is example that must lead the way.

"Gold and silver make it possible for the child to say, 'I do not need He Who Is, for look what I have that I have gotten without He Who Is!' And while that child is to be pitied, what will we do with that child's children?" Berechiah shook his head. "The spoiled child can be poor or can be without need; both are spoiled and both forget He Who Is. If you do not contain the child, the adult will not be contained. Correct your child as you want your great grandchild to be corrected. If my son sins, do I not correct him and chastise him? If I do, will not he want to search out the Word and return to our He Who Is? And is He Who Is any different than this? Does not the Almighty chastise us so that we might return to Him?"

"But we must know what is sin! What is it that displeases He Who Is? Where do I find that out? Do I ask the ignorant? Dare I ask the one who is sinning, 'Is this sin that you do?' Will not the sinner who is ignorant say, 'What I do cannot be sin, for it is good'? And will there not be a thousand reasons why it is good? But good is not that which is pleasure. Only the Word is good. Wealth is not good, but looking on the rich and saying, 'You are wealthy' may mean what you see is what you want! Then with whom lies the sin?

"Tell me, what man is there who would not be king?" Berechiah looked around him. "I tell you, the righteous man is the man who would not be king. Where is there a priest who would not be chief priest? And where is there a holy man who would not be a true Prophet? How many pretenders are there in Jerusalem today? Where is there a poor man who would choose not to be a prince? Their hearts are not hearing He Who Is! But why is it that the true Prophet shudders and cowers? Why is it that the true Prophet is not proud? Why is it that the true Prophet suffers? Is not the true king to suffer? And is not the true prince in pain with what he sees and knows? You see my authority and say, 'He is proud.' No, that is your thought and your jealousy. I wear authority in my clan humbly. Do I take advantage? Where are my concubines and my whores? Where is there a complaint against me?"

Then another said, "Let us kill and take back the land that the *nokri* now have in Judah."

Berechiah said to them, "Our fathers came to this land and took this land and it was given to us by He Who Is. But He Who Is has taken away our inheritance for now, so we must be careful. If my grandfather had a valley with a *wadi* through it, and he said, 'Let me sell my fields and purchase this vineyard,' and he did so and sold it to a *nokri*, then I enjoy only the vineyard of my father and eat its fruit and drink its wine. But my grandson sees the valley of my grandfather, and says, 'Come, we need more. Let us take back this valley which was our fathers' in the land of Judah, which He Who Is has given to us,' and by the sword it is taken back from the sons of the one who purchased the valley. Will it not be right that their sons will come up and hold a knife to the throat of my great grandchildren forever? For are we then not thieves and liars? For we have taken back that which we sold and we have taken back that which was taken from us by He Who Is. If we do not act righteously in all things, will He Who Is be fooled by our trickery or our short memory? The memory of what has been done must be forever! Be careful when you take back! What you may take back may simply be theft, and it would be held against you and your children to come."

So many left Berechiah, for they were displeased with what they heard. But there were those who remained and asked of Berechiah, "What is it we are to do?"

Berechiah said, "Let us prepare. We need to prepare to face the horns of Ba'al, to fight the forces of order, and fight the forces of chaos. For the Holy One of Israel has told us to stay in this land. If we are to stay in this land, we must protect ourselves, our families, our clans, and the faithful remnant. In a time of war we must do war and prepare for peace; in a time of peace we must remember both the forces of order and chaos and prepare for war."

Then Berechiah made agreements with the clans and with the men of war, and he departed from Hebron. With him were Malluch, the counselor, Etutu-Ebuh, the Sukkiim, Nathan, his son, Mikaiahu, his son, Elkanah, his son-in-law, servants, family, and clan.

As they approached En-Gannim, they saw black smoke rising from the city and from the valley. Berechiah the Zadikite went to En-Gannim and saw it burning. He saw the dead and the wounded and heard of those carried off. Berechiah went to his house and saw the flames and the dead, the slaughter of his cattle, and the burning of his *dagal*.

And Berechiah found the bodies of Nathan's wife, Deborah, and Cushi, their son. She was violated and died in great pain. He found Jehoshua, his son, and Naomi, wife of Jehoshua, and Hannah, their child. Berechiah also found Haggith, his daughter, wife of Elkanah, as well as Hilkiah, their son, and Berechiah, their second son, all slaughtered after being made sport.

And Berechiah removed his cloak and was naked before the Almighty and wept. He wept for his loss, for his wife, Rizpah, whom he could not find, and for the grandchildren whom he could not find. Berechiah took a knife and slit his arms, and blood came upon his chest. Berechiah swore an oath against the Moabites who did this thing, and he cursed the Moabites.

And Etutu-Ebuh departed immediately for Egypt. He took the burned *dagal* of Pharaoh with him, and he dipped it in the blood of his great grandchild and swore that he would see the face of Pharaoh before it was crust. He took horses and servants and departed.

Those who saw Berechiah the first day were awed by his scars and skin markings, for he had never been naked before them. Berechiah did not move that night and the next day he mourned with his clan. His messenger departed to the corners of Israel. And the Rechabites came to En-Gannim and the clans, friends, and servants of Berechiah, and all those who had

BERECHIAH

found a helping hand in Berechiah came to him. So Berechiah found at his door a great army. There were five thousand men with sword and bow and two thousand with horse and five hundred with chariot.

Berechiah the Zadikite cried out these words, "Hear, O Holy One of Israel! I curse the Moabite, I curse the sons and daughters of the Moabite, and I curse their land and all their cities! May they die by the sword, now, in my lifetime, before I lose my sight! Hear me! Elohim!

"Did not Jeremiah say this Word? Did he not say:

'Against the Moab the Holy One of Israel has spoken!
   Woe is upon Nebo for it is to be laid waste,
      Kiriathaim will be put to shame;
         Misgab will be shamed and horrified.

No one will praise nor see Moab again!

Come! Destroy her and cut her off from being a people!

Now, O Holy One! Elohim! Adonai!
   Now is the time! Do not wait any longer!

Let the spoiler come and fall upon every city!
   The valley and plain shall be destroyed!'

"The Lord has spoken! Let Pharaoh and Nebuchadnezzar hear this Word! And let my curse be heard in all lands!" So said Berechiah, Nagid of the Zadikite.

And as the *hoshen* of Berechiah was being placed on him, Shelumiel the Rechabite came from the hills near the desert, and with him were Rizpah, Hananiah, and Elisha, sons of Nathan, Rachel and Jesse, the children of Jehoshua and Naomi; Rizpah, the wife of Mikaiahu, and their wet nurse, servants, and clan. And Berechiah wept at the return of his wife. He heard how they had been in the fields and had seen the burning and had fled to the mountains and found Shelumiel the Rechabite tending his flock, and how they hid in the mountains.

While there was rejoicing, there still was great sorrow.

And Berechiah sent a messenger to Nebuchadnezzar bearing blood on his *dagal*, and the messenger said to Nebuchadnezzar, "The jackal Moab has come to feast on the Lion Judah, but the Lion is not dead. The Lion Judah is entering the land of the Moabites to cause compensation. Did Nebuchadnezzar not also pledge to protect the wounded Lion? The Lion will soon use its Claw on Moab."

ROBERT HERMANSON

Word was brought to Berechiah that the Moabites had entered Judah with two armies to the North and two to the South. Berechiah was told that the two armies of the South were separated by three days march. One was about to attack Beer-sheba, and the other was approaching Hebron.

Then Berechiah went to Beer-sheba and found the Moabites awaiting surrender of Beer-sheba, drunk with their success. Berechiah placed his bowmen and swordmen on two walls of the valley of the way to Madmannah, and sent his chariots and horses to the south around the city, and in the evening they charged the Moabites, making noise and beating their chariots, shouting and scattering the horses, so that the Moabites fled from their tents up the valley toward Madmannah. The bowmen of Berechiah used their bows to advantage and there were none remaining to reach Madmannah. There were no Moabites to send a message North. Berechiah ordered that his soldiers take the weapons of the Moabites, but leave the booty, and they took their arrows and swords, and their horses and chariots, and they marched to Hebron.

At Hebron, Berechiah found the second force from the South. Berechiah attacked from the North in the evening, and the Moabites collapsed and fled. Berechiah sent his bowmen and swordmen after them, and they slew the Moabites. Berechiah took a soldier of the Moabites, and fed him but would not clean his wounds, and Berechiah said to the soldier, "Is it not your duty to flee to the North to warn the two armies of the North that Berechiah, the Claw of Judah, Prince of Israel, claims victory over the armies of the South? Here is the *dagal* of your people, for they are no more. So hear the word of Berechiah: 'Leave Judah!'"

The soldier left the presence of the army of Berechiah and he went North, first to Anathoth and then to Riblah. The commanders of the two armies of the North believed the soldier and withdrew across the Jordan River to enter the land which was once of Reuben and the Ammonites.

But Berechiah had placed his bowmen and swordmen at the hills of Pisgah, and hid his chariots and horses. When the Moabites approached the city of Beth-peor, they found the city gates closed and they heard the chariots of Berechiah and the horsemen. The Moabite commanders said, "Let us retreat down the coast of the Salt Sea to Zerethshabar."

And Etutu-Ebuh reached Berechiah with two thousand chariots and two thousand horsemen from Pharaoh.

Berechiah flew his *dagal*, the *dagal* of all the clans, and the *dagal* of Pharaoh. He had the chariots and the horses attack with great noise and dust clouds rising. The Moabites were afraid, for they saw the *dagal* of Berechiah, the *dagal* of Pharaoh, and the taken *dagals* of Moab of the two armies of the South. They fled and were met with the bowmen and swordmen of the clans. The captains of the Moabites were found out and taken to the encampment of Berechiah.

Berechiah

Berechiah, Nagid of the Zadikite, said to the captains, "Go to your people and tell them of the death of their sons and that it was a just death for the murder they committed in Judah! Tell them to prepare to defend their cities, for Berechiah is about to enter Moab. There are no more young men to defend your cities, for all have perished. So fear when you see the *dagal* of the Zadikite and the *dagal* of the Rechabite, for your death is near."

The captains were dismissed and returned to Moab.

But the Moabites were not afraid, for they said, "Does Berechiah have fifty thousand to descend upon us?"

Berechiah encamped against Kir of Moab and minor cities and, while the Moab were safe, they could not go out nor in. And Nebuchadnezzar sent up his army to Moab and found the army of Berechiah encamped.

The captains of Nebuchadnezzar said to Berechiah, "Is this not for Nebuchadnezzar to complete? Is it not time for you to return home?"

Berechiah returned to his home, to his wife, and to his children. The clans returned to Judah, and the Egyptians returned to Pharaoh.

And in the fourth year from the fall of Jerusalem, Moab was no more. The Word from Jeremiah was determined to be true, and the curse of Berechiah was feared.

But Berechiah returned to his home outside En-Gannim, bearing the body of Etutu-Ebuh, his father-in-law, for he had died of wounds from the Moabites. Rizpah, the wife of Berechiah and the daughter of Etutu-Ebuh, mourned his death, as did Berechiah and all their children and clan. An Egyptian of the Sukkiim replaced Etutu-Ebuh.

And the time came that Malluch fell ill, and was sent into his house to his wife, and he slept with his fathers. Berechiah mourned the loss of his counselor and friend. All the Rechabites mourned the loss of Malluch, Possessor of the Word.

For a few years one could walk to Jerusalem from En-Gannim. But the wicked only need the night to gain courage.

Then the governors of Bab'el who knew not Berechiah the Zadikite, bandits and marauders and those that kill for pleasure came. Judah was again in chaos. The people were weak, and evil multiplied upon the people.

There were righteous men in Israel, but they were few. And Berechiah called for an accounting of the clans and the righteous at Hebron, but few came. The righteous were afraid, and there was no recourse. The righteous continued to pray to He Who Is and to worship and to remain faithful. But the wicked prospered and considered that no one could see their ways.

And Berechiah retreated to protect his clan and his family. An exact accounting of the Rechabites and the Zadikites could not occur, but Berechiah met with Jaaziniah as he was departing from En-Gannim. And they remained as brothers in righteousness and faithfulness.

Still Berechiah continued to go up to Jerusalem to worship as required and as was his custom and need. No one could hold him back from the appointed festivals.

Within the Temple ruins he prayed and he wept...and he worshiped.

BOOK THREE

✶ ✶ ✶ ✶ ✶

The Word has been proclaimed. The story of the Ancient One, Berechiah, Nagid of the Zadikite, the Claw, has been recounted. And now, dawn approaches.

Chapter Twelve

✳ ✳ ✳ ✳ ✳

Return to Jerusalem

It was the blast of the yobel that awakened Shemaiah. The blast spoke only of sunrise. His guard had done as commanded, and all were safe through the night. The Ancient One, Berechiah, Nagid of the Zadikite, the Claw of Judah, son of Obadiah, servant of Josiah the king, friend of Pharaoh, remained alive. The strength of the old goat, the Ancient One, continually surprised Shemaiah. There was no changing the end: The time was near, and there was an emptiness entering the stomach of Shemaiah—a loneliness, a hopelessness, a fear. This grandfather was more than grandfather. He held the clan together; he had protected Judah from all that was evil, and now, that honored and righteous warrior approached death.

The wounds of all were treated again by Amoz, third son of Elisha, second son of Nathan, firstborn of Berechiah. It was he who had remained up all night with Berechiah; he who had learned the treatments of Rizpah, his grandmother, born out of Israel and her own people, the Sukkiim, and the Chabash of Israel. His attendance had soothed the pain of Berechiah, but little else. Berechiah slept, he dreamed, and shouted out through the night as he saw old friends and enemies and fought long-forgotten battles.

The men and boys and strangers gathered together in the night to tend to their wounds and to hear the stories of Obadiah the Zadikite, father of Berechiah, and friend of Berechiah the Rechabite. They had heard of the great king, Josiah, of his reforms and his faithfulness and righteousness, and of his death at Megiddo. They had heard of all that this Zadikite, Berechiah, had done: his service to the people of Judah and all Israel; his sons and daughters, all thought to be dead; his grandchildren and great grandchildren; his sister, Deborah, and her husband, Lemuel; his service to Obadiah the Zadikite; and Lemuel's return to his family at Tirzah among the Zadikites of Samaria.

It was the story of Abraham and Isaac and Jacob, and the Word and the words of the story of the Zadikites and the Rechabites and the Prophets. It was their story. It was them. And here was one, spoken of in the story; here he was, in the flesh, loved and dying. Each knew his responsibility and path. Each heard the story and remembered, for each knew that he could someday be as the Ancient One: protector of the Possessors of the Word and protector of the faithful. Was there a choice? No, not for the Zadikites nor the Rechabites.

Nearby there was one not of Israel, but of the pharaohs of Egypt. He stood over Berechiah and had slept. He, too, knew the end was near. He knew that the command of Pharaoh Necho was about to be completed and he would be released from his charge and oath.

It was at dawn that Berechiah the Zadikite had awakened and asked for drink and it was provided. He asked for his captain, and Shemaiah came to him. He asked that the Egyptian be presented, and the Egyptian knelt down to Berechiah and saluted him and kissed him.

Then Berechiah said to the Egyptian, "Go, my friend, to Pharaoh, great grandson of Necho, friend of the Zadikite and Rechabite, and say to Pharaoh: 'This day has Berechiah, son of Obadiah, the Claw, servant of Josiah, king of Israel, whom Pharaoh Necho slew, died, and the pharaoh of Egypt is free of the oath committed by Necho your father. He has died of wounds from those now dead. Great men win wars and lose wars, but it is only in the value of their word that we find honor.' Tell Pharaoh: 'You and your fathers are honored for their word held until the end. Will we not meet again across the great divide? Thanks be to He Who Is!'"

The Egyptian heard the words of Berechiah and said to Berechiah, "I will look on from afar and hear your words as you are approached by the one whom you call the Angel Abaddon. When I hear the yobel mourn, I will return to Egypt and tell Pharaoh as you have said."

And Berechiah said to the Egyptian, "If you wish, you may return to this people whom you have watched and protected, and you will be provided with a wife and a place amongst the Zadikites of En-Gannim, or you may camp with the Rechabites."

"You have honored me, Ancient One, great among all men. I will return, if such is granted by my Pharaoh, whom I do not know. It was his father who sent me here to you. He may have forgotten the services I have rendered and demand more of me."

"Go when you choose, and may He Who Is be with you."

And Berechiah said to Shemaiah, "Listen to my word this day. You will order all the Zadikites and Rechabites with us to depart for the caves where I have left my beloved Rizpah. Once there, send out messengers to all of Israel and call the *zaqen* of the Zadikites and the Rechabites who are still in the land; call them to En-Gannim. Shemaiah, son of my son, you must take my *hoshen* and shield and sword and put them on.

"When the *zaqen* come, say to them, 'Hear, *zaqen* of the Zadikites: Berechiah, the son of Obadiah, has requested your agreement to the appointment of Shemaiah as Nagid of the Zadikite. For our people Shemaiah will be as was Berechiah and Obadiah and Amoz and Hezekiah.' And when they receive you, speak to them immediately of the Possessors of the Word. For such of us cannot remain together. They must be sent out. And it will be Haggai who will remain with you. You will not treat him differently but you will know and see why he is of service to you.

Berechiah paused. "It will be for you to protect and judge and worship and guide and lead. On you will be the righteousness of the Zadikites and protection of the Rechabites. Take my *urim*—not that it has helped me this day—and hold it in your breast. Remember what is, is the Word. Each one you see here must know the Word, for each one here may be the last and only to teach the next generation. Who are we without the Word and our Story? Now, take my *hoshen* and shield and sword and armlets and put them at my feet, and call to all mine to come to me."

So Shemaiah did as he was told, and all came to Berechiah and Berechiah said, "Hear me, Zadikites and Rechabites, faithful and righteous of Israel. I, Berechiah, now assign to you, Shemaiah, to be Nagid of the Zadikites upon my death. I now tell him to take my *hoshen* and place it upon his breast, and may you remember whose heart this *hoshen* has protected. Take the shield and know that it is a gift of our He Who Is, as it has protected your fathers. Take the sword, and may it protect Israel and slay the enemies of Judah as it has for your fathers and their fathers before them! Honor Shemaiah as you have honored me."

And Shemaiah was honored by the words of the Zadikites and Rechabites present.

Berechiah continued: "You will depart from here and go immediately to my wife. Then you will report to Rizpah all that has happened, but you will not speak of me. You will speak of Johanan and the boy Obadiah. But it will only be Shemaiah who will approach her wearing my *hoshen* and with my sword in hand. You, Shemaiah, will say, 'Rizpah, most beautiful of all women, Berechiah, your faithful husband, now rests with his fathers. And he says to you: 'Let no man warm your bed or be your husband, for you need no more children! Only Berechiah can warm your bed!' Tell her...tell her of my love."

BERECHIAH

Then Shemaiah asked, "But what of you, Ancient One?"

"Send these on their way first, and then I will tell you what will be done with me," said Berechiah. "You remember my words and my will?"

"Yes, Ancient One. Is there more?"

Berechiah replied: "Yes, bring with you Haggai, and the Egyptian will come. And bring a horse for each of us."

"But can you ride?"

"You will tie me to the horse until the spring of En-Rogel. Then I will walk to the gate by which the Zadikites and Rechabites enter Jerusalem. You will stay on the far side of the Valley of Hinnom! You will see what needs to be seen and then depart!"

And it was done as Berechiah had said. All departed to see Rizpah, and their hearts were heavy. When Haggai turned back his eyes from those that left, there were tears in his eyes. He would be, he thought, better at the heart of Rizpah. What would she think and do and say?

Then the Egyptian and Shemaiah placed Berechiah on horse and tied him there, and they rode to the spring of En-Rogel. There Berechiah dismounted his horse. He took the sword of the Egyptian and opened the wound on his side. Then he took blood and stroked the Egyptian so that his blood shone in the sun.

He sent Shemaiah, Haggai, and the Egyptian to the hill facing the gate and had Shemaiah blow the yobel. Then Berechiah went across the Valley of Hinnom to the gate, to the ruins of Jerusalem.

When he was near unto the gate, he turned to the valley and said, "Here am I, enemies of Israel! Come and slay me! For I am the son of a wandering Aramean! Servant of He Who Is! The son of the great warriors of Israel, servant of the people and of kings! Here I am! Berechiah, the Claw of Judah, son of Obadiah, son of Amoz, son of Hezekiah of the Zadikite! I have eaten with Pharaoh and I have supped with Nebuchadnezzar! I have cursed and it was as I cursed! I have been faithful and righteous! I have been Blessed of the Holy One of Israel! Come, enemies of Israel! You have wounded Judah! You have destroyed our house of worship! Now destroy me! But know, you will never destroy us!"

Berechiah heard only the splitting of air.

Pf.f..ffft...

Pf.f..ffft...

Pf.f..ffft...

Three arrows were shot from inside the walls of Jerusalem. Three arrows struck Berechiah: two in the back, one in the throat.

Arms outstretched, Berechiah fell forward and died.

Across Hinnom, Shemaiah took the yobel and blew the yobel to mourn the death of a servant of the Almighty.

As instructed, the Egyptian returned to Pharaoh and one day returned to the tents of the Rechabites.

And Haggai and Shemaiah returned to the caves of En-Gedi. Shemaiah went to Rizpah. When she saw him coming with his arms outstretched, she fell down and was wounded. Shemaiah spoke the words of Berechiah to his Rizpah. She smiled in her heart, but could not rise, so that Shemaiah carried her to her bed, which remained cold. And the Angel Abaddon visited her in the night, so Shemaiah buried Rizpah and mourned. And he led his people to safety, along with those Rechabites remaining in attendance. The Zadikites and Rechabites prepared to depart from En-Gedi, going to where Isaiah had found refuge.

Soon after a prince approached the gates of Jerusalem with his party and saw the many wounds on the body of the dead man at the gate, and the party of the prince passed by without stopping at the body. Was this not the party of Zerubbabel, grandson of Jehoiakin, that passed through the gate?

Observing the body, the prince said, "Can there have been any good remaining in Judah?"

And the party entered Jerusalem, where the Prophets continue to weep and the people continue to mourn and worship. And the dust from the bones of Berechiah blew into and out of the city of Jerusalem.

And now, where are the Zadikites and the Rechabites to be found?

The End

*a*DDENDUM

✻✻✻✻✻

1. Historical Setting
2. Maps
3. Zadikite Genealogy
4. Glossary

Historical Setting

✺ ✺ ✺ ✺ ✺

A tale is a tale is a tale—a story in and of itself! Yes, that may be. But if it is, this is not a tale, because it is necessary for you to bring to this fiction an awareness of at least some Biblical historical facts. An active faith will also help in your understanding certain imperatives. For those not so prepared, be aware that issues of faith creation or encouragement will not be addressed here, but some of the historical context into which we plunge will be provided. Overall, one is encouraged to become familiar with the accounts of Scripture found in the following books:

1. II Kings, Chapters 18-25
2. II Chronicles, Chapters 29-36
3. Jeremiah (Yes, the whole book! But pay particular attention to Ch. 35)
4. Daniel, Chapter 1

Remember, the Northern Kingdom, Israel, fell in 724 B.C., and its last king, Hoshea (or Hosea), was taken into captivity to Assyria. The kingdom of Judea continued. The royal lineage of Judah includes:

Hezekiah, who ruled from ca. 720 to 690 B.C., was the thirteenth King of Judah. He was son of Ahaz who had had to make Judah a tributary of the Assyrians. He did evil in the sight of our Elohim. He was twenty-five when he began his reign. Sennacherib of Assyria entered Judah when Hezekiah became defiant, causing great destruction, but he was unable to take Jerusalem. Hezekiah's wife Hephzibah bore the next king.

Manasseh was the next king and he, too, did evil in the sight of our Adonai. He began ruling at age twelve, ca. 699 to 645 B.C., overlapping with his father. The Holy One's anger developed as a result of what occurred during this reign was carried through the next 100 years. Manasseh himself was carried off, repented, and returned to Jerusalem a righteous man.

Amon, the fifteenth king of Judah, was twenty-two when crowned. His servants soon conspired against him and slew him. The people arose and slew the servants. His wife was Jedidah, who was daughter of Adaiah of Boscath. Amon ruled only two tears, doing evil in the sight of Elohim.

Here we have three kings who were terribly destructive of the faith as well as defiant. Out of this history of evil arose a good king, Josiah, son of Amon, who was son of Manasseh who was son of Hezekiah. Consider the politics of the situation! Who would have been pleased? Who would have been unhappy? Consider the implications, as the Holy One was extremely angry with Judah, but here was a "good" and "righteous" king. This is absolutely fascinating and instructive. Josiah began ruling ca. 640 B.C. and ruled until his death on the battlefield of Megiddo ca. 609 B.C. According to II Kings 22:1, he was eight years of age when he became king and he ruled thirty-one years.

With the death of Josiah, Jehoahaz was declared king. He did evil in the sight of the Holy One of Israel, and lasted only three months, as Pharaoh Necho deposed him. He is also referred to as Johanan, spoken about as the first son of Josiah in I Chronicles 3:15. His mother was Hamutal, daughter of Jeremiah of Libnah. Jehoahaz was removed to Egypt where he must have died.

With Jehoahaz deposed, Pharaoh Necho placed Jehoahaz's full brother Eliakim on the throne, naming him Jehoiakim. Jehoiakim ruled from ca. 608 to 598 B.C. He was, for most of his reign, under the suzerainty of the Babylonian king Nebuchadrezzar (or Nebuchadnezzar). This occurred after Nebuchadrezzar defeated Pharaoh Necho (ca. 605 B.C.) at Carchemish when Nebuchadrezzar was not yet king. Nebuchadrezzar ruled ca. 604 - 562 B.C. Jehoiakim did evil in the sight of the Lord. He also had to pay tribute to Egypt and Babylonia.

After a while Jehoiakim became defiant. He died before retribution could be exacted. Soon after his son Jehoiakin was placed on the throne peace was made. But Jehoiakin defied the Babylonians and rebels. Jehoiakin ruled three months, ten days. In that short time he earned a reputation as an evil king. As Jerusalem fell, Jehoiakin, some princes, and 10,000 others were deported to Babylon. It was Jehoiakin's grandson Zerubbabel who returned to reign in Judah after the Captivity.

With Jehoiakim in captivity in Babylon, Nebuchadrezzar placed Mattaniah on the throne as the twentieth king of Judah, renaming him

Zedekiah. He continued the kingly and family tradition (other than Josiah) of doing evil in the sight of the Holy One of Israel. He was the son and full brother of Jehoahaz and Eliakim, and therefore uncle of Jehoiakin. He became king at age twenty-one and ruled for eleven years, from ca. 597 to 586 B.C. His defiance of Nebuchadrezzar led to his defeat, brutal treatment, and the final destruction of Jerusalem.

Upon the defeat of Zedekiah, Gedaliah, son of Ahikam, son of Shaphan, the Scribe of Josiah, was made Governor of Judah. Ishmael, son of Nethaniah, son of Elishama, son "of royal seed," with others, assassinated Gedaliah. Gedaliah was a friend of the Prophet Jeremiah and had protected Jeremiah on many occasions.

With these names and incidents in mind, one needs to superimpose the Prophets on the reigns of the kings. Hosea prophesied during the same period as did Micah. Nahum prophesied most likely during the early to mid years of Josiah's reign. Zephaniah's prophetic work precedes the reforms of Josiah. Jeremiah prophesied through the reign of Josiah, Jehoahaz, Jehoiakim, Jehoiakin, Zephaniah, and the governorship of Gedaliah. Habakkuk prophesied within the time frame of king Jehoiakim. Daniel began with his removal to Babylon when Jehoiakin was deposed by Nebuchadrezzar. Ezekiel also was carried into captivity at that same time. This is simply a brief outline—not all!

The subsequent brief overview may help. Our tale draws structure from the bracketed historical figures as well as their extended families and fictional characters.

Book One (Chapter 1 and 2) begins at the destroyed Temple in Jerusalem toward the end of the Captivity.

A "flashback" story then occurs (Book Two Chapter 3-11) which is placed historically from the seventeenth year of Josiah's reign through (ca.) the Captivity period in Judah.

In Book Three (Chapter 12) we return to the time period of Book One.

Dates	Kings of Judah		Prophets	
		Isaiah		
	Uzziah		Hosea	
				Micah
	Jotham			
	Ahaz			
c. 720-690 B.C.	Hezekiah			
c. 699-645 B.C.	Manasseh			
			Nahum	
c. 638	Amon			Zephaniah
	Our Story			
c. 640-609 B.C.	Josiah			
		Jeremiah		
c. 609	Jehoahaz			
c. 608-598 B.C.	Eliakim/Jehoiakim		Daniel	
c. 598	Jehoiakin			
c. 597-586 B.C.	Mattaniah/Zedekiah			Ezekiel
c. 585	Governor Gedaliah			
	Captivity			
	Zerubbabel			

MAPS
✽✽✽✽✽

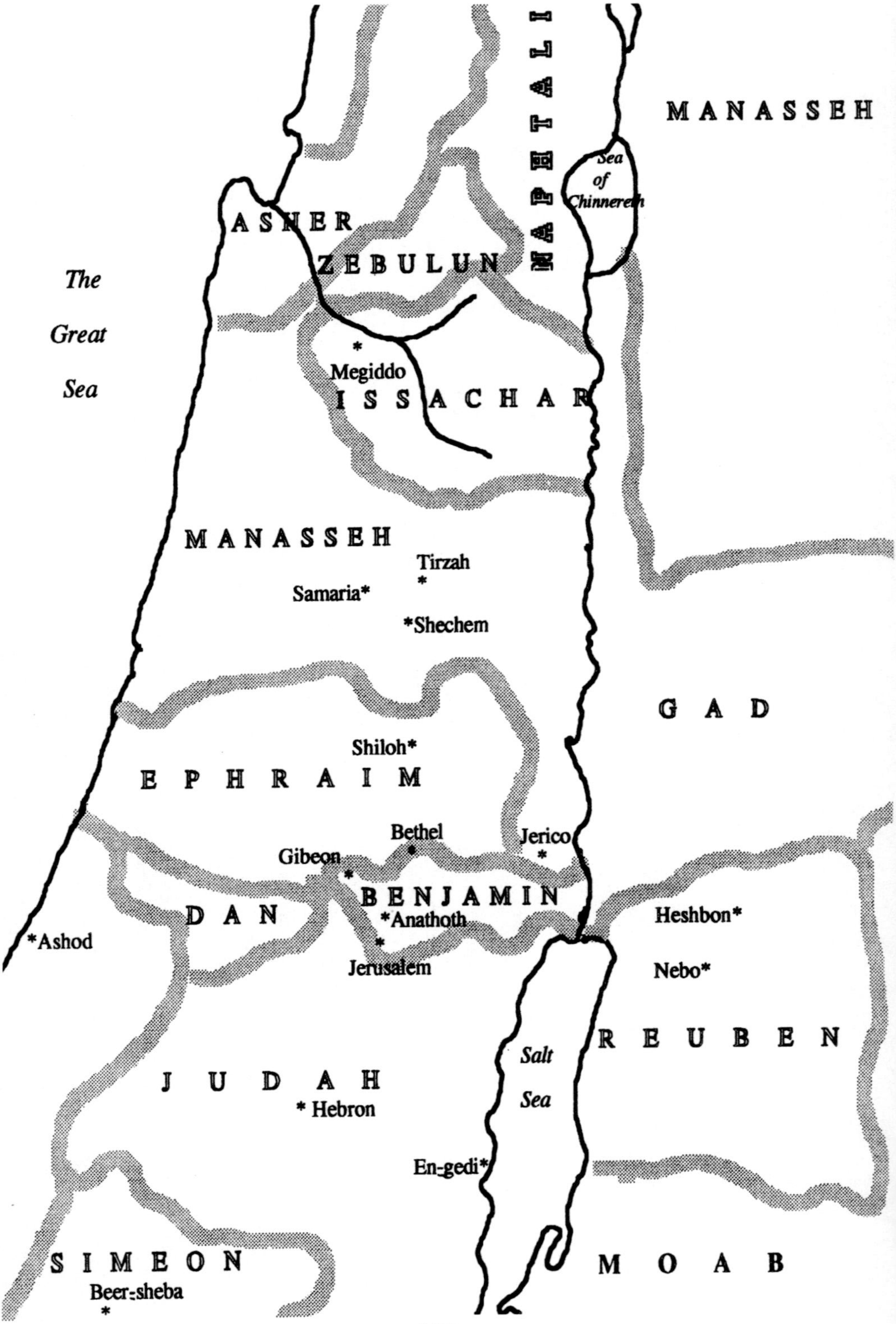
NAPHTALI
MANASSEH
Sea of Chinnereth
ASHER
ZEBULUN
The Great Sea
Megiddo
ISSACHAR
MANASSEH
Tirzah
Samaria
Shechem
GAD
Shiloh
EPHRAIM
Bethel
Jerico
Gibeon
BENJAMIN
DAN
Anathoth
Heshbon
Ashod
Jerusalem
Nebo
Salt Sea
REUBEN
JUDAH
Hebron
En-gedi
SIMEON
MOAB
Beer-sheba

GOMER

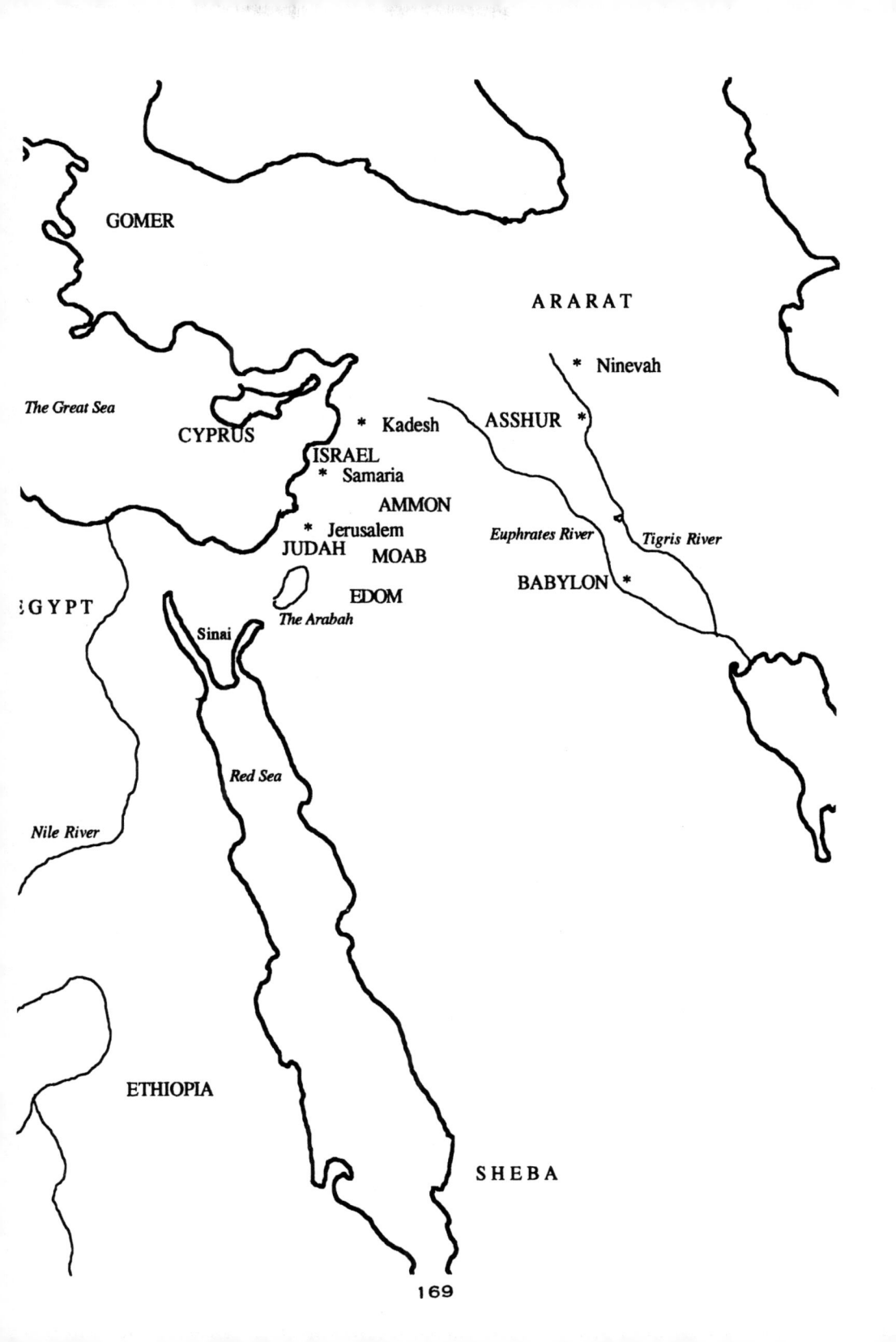

ARARAT

* Ninevah

The Great Sea

CYPRUS

* Kadesh

ASSHUR *

ISRAEL
* Samaria

AMMON

* Jerusalem

JUDAH   MOAB

Euphrates River   Tigris River

EDOM

BABYLON *

EGYPT

Sinai

The Arabah

Red Sea

Nile River

ETHIOPIA

SHEBA

ZADIKITE *G*ENEALOGY

✳ ✳ ✳ ✳ ✳

Progeny of NATHAN THE ZADIKITE
(including the Judean and Tirzah Zadikites)

Progeny of BERECHIAH THE ZADIKITE
(Berechiah is the great great great grandson of Nathan the Zadikite

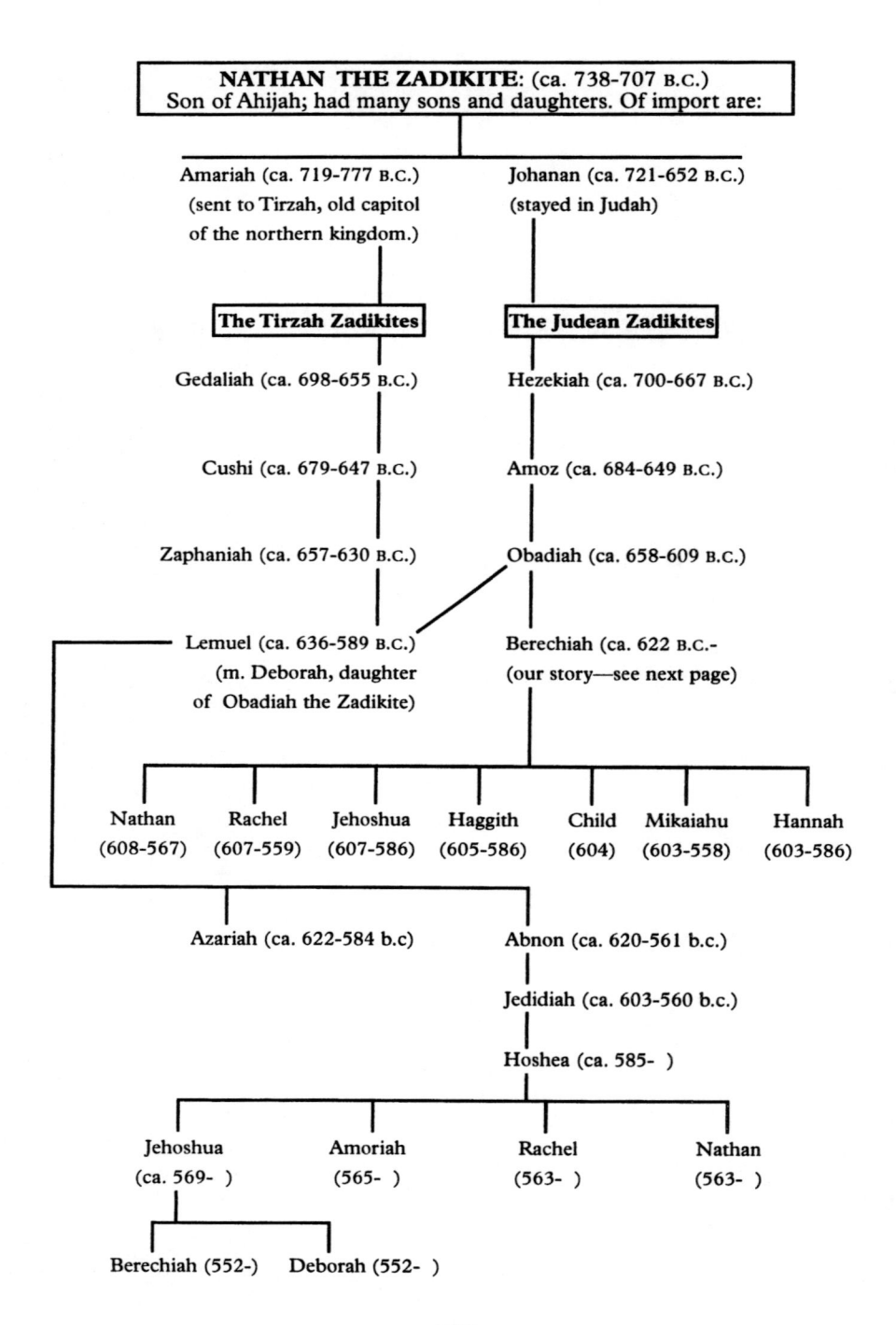

NATHAN THE ZADIKITE: (ca. 738-707 B.C.)
Son of Ahijah; had many sons and daughters. Of import are:

Amariah (ca. 719-777 B.C.)
(sent to Tirzah, old capitol
of the northern kingdom.)

Johanan (ca. 721-652 B.C.)
(stayed in Judah)

The Tirzah Zadikites

The Judean Zadikites

Gedaliah (ca. 698-655 B.C.)

Hezekiah (ca. 700-667 B.C.)

Cushi (ca. 679-647 B.C.)

Amoz (ca. 684-649 B.C.)

Zaphaniah (ca. 657-630 B.C.)

Obadiah (ca. 658-609 B.C.)

Lemuel (ca. 636-589 B.C.)
(m. Deborah, daughter
of Obadiah the Zadikite)

Berechiah (ca. 622 B.C.-
(our story—see next page)

Nathan	Rachel	Jehoshua	Haggith	Child	Mikaiahu	Hannah
(608-567)	(607-559)	(607-586)	(605-586)	(604)	(603-558)	(603-586)

Azariah (ca. 622-584 b.c)

Abnon (ca. 620-561 b.c.)

Jedidiah (ca. 603-560 b.c.)

Hoshea (ca. 585-)

Jehoshua	Amoriah	Rachel	Nathan
(ca. 569-)	(565-)	(563-)	(563-)

Berechiah (552-)   Deborah (552-)

The Family of BERECHIAH THE ZADIKITE and his wife RIZPAH

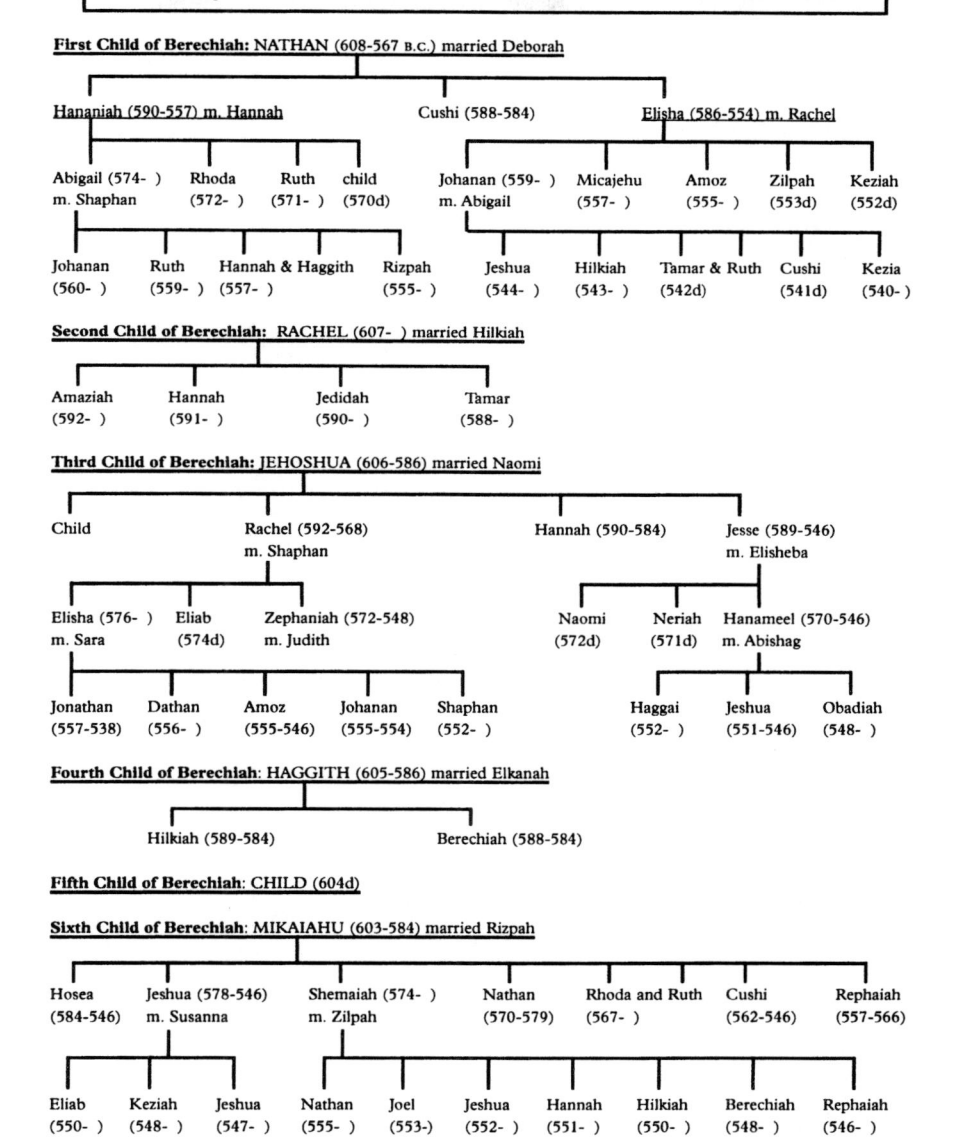

First Child of Berechiah: NATHAN (608-567 B.C.) married Deborah

- **Hananiah (590-557) m. Hannah**
  - Abigail (574-) m. Shaphan
    - Johanan (560-)
  - Rhoda (572-)
    - Ruth (559-)
  - Ruth (571-)
    - Hannah & Haggith (557-)
  - child (570d)
    - Rizpah (555-)
- **Cushi (588-584)**
- **Elisha (586-554) m. Rachel**
  - Johanan (559-) m. Abigail
    - Jeshua (544-)
  - Micajehu (557-)
    - Hilkiah (543-)
  - Amoz (555-)
    - Tamar & Ruth (542d)
  - Zilpah (553d)
    - Cushi (541d)
  - Keziah (552d)
    - Kezia (540-)

Second Child of Berechiah: RACHEL (607-) married Hilkiah

- Amaziah (592-)
- Hannah (591-)
- Jedidah (590-)
- Tamar (588-)

Third Child of Berechiah: JEHOSHUA (606-586) married Naomi

- Child
- **Rachel (592-568) m. Shaphan**
  - Elisha (576-) m. Sara
    - Jonathan (557-538)
    - Dathan (556-)
  - Eliab (574d)
  - Zephaniah (572-548) m. Judith
    - Amoz (555-546)
    - Johanan (555-554)
    - Shaphan (552-)
- **Hannah (590-584)**
  - Naomi (572d)
  - Neriah (571d)
- **Jesse (589-546) m. Elisheba**
  - Hanameel (570-546) m. Abishag
    - Haggai (552-)
    - Jeshua (551-546)
    - Obadiah (548-)

Fourth Child of Berechiah: HAGGITH (605-586) married Elkanah

- Hilkiah (589-584)
- Berechiah (588-584)

Fifth Child of Berechiah: CHILD (604d)

Sixth Child of Berechiah: MIKAIAHU (603-584) married Rizpah

- Hosea (584-546)
- **Jeshua (578-546) m. Susanna**
  - Eliab (550-)
  - Keziah (548-)
  - Jeshua (547-)
- Shemaiah (574-) m. Zilpah
  - Nathan (555-)
  - Joel (553-)
  - Jeshua (552-)
  - Hannah (551-)
- Nathan (570-579)
- Rhoda and Ruth (567-)
  - Hilkiah (550-)
- Cushi (562-546)
  - Berechiah (548-)
- Rephaiah (557-566)
  - Rephaiah (546-)

Seventh Child of Berechiah: HANNAH (603-) married Zerah

- Child (589d)
- Obadiah (588-)
- Amariah (587-)

Glossary

✻ ✻ ✻ ✻ ✻

Glossary of Names and Special Words

Note: "J.": JHVH: Jahweh: Jehovah
(Name never spoken but replaced by Adonai,
Elohim, Holy One, Almighty, He Who Is, etc.)

Abaddon: Angel of Death
Abigail: Source of Delight
Abishag: Father of Error
Absalom: Father of Peace; Father is Peace
Achbor: Mouse
Adaiah: Pleasing to J.
Adonai/Adonay: Lord
Ahab: Father's brother; uncle (paternal)
Ahaz: He Holds
Ahijah: J. is Brother
Ahikam: My brother has Risen
Amariah: The Lord has Said
Amaziah: The Lord has Strength
Amnon: Trustworthy
Amon: Trustworthy; Workman
Amos: Bearer of Burden
Amoz: Strong
Anathoth: Levite city, three miles north of Jerusalem

Arabah: Desert area south and west of the Dead Sea
Asshur: city, fortress of the kingdom of Assyria
Astarte: Goddess of Fertility; female counterpart of Ba'al
Azariah: J. is Keeper
Azor/Azur: Helper

Ba'al: Possessor/Master; chief male deity of Canaan
Bab'el: used to designate main City of Babylonia, which is Babylon
Baruch: Blessed
Benebelija'al: Sons of Worthlessness
Berechiah: The Lord has Blessed
Beth Jesimoth: Town/Place in south of Judah, west of Jordan River
Buzi: Scorned of the Lord

Carshemish/Carchemish: Battle in 605 B.C. where Prince Nebuchadrezzar defeated Pharaoh Necho
Chabash: healer(s)
Chebel: fictitious name coming from Hebrew word meaning 'Sorrow'
Choshen/Hoshen: Breast Plate
Cushi: Black

Dagal: Standard; Pennant; for this story, clan identification worn on the body or draped upon belongings; used as a stole or vestment
Daniel: The Lord is Judge
Dathan: Fount
David: Beloved
Deborah: Honey Bee

Eliab: The Lord is Father
Eliakim: The Lord is Setting Up
Elijah: J. is My Lord
Elisha: The Lord is Savior
Elishama: The Lord is Hearer
Elisheba: The Lord is Swearer
Elizur: The Lord is a Rock
Elkanah: The Lord is Possessing
Elnathan: The Lord is Giving
Elohim: The Lord
En-Gannim: City of south Judah; place unknown
En-Gedi: "Fountain of the Lord"; spring area on the west shore of the Salt (Dead) Sea
En-Rogel: Spring just south of Jerusalem

Ezekiel: The Lord is Strong

Gedaliah: The Lord is Great
Gemariah: The Lord has Completed
Genizah: Temple storeroom for manuscripts
Gracia: Greece

Habakkuk: Love's Embrace
Haggai: Festive (m)
Haggith: Festive (f)
Hamutal: The Lord is Fresh Life
Hanameel: God's Gift
Hananiah: The Lord is Gracious
Hannah: Grace
Haruz: Industrious
Hasrah: Splendor
Hazazon/Hazezon/Hazezon Tamar: Ancient name of En-Gedi: Area of Palms
Hebron: City of Asher
Hephzibah: My Delight is in Her
Hezekiah: The Lord is Strength
Hilkiah: The Lord is Protection
Hophra: Egyptian Pharaoh, c. 588-569 B.C.
Hosea: J. is Help
Hoshen/Choshen: Breast Plate
Huldah: Weasel

Immer: Prominent; also name of priestly family
Irijah: J. is Seeing
Isaiah: J. is Helper
Ishmael: The Lord Hears

Jaazaniah: J. is Hearing
Jachan: Afflicting
Jahath: Comfort
Jahaziel: The Lord will Watch
Jasiel: The Lord is Maker
Jedidah: Beloved
Jedidiah: J. is a Friend
Jehiel: The Lord is Alive
Jehoahaz: J. Upholds
Jehoiakim: J. Sets Up

Jehoiakin/Jehoiachin: J. Establishes
Jehonadab: J. is Generous (see Jonadab)
Jehoshua: J. Saves
Jehozadak: J. is Just/Righteous
Jehudi: Hebrew (m)
Jehudijah: Hebrewess (f) [Jewish]
Jemuel: The Lord is Light
Jeremiah: J. is High
Jeriah: J. is My Foundation
Jeshua: J. is Help
Jeshurun: The Darling Upright; poetic name applied to the people of Israel.
Jesse: J. Is
Jethro: Excellence; Pre-eminence
Jezreel: The Lord Shows
Joah: J. is a Brother
Joahaz: J. Helps
Johanan: J. is Gracious
Joel: J. is God
Jonadab: J. is Generous (see Jehonadab)
Jonathan: J. is Given
Josiah: J. Supports
Jotham: J. is Perfect
Jozadak: J. is Great
Judah: Praise

Keziah/Cassia: Cinnamon; Spice

Lemuel: J. is Bright
Letushim: Oppressed

Maaseiah: J.'s Creation
Malak: Messenger
Malchiel: The Lord is King
Malluch: Counselor
Manasseh: He Who Causes to Forget, Causes Forgetfulness
Masora: Critical notes of the Masoretes within Scripture
Masoretes: Scholars who wrote down Scriptures, tenth to seventh century B.C.
Mattaniah: Gift of the Lord
Megiddo: Battle, c. 609 B.C., where Pharaoh Necho defeated Josiah, King of Judah

Meshullemeth: Friend (f)
Micah: Abbreviated form of Micahjehu/Michiahu: Who is Like J?
Micahjehu: Who is Like J?
Mikaiah: Another form of Micahjehu
Mishael: Who is What Elohim Is?
Mizbeach: High Place; place with simple altar; place of sacrifice

Nachal: Stream in a gorge or hollow
Nahum: Comforter
Nagid: Leader; One Who Goes Before
Naomi: Pleasant
Nathan: Giver
Nazir: One vowed by parents or self to serve J. (before or after birth; sometimes Nazarite)
Nebuchadnezzar/Nebuchadrezzar: King of Babylon for forty-three years; his son followed as N. II
Nebuzaradan: One of the captains of Nebuchadnezzar's army that took Jerusalem
Necho/Neco: Pharaoh of Egypt, c. 510 - 594 B.C.
Nehi: Fictitious name, from Hebrew: 'Wailing'
Nehushta: Support
Nergalsharezer: One of the captains of Nebuchadnezzar's army that took Jerusalem
Neriah: The Lord is Light
Nethaniah: The Lord Gives
Nethinim: Servant or assistant to the Levites
Nokri: Foreigner

Obadiah: Servant of the Lord

Parva'im: Place which provided gold to the Temple in Jerusalem; location unknown
Pashur: Free
Pelatiah: J. Delivers
Perez: Bursting Through

Qadesh: consecration; dedication (Corban)
Qaton: Small, tiny, insignificant

Rachel: Lamb
Ramah: City of Benjamin, on the border between Judah and Israel
Rechabite(s): From Companionship (Rechab); clan beginning c. 925 B.C.

Rephaiah: J. Heals
Rhoda: Rose
Riblah: Bare Place; headquarters for both Pharaoh Necho and Nebuchadnezzar
Rizpah: Burning Embers; burning charcoal; variegate; of many colors
Ruth: Friendship

Samaria: City of Ephraim that became Omri's (and following kings of the Northern Kingdom) capitol when Tirzah was abandoned
Samuel: Heard of the Lord
Seraiah: The Lord is Prince
Shallum: Recompenser
Shaphan: Prudent
Shelumiel: The Lord is Peace
Shemaiah: The Lord is Fame
Sidon: A wealthy seaport city of Phoenicia near present Tyre
Susanna: Lily

Tamar: Palm
Teraphim: Nourisher
Thum'mim: Bag of trinkets under the breast plate; used to discern Will of J. (see Urim)
Tikvath: Strength
Tirzah: Delight; Capitol of the Northern Kingdom until Omri changed its name to Samaria
Topheth: Place where once in the Valley of Hinnom children were sacrificed to Molech

Uriah: J. is Light
Urim: see Thum'mim
Uzziah: J. is Strong

Yobel: Ram's horn

Zadikite: from Hebrew 'tsaddiq,' meaning Just One, Righteous One, One able to cause or give Justice and Righteousness (implying prince, or from the kings) [fictional]
Zaqen: Elder, leader
Zedekiah: The Lord is Mighty
Zerah: Sprout
Zephaniah: The Lord is Darkness
Zerubbabel: Shoot out of Babylon, Begotten of Bab'el
Zilpah: Myrrh droppings